His Fierce Lycan Luna

LYCAN LUNA SERIES

BOOK FOUR

JESSICA HALL

BLURB

Revelations have shattered everything they thought they knew. Ivy, a mere name, is not who she seems. She is Azalea, the long-lost princess of the Landeena kingdom. With this revelation, Azalea not only discovers her true identity but also the dormant Landeena power within her. This power, a force of nature, is the key to everything. Casting off the chains of her former oppression, Azalea emerges as a powerful force, ready to reclaim her birthright and seek justice for the wrongs she has endured.

King Kyson, torn between his obligations and his emotions for Azalea, finds himself at a crossroads. He must choose to support her rise to power or step aside. As Ivy dies and is reborn as Azalea Landeena, she is no longer the submissive figure of her past but a queen in her own right. She challenges everyone around her to stand with her or move out of her way.

Meanwhile, a sinister figure lurks within the castle walls, weaving a plot of revenge. Their actions threaten to either destroy the kingdom and Azalea's rise to power. As secrets unravel and allegiances are tested, Azalea and Kyson must navigate political intrigue and betrayal.

Revenge is in the air, ready to topple one kingdom and wake another from the dead. In the middle of it all, a queen rises, fighting not just for revenge, but for her kingdom.

CHAPTER ONE

GANNON

The steering wheel is cool beneath my palms as I navigate the forested road. Trees, tall and sturdy, flank the path. In the passenger seat, Abbie's outline is motionless against the window, her reflection ghostly as she watches the world speeding by.

I steal a glance in her direction, noting the distant look that clouds her eyes—dulled by shadows I cannot chase away. The silence between us isn't empty; it's laden with the weight of unsaid words, echoes of her pain that neither of us can voice. I grip the wheel a tad tighter, my knuckles betraying the concern etched within me.

I can tell she's lost in her thoughts, probably replaying the horrors she's endured. It's why I'm doing this—taking her away from the castle, from all the memories that haunt her. She needs this break, a chance to breathe, even if she doesn't realize it yet.

We're heading to a secluded cabin I know about, a place used as a safe house in case of emergencies. It's far from everything, surrounded by nothing but nature. I figure it's the perfect spot for Abbie to find some peace, even if it's just for a little while.

"Almost there," I murmur, more to myself than to Abbie, though I hope the words might bring her back to the present. The tires crunch over the gravel as I pull into the last grocery store before we head out to the cabin. Abbie, however, refuses to come in with me and waits in the car.

The bell above the grocery store door jingles as I push it open, stepping into the muted fluorescent lights that flicker casting long shadows between the aisles. The familiar scent of polished floors and fresh produce greets me. I grab a basket.

Each item found its way into the basket with a soft thud—bread, cheese, cans of soup. My mind, however, lingers on Abbie's quiet presence waiting in the car. When I passed the candy aisle, a flash of red catches my eye. I pause, my gaze fixing on the strawberry cloud candies snug between bags of chocolate. They are her favorite; little sugary puffs that might sweeten the bitterness life had dealt her lately or so I hope. I pick up two bags, tossing them into the basket.

Ten minutes later, the cabin comes into view. As we draw nearer, I steal a glance at Abbie. Her eyes wide and watchful—beautiful and wary.

"Abbie," I break the silence as I park the car, "you're safe with me." I turn off the engine, letting the weight of assurance settle over my words. "There's no one around for miles. This is a safe place."

Her eyes flicker to mine, searching for the truth in them, seeking the promise of safety I desperately want to give her. I reach into the back to retrieve the groceries.

Stepping out of the car, I close the door with a soft thud, studying Abbie. She nods in response to my promise, her lips caught between her teeth, betraying her nerves. Together, we climb the steps, and I unlock the door. The air inside is still cold enough to make Abbie wrap her arms around herself. Without hesitation, I slip off my jacket and place it over her slender shoulders, the fabric swallowing her frame.

"Let me get some wood for the fire," I say, moving toward the pile of logs stacked by the hearth. I'll need to chop more up. This won't last the night. Kneeling, I can feel the weight of her gaze on me.

I turn back to see her perched delicately on the edge of the rustic bed, the room's centerpiece crafted from thick, interlocking logs.

"Only one bed?" Her inquiry is faint, almost lost in the vast silence that fills the space between us.

Her heartbeat is a rapid flutter, an undercurrent of fear I can sense as surely as the chill in the air. It pulls at something deep within me, a desire to protect, to soothe her.

"Abbie," I begin my resolve firm, "you take the bed. I'll be fine on the couch."

I move closer, the floorboards creaking underfoot as I approach her. The cabin seems to close in around us, the simplicity of the space magnifying her unease. My fingers find her chin, lifting it gently so that her eyes, wide and brimming with unshed fears, can meet mine.

"Have I ever given you a reason to fear me?" My question hangs in the air for a moment.

In the silence that follows, she offers me the barest shake of her head. That small gesture, devoid of words yet heavy with meaning, unties a knot in my chest, releasing a breath I hadn't realized I'd been holding.

"Then don't start now," I tell her. "I'll sleep on the couch."

Abbie's gaze drops to her trembling fingers, interlocked and resting on her lap. I observe the subtle shift in her posture, the slight nod that is her response—a silent acceptance of the arrangement.

The room grows quiet, save for the settling of the old wooden beams and the distant whisper of wind through the pines outside.

I watch as she draws a deep breath, seeming to gather the scattered pieces of herself, finding some measure of control.

"I need to gather more wood. I'll be outside," I tell her.

Stepping into the crisp air, I let the screen door close gently behind me; its soft click punctuates the silence within. The axe rests in the same place I left it months ago, against the chopping block, its handle roughened from years of use.

I roll up my sleeves, feeling the chill bite at my skin as I grip the wooden handle. Grabbing a log, I set to work. Each swing is a release of pent-up tension, the blade splitting through the logs with satisfying thuds that echo in the quiet forest clearing.

With every piece of wood I stack, my thoughts drift back to Abbie and I lose myself in the task. The muscles in my arms burn with exertion, mirroring the ache in my chest for her suffering. She needs time and space.

The scent of pine needles and freshly split wood mingles in the air, a natural balm to the senses. I've always loved being outdoors. I glance towards the cabin when I hear movement inside the large cabin.

CHAPTER TWO

ABBIE

Standing on the porch, I tug Gannon's jacket closer around me, feeling a chill despite the sun. The sound of the ax hitting wood punctuates the surrounding silence. Curiosity gets the better of me, and I step forward to see Gannon working, his back glistening with sweat under the effort, his shirt discarded somewhere out of sight. A huge pile of wood is already chopped, and I can't help but let my eyes wander over his muscular body, noticing scars that mar his chest. I've never seen him like this, so focused, so... captivating.

I lean over the porch rail, where curls of wood shavings lay strewn about like the aftermath of a silent storm. There appears to be a method to his movements—raise, swing, impact—a dance of strength and purpose that left his broad back shining with sweat.

The sharp lines of muscle shift across his torso with every movement, drawing my gaze in a way that felt both invasive and admiring. Scars lace his skin, etched into the tanned flesh of his chest.

A flush of embarrassment warms my cheeks when he turns suddenly, catching me in the act of staring. My eyes dart away, seeking the wooden steps as I descend and perch on the top one, hugging myself tighter, trying to stop the cold chill seeping into me.

"Come here," Gannon's voice breaks the silence, soft yet somehow reaching me clearly. I hesitate, swallowing hard as I glance up at him. The world around us feels almost unnaturally quiet. He gestures for me to come closer with a finger to his lips, signaling me to be quiet. With reluctance, I stand and walk towards him, and he pulls me close by the waist, pointing towards something in the trees.

I follow his gaze to spot a mother deer and her baby. We watch in silence until the wind shifts and the mother's head snaps towards us, her and the baby darting away through the trees. A smile finds its way to my lips, a rarity these days, and I look up at Gannon, who brushes my hair behind my ear with a gentle touch.

"Finally, a smile," he says, his voice warm. "See, there is good, Abbie. You just need to find it." After watching the deer disappear, Gannon starts gathering the wood, and we head inside. He gets the fire going.

The warmth from the freshly kindled fire wraps around me as Gannon painstakingly stacks the last few logs beside the hearth. The glow illuminates his features, casting shadows that play upon the rugged lines of his face. He catches my gaze.

"Did you see the bathroom?" he asks suddenly, an undercurrent of eagerness in his voice.

I shake my head, curiosity tickling the edges of my wariness. His hand finds mine, calloused and warm, and with gentle force, he leads me down the hallway. The door swings open to reveal a space bathed in soft light, the centerpiece being a vast spa bath sitting beneath a huge skylight.

My breath escapes in a hushed gasp, but the awe quickly turns sour as my eyes catch the unavoidable reflection in the mirror. A shiver claws up my spine, and the room seems to close in around me. My scars, usually hidden beneath layers of fabric, peek out reminding me this is just the illusion of safety.

"Abbie?" Gannon's voice pulls at me, laced with concern.

Panic blooms in my chest, wild and desperate to escape. I start to retreat, every muscle tensing to rush out, but his hands are there, firm on my hips, halting my movement. "You will not hide here," he says, a command woven with the gentleness of his voice.

My head shakes involuntarily. The thought of confronting my marred reflection, the visual of my fractured past, is unbearable.

Gannon seems to sense the turmoil within me; he slides the jacket from my shoulders and presses a reassuring kiss to the exposed skin on my shoulder. His fingers brush the hem of my blouse, inching towards the ghosts that haunt my flesh and my mind.

"I don't want to see," I whisper.

His touch pauses, and for a heartbeat as his eyes dart to mine.

"Then close your eyes. I'll tell you what I see," Gannon murmurs, his voice soft as a feather drifting through the air. It's almost too much, that voice, carrying with it the promise of an acceptance I've never dared to give myself. Tears brim at the edges of my eyes. My breath catches in my chest, my heart pounding against my ribs like a hummingbird's wings.

I nod, a mere dip of my chin, and let my eyelids fall. Darkness cradles me, and I'm grateful for it. Grateful not to witness the slow reveal of my damaged skin, the map of my pain laid out for him to see.

As Gannon's hands slide over the fabric of my clothing, every touch is a whisper against my fears. His fingers graze the blackened mark on my neck, and a sharp intake of breath escapes me. The memory of fire licking at my flesh rushes back. I hate that mark and how much control it has over me. I despise what it represents.

But then, there's Gannon again—his presence a balm, his voice pulling me from the confines of my mind. "I see a woman who doesn't know how beautiful she is," he says, and the warmth of his breath tickles my ear.

"Her scars are not something to hide." His tone reverberates with conviction, a stark contrast to the quiver that threatens to break through my resolve. "They tell a story of what she's overcome."

Gannon's touch is careful and reverent as if he knows he's not just peeling away layers of clothing but layers of my past.

"I've overcome nothing," I whisper back, my voice shattering the silence.

"That's what you think," he replies. His hands pause on the small of my back, warm and steady.

The air between us charges with something unnamed, a current that buzzes through my veins, filling spaces hollowed out by years of self-loathing.

And for a moment, just a fleeting moment, I allow myself to believe him. With his hands on me and his voice a soft caress at my ear, hope flickers—a delicate flame in the space that holds my fears.

Hope feels dangerous to me. It threatens the walls I've built, the safe cocoon of darkness where I've hidden. Yet here, in this sliver of time, I cling to it, and the possibility that there might be beauty in the scars. Strength in the pain and a future where I see myself through eyes not clouded by the ashes of my past.

As Gannon continues, his voice is a gentle caress in the silence of the room.

"This lash here," he continues, his fingers hovering over a scar, "it tells me you've faced unimaginable horrors and yet, you've emerged stronger. Your strength is breathtaking."

"That's not strength Gannon," I murmur.

"Really, because all I see is a woman who is still alive despite everything she has been through." I shake my head yet he ignores me.

"These bite marks," he says, his voice filled with reverence, "they're proof of the battles you've survived. You're a survivor, Abbie, in the truest sense."

"Your eyes," he marvels, "despite the darkness they've seen, they hold a light that's purely yours. A reminder that there's beauty even in pain."

"Your hands," he notes, gently taking them in his, "they've clung to hope when despair seemed the only option, yet still, you fought. It doesn't matter whether it was for you or Azalea. You held on even though you preferred death."

Tears blur my vision; I didn't hold on. If only he knew how many times I tried to end it, yet fate chose torture, not freedom for me.

"This mark on your neck," he murmurs, "while it might seem a reminder of Kade, but to me, it's a reminder that not even a mate bond can get between me loving you."

"You've been to hell and back, yet here you are Abbie. Don't let what they did to you be the only way you see yourself."

That's easy for him to say, all I see is them when I look in a mirror.

"Your heart," he says, his voice barely above a whisper, "it's seen the depths of human cruelty, yet it's filled with an unparalleled capacity for love and forgiveness. It's the most beautiful thing about you."

"And your soul, Abbie," he concludes, "despite being fractured by torment, it's not dimmed. It's tragically beautiful, and there's nothing more captivating than that. Nothing more captivating than you."

A lump forms in my throat at his words. He must be deluded to think I am the least bit captivating. I'm frightening, yes, but certainly not captivating.

CHAPTER THREE

GANNON

The evening unfolds with a gravity that weighs heavily on my heart. Abbie sits across from me, her usually radiant face now clouded with doubt and self-loathing. I know she doesn't believe my words; the compliments that I bestow upon her seem to dissolve before they can truly reach her heart. But I'm determined, resolved to remind her every day of the beauty I see in her until she sees it in herself.

Still, I can't help but feel a pang of sadness as I watch her pick at her fingers. I wish she could see herself through my eyes, see the way her laughter lights up a room, the way her eyes sparkle when she talks about her passions, the way her heart is so full of love for others.

But tonight, she is lost in her own darkness, unable to see the light that shines within her. And so, I continue to speak words of love and admiration, hoping that someday she will believe them and see herself as the beautiful, deserving woman that she truly is.

As the sun dips, leaving the sky draped in darkness, I prepare the spa bath, adding oils that fill the room with a soothing scent. With a deep breath, I shed my clothes but keep my boxer shorts on, understanding Abbie's fragile state and not wanting to alarm her further. Gently, I lead her into the warm water, positioning her between my legs. The moment her back meets my chest, she shudders, a gasp escaping her lips as her body goes rigid in my embrace.

I reach for the soap, intent on washing her, but she stops me, her hands trembling as they grip my wrist to stop me. "I will never hurt you," I whisper, my voice laced with a sincerity born from the depths of my soul. "I would rather rip out my own heart than ever hurt you."

Her hand trembles but eventually loosens its grip as I move the soap over her skin, carefully avoiding the areas that might trigger her.

After a few moments, her hand falls limply into the water, and she allows me to clean her, though I meticulously avoid touching her in any way that might cause distress.

Next, I shampoo her hair, my fingers working gently through the strands, washing away the grime of the day. When we're done, we soak in the silence that blankets the room, the warmth of the water encasing us both until it gradually turns cold. With a sigh, I pull the plug, turn off the jets, and wrap her in a towel, leading her back to the room where the fire crackles invitingly.

Abbie quickly dresses and grabs a blanket, moving closer to the fire. She sits there, staring into the flames with a vacant expression that chills me to the bone. After a while sitting in silence, eventually, I decide to cook dinner.

It's hard for me to sit still in the silence. As I cook in the kitchen, the aroma of sizzling steak fills the air. I call out to Abbie, asking her how she likes her steak cooked, but there is no response. Concern gnaws at my insides as I peer around the corner to find her sitting in front of the fire, staring into its mesmerizing flames as if transfixed.

Then, I see it—her hand outstretched toward the flames. "Abbie!" I boom, and she jolts back to reality, her hand jerking back from the fire. I rush to her side, clutching her hands and turning them over to inspect for damage. Her fingertips are burned. "Why,

Abbie? Why would you do this?" I demand, my voice a mix of frustration and concern.

She says nothing, her eyes brimming with unshed tears. I curse under my breath, dragging her to the sink to run her hands under cold water. *Where has my Abbie gone?*

"Why would you burn yourself?" I ask again, grabbing her face gently, forcing her to meet my gaze. Tears blur her eyes, and my heart breaks for her.

I pull Abbie into my arms, holding her tight against me as she sobs, her body shaking with the force of her emotions. I can feel her guilt radiating from her, and it breaks my heart to see her in such a state.

As Abbie's anguished cries fill the cabin, my heart shatters into a million pieces. "Pain is in your head," she tells me, her voice breaking. "Physical pain is nothing but this," she clutches her chest, "this inside me, it's unbearable. It hurts, Gannon. It's an ache that never stops. You say I'm good, but I'm angry. I'm so angry, Gannon. I want them to hurt like they hurt me."

"They can't hurt you anymore Abbie. They're dead," I try to remind her.

But she breaks down even more, pulling at her hair, yanking it as if trying physically to remove her torment. "They aren't dead, Gannon! Can't you see? They haunt me!" she screams, her voice filled with despair.

"They live, Gannon, they live," she repeats, clutching her head, her memories haunting her in a way that makes me feel utterly helpless. Then, she starts chanting a call for Azalea, almost like she is repeating a mantra before she starts rambling. "More than my life, more than my life, more than my life. But I don't want this life. She made me promise," Abbie sobs, lost in her torment.

In a panic, I let her go, my eyes darting around the room until they land on a knife in the kitchen. Snatching it, I move toward her with determination, thrusting the knife into her hand.

"That's right, more than my life, Abbie." I press the knife, now clasped in her hand, against my heart. "You want to end it, you end me too. Do you hear me?"

Abbie's sobs turn into gasps of shock as I press the knife against my chest, daring her to end my life along with hers. She looks at me with wide, tear-filled eyes, and I can see the terror in her expression.

"Come on, Abbie. Do it," I goad her, pushing the blade closer to my heart. "End it all."

Her grip tightens on the knife, trembling as she struggles with her emotions. "Stop," she pleads, her voice cracking.

"You want it to stop? Then make it stop," I demand, my voice shaking with emotion. I don't know if this is the right thing to do, but I can't just stand by and watch Abbie hurt herself anymore.

For a moment, we stay frozen in that position, our bodies tense and our eyes locked. The tip of the knife presses against my chest, over my heart.

"My heart isn't worth beating if yours isn't. More than my life," I repeat her words back to her, my voice firm yet filled with an emotion I can barely contain.

"So, what's it gonna be? Are you going to kill me? Because I can't live without you. My heart only beats for you."

Her lips quiver, tears streaming down her face as she looks at me, the knife trembling in her grasp. The weight of her decision hangs in the air between us, a palpable tension that threatens to consume us both. In this moment, I realize the depth of her pain, the darkness that she's been fighting alone.

But she's not alone, not anymore. I'm here, willing to bear the burden of her pain, to stand by her side through the darkness until we find the light together. "Abbie, please," I whisper, my voice breaking with the intensity of my plea. "I need you more than my life. We can get through this together."

Finally, after what feels like an eternity, Abbie lets out a sob and drops the knife to the floor.

"I can't," she cries out, falling to her knees as tears stream down her face. "I can't do it."

Without hesitation, I drop to the ground beside her and wrap my arms around her trembling form. It breaks my heart to see her like this - so broken and vulnerable.

"It's okay," I whisper soothingly into her hair as she clings to me for dear life.

"You're not alone, Abbie. You'll never be alone again," I promise her, my voice steady.

I love her, and I'll do whatever it takes to see her smile again, to see her realize how truly beautiful and strong she is.

CHAPTER FOUR

AZALEA

Two days have passed, and I never thought I would be so relieved for Kyson to be out of the castle. He has been driving me up the wall, constantly watching my every move and forcing vitamins down my throat. It has only been a week since we found out about the pregnancy, and he's already becoming overbearing. He had explained that one week in human pregnancy equated to three or four weeks for Lycans. But if it's only been a week, I dread to think about what a fortnight will bring. Nevertheless, there is a silver lining to his absence – Abbie will be returning tomorrow. The prospect of her company brings a welcome relief to the monotony of castle life, especially since Kyson had forbidden me from helping Peter, the stable boy, or assisting Clarice. I might die of boredom before he gets back.

When I wake up to find him off on business, I feel relieved. This relief is short-lived, however, when I find out, he assigns me a babysitter in the form of Liam. Liam is... let's just say... eccentric. Despite his disturbing sense of humor, he has a way of entertaining Dustin and me, who doesn't seem to mind his presence either.

"My Queen," Liam greets as he walks into the room. I roll my eyes playfully and scoot to the edge of the bed upon seeing him enter. In his hands are the dreaded vitamins and a green, chunky-looking smoothie that Kyson has been making me drink three times a day. The concoction tastes absolutely dreadful. "Bottoms up," Liam says, holding out the glass of green sludge and the pills.

"I think I'll pass on that," I reply with a smirk.

"Your royal pain in the ass instructed me to ensure you drink this lovely concoction that looks like snot and baby shit, my Queen," Liam says as if he is getting some sort of pleasure out of making me drink this. "It can't be that bad," he adds, thrusting the cup toward me.

"Have you tasted it yourself?" I ask skeptically.

"No, but I watched him make it before he left, and he was very insistent that you drink this lovely glass of vileness," Liam explains.

"What he doesn't know won't hurt him or my stomach," I reply, cringing at the thought of the taste. It's a flavor that's hard to forget.

"Just take a sip, and I can say I witnessed you drinking it," Liam suggests. I raise an eyebrow at him – he will have to pin me down to get me to drink that.

"If you can stomach it, then I'll give it a try," I challenge. Liam shrugs and sighs, holding the glass up.

"There's not much I haven't had in my mouth, my Queen, but if it gets you to drink it, I'll have a little sippy sip," he says, bringing the glass to his lips. He tips it back, taking a mouthful. I watch as he struggles to swallow, covering his mouth with his fist as he gags and coughs dramatically. He forces it down, looking as though he is swallowing a golf ball, and appears visibly pained. Just as he continues sputtering, Dustin walks in carrying my breakfast tray.

"Good God, that tastes worse than that prostitute I went down on," Liam gasps, shaking his head. Both Dustin and I recoil in disgust. "What? The woman could have told me. How was I to know she was a hooker, and I was her fifteenth client for the day?" he mumbles the last part. My face twists in disgust, and so does Dustin's. We could have definitely gone without that information.

"Wait, if she was a prostitute, how did you not know?" I ask, genuinely curious.

"To be fair, I was pretty drunk. I thought it was a hotel. Turns out, instead of a mint on my pillow, it had a woman," Liam explains, taking another sip of the drink as he rambled on. Suddenly, he heaves, spitting the green substance all over Dustin. Dustin tenses, his face covered in the repulsive liquid, while Liam drops the glass onto the tray Dustin is holding. Frantically, Liam digs into his pocket and pulls out a small glass bottle that fits in the palm of his hand. The potent scent tells me it's liquor. He quickly downs its contents, gulping it until the bottle is empty.

"Ah, nasty," Liam said, wiping his mouth. I pressed my lips together, trying not to laugh at the horrified look on Dustin's face as he stood frozen in shock. Finally turning his head, Liam noticed that he had spat the drink all over Dustin and choked on his laughter before regaining his composure as an enraged Dustin glared at him.

"Well, that shirt was damn ugly anyway. All good. I'll get you cleaned up," Liam said nonchalantly, taking out a handkerchief to scrub Dustin's face.

Dustin growled in frustration. "It's my uniform! And you're wearing the same one," he snapped as Liam cleaned his shirt and face.

"One sec," Liam said, licking the handkerchief wrapped around his finger before scrubbing at Dustin's chin.

"They're good as new," Liam exclaims.

"You did not just clean me with your spit," Dustin snarls.

"Ah, come on, Dustin, not the worst part of me you have had on your face," Liam says, and Dustin's face turns bright red. He shoots Liam a look.

"Liam!" Dustin snaps.

"What, I was just saying," Liam shrugs.

"Little sensitive this one," Liam says, sending me a wink.

"Do you have no manners? She is the Queen. You can't speak like, ah," he thrusts the tray at Liam before storming out.

"Wonder what crawled up his ass... besides me, of course," Liam muses, watching Dustin leave. Unsure of how to respond, I simply shake my head and wander off to the bathroom, leaving Liam behind. After a quick shower and change of clothes, I feel refreshed and ready to find something to occupy my time.

As Liam escorts me downstairs, the castle seems unusually quiet. Most of the guards had accompanied Kyson on a raid of a nearby pack, leaving only a handful behind to secure the castle, which is locked down like a fortress in his absence.

"We could go for a walk in the gardens, my Queen. The King doesn't..." Liam begins, but his sentence is cut short as he suddenly grabs my shoulder and pulls me back. Within seconds, he presses me against the wall, covering my mouth with his hand.

My heart races, pounding erratically in my chest as I stare into Liam's eyes. I have never seen such a serious side of him, which makes me all the more worried. The playful man I have grown accustomed to is gone, replaced by a darker, more sinister version, alert and instinctual. His eyes flicker strangely, a sadistic gleam reflecting in them as they darken. I see his canines extended past his top lip. I hear Clarice's frantic voice echoes down the hall before the doors adjacent to the staircase burst open. Liam pushes me further behind him as men in armor flood the halls from every direction. My hands tremble as I cling to the back of Liam's shirt, wondering what is going on.

Guns raised, four other men – unmistakably Lycans – clad in suits enter the foyer. Clarice rushes in after them, her voice filled with anxiety.

"May I ask what this is about, Mr. Crux?" Liam inquires, motioning for Clarice to join him with a subtle gesture of his hand. She hurries to his side, whispering something urgently. I catch only the tail end of her sentence, mentioning how the guards had been taken out. Nervously, she glances at me from behind Liam. He nods, but his eyes remain fixed on the armed men surrounding us.

CHAPTER FIVE

AZALEA

The mindlink crackles open as Liam desperately calls for the guards, his voice filled with urgency, increasing my heart rate and panic. But there is only silence in response. A disconcerting silence hangs heavy in the air, causing a knot of unease to form in the pit of their stomachs.

Yet, despite the lack of any answer from the guards outside, Kyson opens the mindlink, and his voice flits through our heads.

'What is it?' Kyson asks, his voice laced with concern and a touch of apprehension.

'The council is here. Get home. Now,' Liam's voice comes through the link, tinged with a mix of frustration and desperation as his head turns, taking in all the council members and guns trained on us.

'Don't let them in. I am on my way,' Kyson responds.

'Too late.'

'Azalea?'

'Get here, Kyson. I am all that is left,' Liam growls, his words laced with fierce protectiveness as he slams shut the mindlink, cutting off any further communication.

As Liam takes a deep breath to steady himself, he walks down with purposeful strides to confront the unwelcome visitors, standing in front of me still, he pushes me further behind him.

"How may I help you, gentlemen?" Liam asks, walking down to greet them.

"We have had a complaint," the tallest member of the council states coldly, his voice dripping with authority and superiority.

"So you thought you would break into the Kingdom? The King isn't here, so I am sure we can reschedule," Liam retorts, a bit of his humor slipping back into his tone. The tall council member matches Kyson's height effortlessly; his obsidian eyes fixated on Liam with an unsettling gaze. He then peers behind Liam, his gaze finding me, and he stares at me curiously, giving the air a sniff.

"Clarice, take the new girl upstairs," Liam commands, but the tall council member steps forward, causing Liam's hand to instinctively fall on his chest, a silent warning.

The energy in the air shifts, crackling with tension as Clarice grabs my arm, pushing me up the stairs. The man's presence is foreboding, commanding attention and respect. He steps forward, disregarding Liam's attempt to redirect him.

"She remains. We aren't to see the King but to find two women, an Abbie and the Queen."

"As I said, the King isn't here, and neither is Abbie, and neither is the Queen," Liam growls, looking at the man whose gaze has not left me. His eyes then dart back and forth between the council member and the men surrounding him, their guns glinting ominously in the dim light when one presses against his chest.

The man watching me tilts his head to the side. "Now that would be a lie because she reeks of the King's scent," he growls.

"And as I said, the King is not here, so I will escort you off the premises, gentlemen. No need to frighten everyone here," Liam retorts.

Clarice's grip on my arm tightens, pulling me further away from the unfolding confrontation. Fear courses through my veins like venomous poison, constricting my thoughts and actions making me sluggish, and I follow her when another voice fills the room.

Just as Liam is about to make his next move, another voice cuts through the chaos, commanding attention and freezing everyone in their tracks. The sheer force behind it sends shivers down my spines.

"She goes up those stairs, shoot him, and the woman," the voice echoes through the room, its authority leaving no room for argument. Clarice gasps, her eyes wide with terror as they meet mine, silently conveying the gravity of the situation to not move right now.

"Clarice, take her upstairs," Liam orders, his voice filled with a dangerous edge. I swallow, turning my attention back to these men surrounding Liam.

"What is this about?" I demand, and the man smirks as my command rolls over him but has no effect. He looks amused at my attempt.

"If you would come with me, my Queen," he says with a mocking tone, his words dripping with falseness.

"She is not going anywhere with you," Liam snarls, stepping into the council member's path and placing a firm hand on his chest. The tension in the room intensifies as the other men surrounding Liam move closer, their guns pressing against him. A palpable sense of danger hangs in the air, threatening to explode at any moment. The men holding guns step aside to allow the other three men into my line of vision, all of them dressed impeccably in tailored suits.

"You must be Azalea. I see you have met Mr. Crux. I am a council elder. My name is Denali," he says.

This man, Denali, oozes authority, and is clearly the one in charge. He smirks, his cold blue eyes looking up at me as he sweeps thick blonde hair from his face. He also speaks with a thick accent I can't quite place.

"And this is my brother, Larkin," Denali says, motioning towards the man beside him in a tailored blue suit, his blonde hair tied neatly at the nape of his neck. Larkin possesses the same cruel, sharp features as Denali, a mirror image of him.

"And this is Kendrick," he says, motioning to the last man who is missing an eye. A long, jagged scar stretches from his hairline to his chin, his lips twisted into a permanent snarl. He moves forward with an unsettling grace, his one-eyed gaze fixated on me with an intensity that sends shivers down my spine.

He takes a step toward me, and Liam moved quickly, stepping into his path and grabbing the front of his suit jacket.

"Touch her, and I will remove your other eye," Liam snarls, his words laced with a lethal promise. Kendrick responds with a snarl of his own.

Denali intervenes quickly before the tension can escalate further. "No need for that, Liam. You are outnumbered. We are here for the rogue girl and the Queen. There is no reason for things to turn messy," Denali states calmly, his voice carrying an air of authority that brooks no argument.

"Not without the King present," Liam retorts, turning his attention squarely towards Denali.

"We are well within our rights to enter. As council members, we have immunity into any pack, even the King's Pack. We also have a warrant and an entire pack to back our claims. She will be given a chance to have her say, but for now, she must come with us," Denali states with an air of finality, his words leaving no room for negotiation.

"What claims?" Liam demands.

"There are only two laws that are upheld to this degree, Liam. You know that, so if you would follow me, Queen Azalea, we can settle this and bring the other girl," he says, motioning toward me.

"Abbie isn't here," I tell him.

"Very well, this won't take long, we brought the truth serum, so it should be settled quickly," he says, motioning for his men.

Liam growls, and all hell breaks loose. The tension in the room reaches its breaking point as the men surrounding Liam tighten their grip on their guns, their fingers itching to pull the trigger.

A sudden racket of gunshots and chaos erupts, tearing through the air like thunder. Liam's body shifts in a blur of motion as he fights against an overwhelming number of guards. But my attention is torn away from the unfolding battle as Clarice grabs my arm, pulling me desperately up the stairs to safety amidst the confusion.

The sound of gunfire and screams reverberates through the castle, haunting my every step. Panic courses through my veins as Clarice and I race away, searching for a hiding place. My heart pounds in my chest, my breaths coming in ragged gasps as I struggle to comprehend the magnitude of the situation.

'Kyson!' I scream through the link, my voice filled with desperation and terror.

'An hour out, fucking pull over!' Kyson's voice crackles through the link. *'Hide. I will find you,'* he promises. I feel him shift through the bond just as Clarice stuffs me into an unfamiliar room. She looks around, and so do I as I hear footsteps. My entire body shakes, and I find myself in the forbidden room across from Kyson's old quarters.

"Stay here. I will lead them away," Clarice whispers urgently.

"Lock the door," she says, cracking the door open and peering out. I move to go after her when she slips out and shuts the door. I quickly lock the door and glance around toward the window. Hundreds of people stand out front the gates, and I step back so they won't see me.

'Where are you?' Kyson says through the link.

'The room across from your old Quarters,' I tell him, watching in horror as I see Dustin lying unconscious on the cobble driveway along with a heap of guards. Men are handcuffing their hands behind their back, all of them unconscious with darts sticking out of them. I hear a barrage of yelling, without being able to clearly make out what they're hearing. Liam is being dragged out, fighting against his restraints, his body twisting and arching as he's forced to shift back.

Multiple darts are in his back, legs, and neck when a guard wearing black camo lifts his gun and shoots him in the chest three times with more darts. His legs go out from under him and drench his entire body in blood. Just then, I hear a shrill scream; a female's scream. .

I watch petrified as Clarice is dragged out kicking and screaming with the two boys she had taken in. Denali wipes his face with a handkerchief as he walks out toward the gates when I spot her. *It's her... the woman who stood watching after Kade was killed.*

She is attractive but haughty and menacing. Denali talks to her through the gate, though I can't make out what he's saying. Three other men also stand off to the side, watching him before he turns around. The man with the missing eye wipes the blood off his face before snarling and kicking Liam in the stomach. My hands cover my mouth, and I am so consumed with fear that I've forgotten Kyson is still talking to me through the link.

'Azalea!' he snaps. Denali turns around before reaching for a microphone from one of his guards. He turns to face the castle, bringing the microphone to his mouth.

"Queen Azalea, you have been summoned by the council, so you need to step outside," he says slowly. He looks up at the windows, and I remain back out of his line of vision.

"You have two minutes to step out, or we will use deadly force, beginning with..." he looks around before one of the guards grabs Oliver.

At this, Clarice loses it. She writhes free and lunges towards the guard when Mr. Crux punches her in the stomach, knocking her to the ground.

"Two minutes or the rogue boy dies."

'Azalea!' Kyson snaps at me.

'They're going to kill them if I don't,' I whimper.

'Don't you fucking dare.'

'They have Oliver.'

Azalea, I am not far out. Remain where you are,' Kyson says as I watch in horror as they push tiny Oliver to the ground on his knees. Mr. Crux pulls a pistol from inside his jacket and presses it to his head.

"Two minutes Queen Azalea, I can not kill any Lycan here but a rogue, even a child I have the authority too."

'I have to go,' I tell Kyson.

'No, remain where you are,' he orders and I grit my teeth.

'How far out?'

'20 minutes.'

'It's too long,' I tell him, forcing his command off.

"One minute," Denali calls over the microphone, and Oliver cringes away from the gun held to his head.

'Azalea?' Kyson says, his panic smashing into me.

Mr. Crux presses the gun to Oliver's temple, and I rush toward the window, throwing it open.

"Wait, I will come down," I scream to them. Mr. Crux lifts his head to look at me while Mr. Denali smirks.

"We thought you would change your mind." He nods toward some of his men, who race toward the castle.

"They will meet you at the foyer doors," Denali called through the microphone, and I nod, moving back inside the window. I glance around at the baby's room. One that was made for me had Kyson found me when my parents were killed. Yet it offers no protection for me now. Swallowing down the bile in my throat, I move toward the door and open it.

CHAPTER SIX

AZALEA

The moment I step out of the safety of the castle doors, I am surrounded and dragged out of the castle, my heart racing. I fear more for the life of my unborn child than my own. The guards have me in a tight hold, and I struggle against them as I am led to the front of the castle. Kyson's voice is constant in my head, urging me to stall them. His fear is potent, and I wonder what sort of history he has with the council that they would be daring enough to go against the Lycan King.

"Azalea, my Queen. So lovely for you to join us," Denali purrs, causing my skin to crawl as he approaches closer. He clicks his fingers at one of his men, who shoves me toward the iron gates and handcuffs my wrists to the solid bars. My heart skips a beat as everyone takes a few steps back as they watch beyond the gate.

"Fear not. You will have your say. We just have a few questions for you. This is merely a precaution," Denali says, gripping the back of my neck to turn my face toward his.

"Precaution?" I scoff, glaring up at him. "You have me handcuffed and surrounded by your guards. I think that goes beyond a mere precaution."

Denali's grip tightens on my neck, cutting off my air supply. Panic sets in as I struggle against my restraints, but it's no use. His hold is too strong.

"You are in no position to sass me, Queen Azalea," he growls, his face inches from mine. "You may be the Lycan King's mate, but you are still a member of our council and are expected to follow our rules."

"I am not a member of your council," I shoot back, gasping for breath as his grip loosens slightly.

"But that is where you're wrong, even the King's mate is expected to uphold the laws of our people."

"Are you really that gutless that you had to wait for my mate to leave?" I ask him, and he laughs sadistically.

He steps away, and I can see Oliver kneeling next to Clarice, crying, huddled in Logan's arms. I turn my attention back to Denali, who sneers at me.

"It is a mere coincidence that the King wasn't home. We were sent the report and investigated; this is just a questioning."

"If that is all it is, why did you feel the need to take out my guards and handcuff me to a damn gate?" I spit back at him.

"Because we are aware of the pact the guards hold, they will fight. We haven't hurt them, just made them more compliant," he states.

"What pact?" I asked, a little confused.

"The King never told you?" he asks, and I glance around at the crowd of onlookers watching me. "Regardless, I am here to administer the serum, ask the questions, and choose *punishment if necessary."*

'15 minutes, love. Keep stalling. Leave the link open, so I can hear what is going on. Help is coming,' Kyson says in my head. I swallow when Mr. Crux approaches with a vial.

'Landeena people, head to the castle your Queen needs you,' Kyson

calls through the link. I don't have time to process his words. The town is a good 15 minutes away. What would the people do if they got here?

"What is this about?" I ask, knowing full well by the woman standing on the other side of the gates watching me. Denali follows my gaze and motions for one of the guards to let her in. The gate opens beside me, and the smug bitch steps inside, her heeled boots clinking on the stone driveway before they close it. She moves behind me and stops beside him, folding her arms across her chest.

"Cassandra," I snarl.

"So you do know each other, wonderful. Cassandra here says you commanded Abbie to reject her husband, Alpha Kade and made him accept the rejection; she also claims that you also stole the pack's future Luna," Denali says.

"That is not true. Abbie tried rejecting him. He was abusing her," I tell Denali before glaring at Cassandra. "With her help," I growl.

"That wasn't what I asked. I asked if you abused your power as the King's mate and broke a sacred law regarding mate bonds?"

"As I said, he was abusing Abbie. He sexually assaulted her."

"And where is Abbie to verify this?" Denali asks, tilting his head toward me. He nods to Mr. Crux, who moves toward me with the vial. I clench my teeth together.

'Kyson!' I rush through the mindlink.

'Any minute,' Kyson replies when Denali grabs my hair, ripping my head back while Mr. Crux pinches my cheeks, stuffing the vial in my mouth. Denali checks his watch while I cough and gag at its taste. Yet it tastes familiar in a way. It almost reminds me of Kyson.

'You can fight the effects,' Kyson links to me. *'Focus, love, that serum is made from my blood. You can resist it.'*

A minute or so goes past, and Mr. Crux nods to Denali.

"Did you command Luna Abbie to reject her mate, Alpha Kade?" Denali asks. I grit my teeth. Fear so palpable it made goosebumps rise on my skin as the urge to answer rolls through me, making my body tense.

'Nearly there, fight it,' Kyson snarls when I hear a commotion outside the gates. Denali glances out the gates to the cobble road where Kade's pack stands. He waves some of his men to sort out whatever is happening, and they rush out the gate and down the road.

"Answer me," Denali demands. I don't know what Kyson had meant about fighting it. Fighting against it is causing me to break out into a sweat, my stomach twisting painfully. Is this bad for my baby?

"Yes," I gasp. Meanwhile, fighting breaks out outside the gates and down in the gully before the driveway. Denali looks toward the commotion outside the gates.

"Enough proof, bring the whip," he says, wandering off to talk to someone behind me. I look over my shoulder, twisting my neck to see what is going on behind me. I gulp when I see the barbed whip in the man's hand.

'Tell them I commanded you to,' Kyson yells through the bond.

'I can't,' I say.

'You can and fucking will, you're pregnant Azalea, tell them I commanded you to.'

I try to open my mouth to lie, yet whatever the truth serum contains does not allow me to breathe a lie.

'Azalea!' Kyson booms in my head. I choke on the words, trying to spit them.

'Don't you dare fight me. I'm sorry, love, I have no choice,' he murmurs when I feel his command smash me through the bond and mindlink. It rolls over me, causing crippling pain as he orders me to blame him.

"Kyson ordered me to do it," I blurt. Mr. Crux grips my face, and Denali comes back over.

"Excuse me?" Denali asks.

'Say it again!' Kyson commands through the bond. Sweat glistens on my skin and I feel like I'm going to be sick.

"The King ordered me to command them," I choke out, gasping

for air. Denali and Mr. Crux look at each other before turning to Cassandra.

"Is what she says true?" Denali asks her. She opens her mouth and closes it.

"Well?" Denali snaps.

"I...I don't know. I only got there to see her command them both. What does it matter? She still did it," Cassandra says in her nasal voice.

'Good girl,' Kyson says, letting the command slide off me.

CHAPTER SEVEN

AZALEA

Denali and Mr. Crux talk among themselves while Cassandra digs a pack of smokes out of her leather jacket.

"How could you, after everything you did to her?" I ask Cassandra. She pops her hip, lighting a smoke before stepping closer.

"My husband is dead because of her. Your mate killed him. I now have to raise my kids without their father because of that bitch," Cassandra spits at me. I growl, my canines slipping past my gums as anger courses through me. She turns to face the council members who are now whispering among themselves behind me.

"She still commanded them, but I have one more question before we proceed."

I turn my head, and he steps closer.

"Did you know it was against the law to break a mate bond against their will?" Denali asks. My brows furrow, wondering why he is asking. I fight the urge to answer instantly.

"Yes," I breathe.

"And you still did it?" Denali asks.

"He was hurting her, so yes."

"Well then, regardless of whether the King commanded you, you knew better. Being his mate, you are capable of fighting his commands, therefore will be held accountable," Cassandra smirks at his words puffing on her cigarette.

"What are they going to do to me?" I asked Mr. Crux, who was still standing beside me. Though I already knew by the whip in Kendricks's hand. My heart raced a little faster when Mr. Crux started ripping the back of my dress open.

"You broke a sacred law, you may be the King's Mate, but you abused your authority, so you will be punished. 1000 lashes, or until Cassandra deems fit," he chuckles. "About time the King is held accountable for errors," Mr. Crux sneered. I swallowed and chuckled.

"Silly girl, just because you're the King's mate, that doesn't give you the power to break the law,"

"He was abusing her," I scream at him.

"And where is your proof?" Mr. Crux demands.

"Ask me, or is your truth serum, not 100 percent," I spit back at him. He grips my chin, pinching it tightly.

"Truth or not, you broke the law. We uphold it. We were looking for a reason to take him down, but if we can't, you will do," he laughs.

"Coward," I retort. Mr. Crux grips my hair, yanking my head back painfully.

"Oh, Kendrick will. He won't hold back, not after the King took his sight."

I swallow, and my breathing becomes a little harsher.

"Your people are coming. Tell them who you are. It will buy you some time, I didn't want to risk it but we have no choice."

"What?"

"Your parents-"

I don't get a chance to listen to what he says when I feel the crack of the whip bite into my flesh, making me scream. Hooks slash up my spine and dig into my shoulder. My scream reverberates around the castle grounds when he rips them out.

My knees buckle underneath me. My blood sprays across those on the other side of the fence when all hell breaks loose. Kade's pack starts running toward the fence, suddenly trying to get in. My knees drag across the ground from the force of the gate being pushed inward. I can't see past them to see what is happening and don't even care when the whip tears into me again.

Gunshots ring out, and I hang limply in handcuffs, my wrist bent backward painfully and on the verge of snapping under my weight. I feel the barbs tear out of my skin, ripping my flesh away. My head feels too limp to hold upright and all I can think about is the pain radiating through my back when someone's head is shoved through the iron-barred gates beside me. I blink deliriously, finding it odd. How did it fit through the bars?

Screams ring out loudly, but all I can do is blink at the man's head stuck between the bars. It takes me a few moments to realize that the bottom half of his body is missing. My head rolls to the side, and I see the men in armor backing up, guns trained down the driveway as they fire. I thought my eyes were deceiving me when I watch around 50 Lycans ripping into Kade's pack members and the council's men, ripping them limb from limb. People run everywhere to escape as chaos breaks loose.

I can't tear my gaze away from the horrors on the other side of the gate, my eyes wide, and I feel sick to my stomach. Hearing screaming, I turn to find Cassandra. Her hands cup her mouth as she watches, helplessly, as her pack is torn to shreds. Suddenly I drop to the ground, and I don't even realize someone is uncuffing me. My body is limp as I stare around at the slaughter. Hands grab me, ripping me against someone's chest. My back arches as I try to get the pressure away from my back.

Seconds later, the iron gates burst open. And there's a knife pressed to my throat by the person holding me. Out of the corner of my eyes, I see a group of Lycans stalking into the castle grounds.

I am vaguely aware of Kyson talking to me, yet I cannot understand what he is trying to tell me.

"Get the car ready?" Denali says. The Lycans circle us before dropping on their knees around us. The whole thing is surreal as I look around, trying to figure out what is happening, when I notice Dustin roll over as he starts to wake.

"Take so much as one step toward us, and I will kill her. You have all just interfered with the council. There are severe penalties for obstructing justice," Denali says, walking past me to address the Lycans kneeling. They growl and snarl, watching him. But the council members are all Lycan, and I feel his aura demanding them to submit, forcing them to remain where they were.

"Now, I am willing to let this slide, so back up," Denali ordered.

"She may be King Kyson's Queen, but she will be held accountable for her actions," Denali snarls, causing Dustin to laugh maniacally.

Denali turns his head to look at him as Dustin sits up, his arms still cuffed behind his back. He starts ripping at his handcuffs, once, twice, thrice, and I hear his wrists snap and shoulders dislocate before he rolls his shoulders, bringing his hands around to the front. Kendrick runs at him, but Dustin moves quickly, sweeping his legs out from under him and pivoting on his knee, so he was suddenly on Kendricks's back, his knee pressed to the back of the man's neck.

"And who are you? Let Kendrick up now," Mr. Crux growls, dropping me at Denali's feet. Dustin rebreaks his wrist before gripping Kendricks's hair and ripping his head back.

"No, wrong question Denali. The question you should be asking is, who is Azalea? Does her name ring any bells to you?" Dustin sneers.

CHAPTER EIGHT

AZALEA

Denali towers over me, his gaze piercing and menacing. Meanwhile, Cassandra trembles behind him, clutching the back of his suit jacket for protection. With a forceful shove, Denali pushes her aside, causing her to stumble and fall onto the ground. A sharp shriek escapes her lips as she lands hard on her backside.

Kendrick, desperate to intervene, attempts to shift his position underneath Dustin's knee. But before he can make a move, Dustin emits a low growl, grabbing Kendrick's head and twisting it forcefully towards him.

The sight is too much for me to bear. My stomach churns, and I felt an overwhelming urge to vomit. As my body convulses, Dustin snaps Kendrick's neck with a sickening crack. Rising to his feet, he casually wipes his hands clean and removes the darts embedded in his legs and chest.

Dustin's voice cut through the tension like a knife. "Does the name Azalea Ivy Landeena ring any bells for you?" he asks, his gaze shifting between Mr. Crux, Denali, and the other man named Larkin.

I lay on the ground, my blood pooling around me, struggling to keep my eyes open as waves of dizziness washed over me. The presence of Kyson, growing closer by the moment, is the only thing keeping me from succumbing to unconsciousness.

"The Landeenas are dead," Denali declares, though there is a slight falter in his usual confident demeanor. He's uncertain; his eyes darting between Dustin and me. I can't comprehend why my heritage matters to the council or what significance it holds in this escalating confrontation.

"Ask her who her mother is," Kyson's voice rings out, causing me to turn my head towards him. When our eyes meet, a feral growl escapes Kyson's lips, sending shivers down my spine. The Lycans surrounding us instinctively step aside as Kyson storms through the gates, his gaze fixed on Denali. He approaches him with a predatory stride, treating him as nothing more than prey. With a swift motion, Kyson grips Denali's throat, cutting off his breath.

"You dare enter my Kingdom unannounced and attack my Queen," Kyson roars, his voice filled with fury. Denali struggles to breathe, clutching at Kyson's hands in a desperate attempt to free himself.

"The law states we can enter," Denali chokes out, his face turning an alarming shade of purple as Kyson's grip tightens. Kyson glances at Dustin, who rushes towards me, pulling me up so that I am sitting upright.

"Your laws are nothing but bullshit, and you know it. She told you that I ordered her to command them, and yet you still laid your filthy paws on my mate," Kyson snarls. Mr. Crux reaches out, attempting to calm the situation.

"Crux, I'll give you two seconds to correct that mistake," Kyson warns, causing Mr. Crux to hastily retract his hand and back away in surrender. Kyson locks eyes with him.

"You will mind your tongue when speaking of my mate. Now, as I was saying, Denali, you are hereby sentenced for treason," Kyson growls, releasing his grip on Denali. The council member falls to the ground at Kyson's feet, gasping for air and clutching his throat.

"Treason!" Larkin exclaims, rushing forward. However, upon meeting Kyson's fierce gaze, he freezes in his tracks.

"Now, let me introduce my mate," Kyson declares, motioning towards Dustin. With great care, Dustin scoops up my bloodied body into his arms, cradling me against his chest. He crouches beside Denali, who lifts his head to meet my gaze, his face flushed and contorted with pain.

"Do you recognize those eyes, Denali?" Kyson asks

Denali gulps, looking up at Kyson with a mixture of fear and recognition.

"You made the grave mistake of assuming my mate was just an ordinary Lycan. Now you will pay for your treason and attempted murder of her majesty Azalea Ivy Landeena, the rightful heir to the Landeena Kingdom. I may be bound by council laws, but..."

"How is this possible?" Denali interrupts, turning to his brother Larkin before seeking confirmation from Mr. Crux.

"That kingdom fell," Mr. Crux interjects, stepping forward.

"Yes, and now it rises," Kyson declares, motioning towards the Lycans who are kneeling around us. A chorus of growls fill the air as they glared at the council elders. My vision starts to blur as my wounds continue to bleed, staining Dustin's clothes.

"Now, can anyone explain why the Landeena bloodline is exempt from the council's laws?" Kyson demands, his gaze shifting between the three men.

Denali swallows, rising to his hands and knees. "Please show leniency, I had no knowledge of your identity," he pleads, gripping my arm in a feeble attempt to plead for mercy. But Kyson swiftly places his foot on Denali's shoulder, forcefully pushing him back. Dustin stands protectively beside me, holding me closer in his arms.

"My King, I swear had I known," Denali stutters.

"No one knew. I knew the hunters would come after her. Only those in my castle knew her true identity, and you have not only harmed my pregnant mate but broke the very laws you are supposed to uphold," Kyson booms.

"We were only-" Mr. Crux says, but one look from Kyson makes him shut up.

"Looking for a way to punish me, I am not stupid. I know the council has been looking for a reason to take me down for centuries. Had she mentioned who she was, I know you would have killed her before I got here, but now that I am. Who dares to answer the question I asked?"

"My King, my brother didn't know. Surely, you can't punish him for such an innocent mistake," Larkin interjects, rushing forward in defense of his sibling. Kyson turns his gaze towards Denali's brother.

"He should have considered the consequences of laying a hand on the Empress of Alpha's," Kyson growls, his foot coming down on Denali's head with a brutal stomp. Larkin wails in agony as his brother's skull is crushed beneath Kyson's unyielding force. Mr. Crux lunges at Larkin, grabbing him before he can reach Kyson. The sight is too much for me to bear, and I lurch forward in Dustin's arms, vomiting as brain matter splatters onto the ground.

Ignoring Larkin's anguished cries, Kyson turns his attention back to me, gently taking me from Dustin's embrace. "Shh, I've got you now," Kyson whispers, his voice filled with tenderness. The sparks emanating from his skin provide a soothing sensation that eases the pain coursing through my body.

"I suggest you leave. Enough council members have died. Dustin, take that bitch to the dungeons."

Cassandra screams and tries to run, but Dustin grabs her quickly, and Kyson turns to the rest of the Lycan still on their knees.

"Kill the lot of them," he says as my head rolls back, and I see what's left of Cassandra's pack start running, their screams ring out loudly when Kyson turns on his heel and walks toward the castle.

Kyson lifts me higher, burying his face in my neck, the sparks from his skin soothe the pain coursing through me.

"Hang on, love, I will take care of you," he purrs.

CHAPTER NINE

KYSON

Azalea whimpers as she jostles in my arms. Her blood streams down my arms as I make my way to the bedroom. I kick the doors open, and they bang against the walls. Dustin comes rushing in behind me, runs past me and toward the bathroom, shoving the door open and turning the shower on.

Not only is she losing an alarming amount of blood, but I know those barbs are dipped in wolfsbane and water-hemlock, which are used to prevent healing. Water pours from the shower head, and Dustin turns to me. He uses his claws to shred what's left of her dress, letting it fall away in tatters to the floor.

"Give her here, you shift," he says, holding his arms out for her. I pass her to him. She's like a rag doll in his arms, her body flopping around as he steps into the shower, forcing her back under the spray to rinse the poison off her while I shift. Using one hand, he turns the other shower head on, turning the head and aiming it at her back. Moments later, Liam runs in, looking worse for wear. I don't even care that they're all seeing her naked. My sole focus is on stopping the wolfsbane from soaking into her system and killing our baby.

"What do you need?" Liam asks.

"Alcohol," I tell him, knowing I am about to ingest whatever was in her system, and hopefully, the alcohol would burn it out.

"On it," he says, disappearing out the door. Dustin's arm moves to the back of her neck and the other under her ass, exposing her back to me, and I waste no time running my tongue over her wounds, healing them and sucking the poison out where the barbs had dug into her flesh and ripped off her skin in chunks.

A growl escapes me, the wolfsbane burning my throat, and I heave, retching when I get a huge mouthful of it. My hand hits the wall, steadying me as I throw up before returning to heal the other two long gashes up her back. Her wounds eventually close, and I know the wolfsbane and water hemlock are gone, or she wouldn't have healed.

My throat is now on fire, and I press my face under the stream, banging my head on the shower head because I am taller than it in this form. Liam rushes back in with a bottle of tequila. Not my go-to, but it will do. He breaks the cap, thrusting the bottle at me, and I grab it, retching again as my surroundings spin. Suddenly, I'm seeing double. My legs give out under me when I am forced to shift back, my ass hitting the hard tiled floor in the process.

"Shit, take her," Dustin says, passing Azalea off to Liam. Liam grabs her, wrapping a towel around her before disappearing out the door as Dustin crouches over my gasping figure. My lungs feel like they have been engulfed in flames, my blood boiling in my veins. He pries my mouth open just as Liam comes in. Dustin pries my eyelids open, his hair and clothes both drenched as he looks down at me. He looks over his shoulder at Liam.

"Azalea?" I mumble.

"Damian just got here. He is with her. He sent for a Doctor."

I nod or try to. Dustin grips my jaw, yet my arms feel numb as I try to lift the bottle to my lips. Liam snatches the bottle from my hand.

"Come on, big fella, down the hatch it goes," he says, tipping the tequila down my throat. I gasp, breathing it in, and choke and sputter as it goes down the wrong pipe.

"Now, now, none of that. Dustin can give you some pointers on how to swallow if needed," Liam mocks, earning a menacing growl from Dustin. Liam pours more in my mouth this time, not waterboarding me with it. I gulp it down, feeling it warm my stomach and entire body. Ghastly stuff, yet I can feel it diluting the poison I had ingested. I feel it working through my system, not that it makes me feel any better.

My head lolls forward as the poison burns out, leaving me shitfaced and on the verge of passing out drunk. Liam slaps my face with his hand, tilting my head back. My eyes try to close, and he smirks, chugging the rest of the bottle before passing the now empty bottle to Dustin.

"Never thought I would see the day when I had to carry you over the threshold bridal style," he chuckles, grabbing me and tossing me over his shoulder, jostling me in such a way that the tequila threatens to come back up. "Hmm, caveman style, what can I say? I am a barbarian," Liam chuckles.

"Pretty fucking ugly bride, though," he laughs, slapping my ass. If I could, I would hit him for that. Damn, this man is a handful sometimes. It's like he doesn't have an off switch. I know he swings both ways, but he really toes the line, that's for sure. He walks out of the room, dropping me on the bed. Meanwhile, Damian comes into view on top of me, chucking a towel over my waist and prying my eyelids open.

"Council," I mutter.

"Gone, those that showed from the pack are dead. Cassandra is in dungeons," Damian says. I sigh.

"Rest. I have everything handled."

"She knows now," I try to tell him, and his eyes dart past me. I try to turn my head to see her, but it feels ridiculously heavy.

"She does, but you have the bond. She loves you, Kyson," Damian says. Yet, that isn't my worry. Once she figures out her Alpha voice, she outranks me. Yet even that doesn't worry me. I could still control her with the calling, the one thing she could never resist. What worries me is her realizing I kept it from her. I'm not even sure why I did that. Probably because I figured she had the power to leave me if she really wanted to.

Empress of Alphas could not be tied by a bond; she could walk away, and I would be destroyed and powerless to stop her. I couldn't lose her. Yet now it would be out, everyone would know, and they would come for her. It was only a matter of time. Her blood was more precious than gold, and if she shares the same gifts as her mother, I know she had one trait of her father's. But if she obtained both, they would come for her. Come for her and our baby. Her blood was the key to putting the werewolf and Lycan species into extinction, or it could be their salvage. If the hunters get wind of her, they will never stop, and without a doubt, I will spend the rest of my life fighting to keep her safe.

CHAPTER TEN

ABBIE

Gannon tells me Azalea has been hurt because of me. Well, he doesn't say directly that it's my fault, but that's how it feels. She wouldn't be in this situation if not for me. The weight of guilt settles heavily on my shoulders as I realize she might have been spared if I had just listened to everybody and never followed Kade. It frustrates me that even in death, Kade's influence lingers, casting shadows over my present, and preventing me from moving on. Gannon's phone rings suddenly, and my gaze darts to where it rests.

Damian's face illuminates the screen, prompting Gannon to pull the car over to take his call. A sense of nervousness grows within me; Damian rarely calls instead of using the mindlink unless it's urgent.

I recall how Gannon reacted when informed about the council through the mindlink, nearly causing an accident. Perhaps that explains why Damian is opting for a conventional call this time. Gannon steps out of the car and perches on the hood while speaking on the phone. He steals a glance back at me through the window with a hint of nervousness before turning away. His voice escalates in tone as he paces away from me, his words muffled by distance.

We are pulled over on a rough stretch of highway, the relentless stream of passing cars causing our vehicle to shudder. Gannon, his frustration palpable, runs a hand through his disheveled hair before turning his gaze back to the car. Sensing the drop in temperature and the gusts of wind outside, I reach over the back seat to retrieve his jacket, my fingers brushing against the cool leather. With a swift motion, I pull it on and step out of the car, yearning to stretch my legs after hours of confinement. The prolonged sitting has left my senses dulled, my rear numb from the seat.

Raising my arms above my head to stretch, I pace around the front of the car while Gannon distances himself, engaging in a heated conversation with Damian. Leaning against the sleek hood, I observe him closely, catching only fragments of his heated argument.

"You should have eliminated her. By doing so, you could undo all that I have painstakingly accomplished," Gannon snaps into his phone, his voice laced with frustration. He abruptly ends the call and growls under his breath before locking eyes with me.

I rummage in his jacket pocket, finding some red sugar clouds. He always had candy on him. Yet, I never see him eat it. I shrug. *More for myself.* I giggle, opening the little bag and pulling one out while he lights up a smoke.

"Everything alright?" I ask him, and he nods.

"It will be," he says, wandering over to me.

"You found my stash?" he laughs, pointing to the red sugary clouds in my hand. I smile, popping another in my mouth.

"You always have them, yet you never eat them?" I chuckle—the tips of my fingers tinged red from digging them out of the bag. Sugar coats my lips, and I quickly lick them, savoring the sweet taste.

"I don't like sweets," he laughs.

"Then why buy them?" I ask.

"I buy them for you. I know they're your favorite," he says, and I let out a breath.

A shudder runs through me as I think of the only time we were offered sweets, and each time it was a lie. I shake the thought away.

"What?" he asks.

"Nothing, you had me worried for a second, I thought," I shake my head, not understanding why my mind went there.

"You thought what?" He asks

"Nothing, it was a stupid thought, just don't worry about it," I tell him. His brows furrow, and he draws back on his smoke, watching me before blowing a smoke cloud in the air. "How much further?" I ask him.

"About three hours. Why, anxious to get away from me?" he chuckles.

"No!" I roll my eyes.

"Come on then, let's go," he says, holding out his hand. I slide off the hood, and he walks around, opening my door. I shake my head, unsure if he just likes opening doors or thinks I don't know how to open them for myself. I shake my head and climb into the car. We drive, listening to the radio for a while. After a while, he seems off, like something is very wrong. His aura is all over the place.

I pull the candy from my pocket again, and he glances at me. "What were you thinking before?" he asks, and I look at him. He points to the bag in my hand. I don't want to answer, suddenly feeling ashamed for even thinking about it. I know Gannon, and he isn't that sort of monster.

"What did Damian want earlier?" I ask, wanting to change the subject.

Gannon glances at me, his hands tightening on the steering wheel. "I'll answer when you do," he retorts, and I sigh. I turn my gaze to the window, watching the scenery go by.

"So?" he asks. I shrug, turning back to look at him.

"When Azalea and I were little, the butcher used to offer us candy to help him in the basement. We never did. He always gave us strange vibes. We always thought there was something off with him, so when he would ask, we used to tell him Mrs. Daley gave us chores, which she did anyway, so it wasn't technically a lie."

"You thought I was a creep?" he asks appalled, as he should be; no one would like being thought of that way, which makes me feel guilty. However, I couldn't help when the memories float in, uninvited.

"No, just when you said you didn't eat candy, it came to mind. It's just where my mind went for some reason."

"Well, I am definitely not a pedophile. That I can assure you, and do you mean Doyle, that same butcher?"

I cringe hearing his name but nod, looking back out the window. All that seems like a lifetime ago, yet at the same time, I will always remember every detail, remember it like it was yesterday; it only needs the right thing to trigger it and bring it to the forefront of my mind.

"He's dead now. You don't have to worry about him," Gannon says, and I swallow.

"It's my fault, though. I went down to the basement with him. I knew I shouldn't have, but Mrs. Daley said she wouldn't feed us for a week if I didn't help him bring the meat down to the freezers." I clench my eyes, my stomach turning.

"I shouldn't have gone down there. We always made sure we were never around and made sure we were busy when the butcher came to drop the meat off. We both knew something was off about him," I tell him.

"Then why did you?" Gannon asks. My bottom lip quivers.

"Because if I didn't, she would have made Ivy, I mean Azalea. We hadn't eaten in three days. Mrs. Daley used to make us share whatever scraps were left over. But this time, we had gone a while without food. There was nothing left over."

"She used food against you?" Gannon asks, and I nod.

"Mrs. Daley said if I helped him stack the freezers, we could make ourselves a plate and eat with the rest of the children, so I went down there. She said we would have got lashings if I didn't. If I had known what was waiting for me, I would have taken those instead, but we were hungry, and Azalea's back was badly torn up already. She couldn't take more lashings, and some were down to the bone. I just didn't expect what I got when I went down there," I whisper the last part.

CHAPTER ELEVEN

ABBIE

"That doesn't make it your fault," Gannon says. "And afterward?" he asks, and I stare, unblinking out the windshield for a second before my gaze goes to my fingers as I pick at the skin.

"Azalea found me afterward. We cooked dinner, and she fed us. We were allowed a bowl of rice to share. Both of us were starving, yet neither of us touched it. That was the payment, a bowl of rice." A tear escapes, knowing my worth to her was a bowl of rice.

"Mrs. Daley then called us ungrateful, and Azalea," Taking a deep breath, I shut my eyes as the guilt rolls over me in waves. Shame stains my thoughts, knowing she bore over half of her cuts that day because of me. "She was punished for our refusal." My voice comes out weaker than intended, "It was supposed to be just five lashes; cruel nevertheless, but more bearable – Mrs. Daley made it forty."

"Was supposed to be five?" Gannon's question pulls me from my haunted memory. A slight nod is all I manage while battling the fresh onslaught of guilt at recalling how much she suffered for me.

"Yes." Swallowing hard, I manage to find my voice again. "She threw a bowl at Azalea when we defied her at dinner. It shattered against her face. The sharp edge left a bloody trail down Azalea's face and cleaved her eyebrow in two." With a shuddering breath, I vividly picture the gnarled cane with its intimidating whip wrapped around the handle – usually brandished exclusively for Azalea.

My own quiet sob breaks through the silence piped in the horror of what Azalea had endured on behalf of my defiance that night – willingly bearing punishment destined for me.

"What happened?" Gannon asks.

"Mrs. Daley gave her the five lashings, but when it was my turn, Azalea..." My face burns with shame at my next words.

"It hurt, I couldn't sit; it hurt too much. Azalea was already hurt, and she still did it."

"What did she do?" Gannon asks. I chew my lip and glance out the window as that night burns through my vision like I was right there all over again, witnessing it.

"She attacked Mrs. Daley so she wouldn't hit me with the cane." Gannon glances at me, probably shocked at what he is hearing because it shocked me back then too. I believed Mrs. Daley would kill her. "Azalea's back was bleeding everywhere, her cuts from the day before had reopened. Mrs. Daley told me to straddle the chair; usually she made us stand for lashings. But she said her back was sore and wanted to make sure we didn't move on her." A startled laugh comes out of me.

"Her back was sore; that woman didn't know the meaning of a sore back," I chuckle.

"Abbie?" Gannon asks, pulling me back from wherever I drifted off. I suck in a breath, remembering I am supposed to be explaining what happened. "I told her I couldn't sit, and she tried to shove me in the chair. When she grabbed me, Azalea slapped her. I was so shocked I just stood there. We were petrified of that woman, yet Azalea slapped her. Mrs. Daley slapped her back, knocking her to the ground, where she whipped her five more times."

I peer out the window, my mind going back to that haunted

place. "But then, when Mrs. Daley turned back to punish me, she got back up and hit her again, this time knocking Mrs. Daley over."

Tears burn my eyes, and I can still see the blood gushing from Azalea's face where the bowl hit her. I had never seen that much blood before. It ran down her arms and legs, staining her clothes. I gave her my own clothes because I couldn't bear to wear them anymore. Mrs. Daley already whacked her good for that before dinner for wasting clothes. Only to suffer more for me.

"Mrs. Daley smacked her head on the coffee table. She had a nasty bump, she then sent me to my room, but I stayed on the stairs. Mrs. Daley said Azalea was going to get 40 lashings for messing up her face before the Alpha visit. But it was so much more than that."

"Forty Lashings?" Gannon asked, shocked. He growls when I nod casually.

"Most of the scars Azalea has are because of me. She always took most of my punishments after that. Mrs. Daley was brutal with her. That night, Azalea collapsed on the ground, and I watched as she just kept whipping her over and over until she wasn't moving. I thought she was dead. I waited for Mrs. Daley to leave, and I helped her clean up as she did me," I tell him. The car is silent for a few seconds until I can't handle his silence or his burning aura any longer.

"So, what did Damian want?" I ask him, changing the subject.

"They have Cassandra in the dungeons," Gannon answers, and I gulp, biting on my lip to stop it quivering.

"It's up to you what they do with her. That's what Damian called about."

"I get to choose her punishment?" I ask, horrified. Gannon grips the steering wheel tighter, his knuckles turning white under pressure.

"You don't have to do anything, you don't want to. You don't even have to see her if you don't want to. I can handle it when we get back but it is up to you," Gannon says. I swallow and nod.

"And the council?"

"Kyson killed Denali and Kendrick. The other two he let go."

"Why would he let them go?" I ask, confused.

"Because Mr. Crux has immunity, despite Kyson hating him. He also left Lark alive to serve as a reminder that no one is untouchable. Denali and Larkin are from very prominent families."

"What do you mean Mr. Crux has immunity?"

"He has immunity because he is Azalea's cousin," Gannon tells me.

"Then why isn't he ruling then?" I ask confused.

"Because he is an illegitimate child to Garret's brother. Plus, Kyson always held out hope Azalea was alive and that one day he would find her. He refused to believe she was dead until he had proof," Gannon tells me.

"What do you mean?"

"The Landeena's kept her a secret. Kyson knew he would be betrothed to any daughter they had, but for some reason, they never told anyone she was born. We never knew until we heard of their slaughter."

"So why did he think she would be alive?"

"Because Landeena's blood is special. When we learned there was a child, and we couldn't find her, we at first thought the hunters took her."

"But if hunters killed them, why would they want to keep the child?"

"Because Landeena's are venomous," Gannon says, and my brows furrow. I look at him, and he sighs.

"Landeena blood is more potent than even the King's," he adds.

"I am not sure what you are saying," I confess.

"They were the only ones that could make a human a Lycan. Lycans like me, can turn a normal werewolf into a Lycan, but the Landeenas could change a human into a Lycan."

His words shock me. "Wait... Does Azalea know this?" I ask, and Gannon shakes his head.

"And you can't tell her, Abbie. Let Kyson do that."

"I am not going to lie to her."

"I'm not asking you to. I'm just saying don't mention it unless she says something; just don't deliberately mention it. Give Kyson a chance to tell her first."

"Why are they different, though?"

"Because they were the first Lycans. They were created by gods, or so the story goes anyway."

"So the Moon Goddess?"

Gannon nods.

"But if hunters wanted to get rid of Lycans, why would they want to become one?"

"Same reason anyone would, to gain immortality. Landeena and Azure blood is the only blood that could make humans immortal. We believe that is why her parents kept her hidden from everyone except those in the castle."

"They were worried someone would try to take her," I state with a sigh.

"And they did," Gannon says.

"So what, she just has to bite them?"

"Yes, there is more to it though. For me to change you, I only have to mark you and...." He pauses for a second, but I note his hesitation when he changes what he is going to say. "It is part of the reason Kyson wouldn't do it. You could sire to him and basically become an extra mate. It's rare for that to happen when you already have a mate, but it has happened in the past," Gannon explains.

"Can Azalea do it?" I ask thoughtfully. Gannon clenches his jaw but nods.

"Yes, but I would rather change you myself."

"I know, but-"

"You think you aren't worthy of me, but you are. I am the one not worthy of you, Abbie. I want to be with you. I don't care about your past or the shit that has happened. I told you I could wait for anything more as long as I can have you as mine. The rest we can figure out. Just let me love you. That is all I am asking for," he says, cutting me off. I can feel his anger simmering below the surface.

CHAPTER TWELVE

ABBIE

Gannon sighs heavily. "I'm sorry. I just want to be the one to do it."

"Okay, I won't ask Azalea," I tell him, and he lets out a breath.

"But-"

"But you still aren't sure you want to be a Lycan," Gannon says.

"No. I was gonna ask if we could do it tomorrow and not when we got back home," I tell him, rubbing my temples.

"Wait. You will do it?" Gannon asks. I look up at him to see his shocked face.

It's true, I had been unsure, even amid the multiple times he asked me. The answer was always no. But in the last day or so, I've been feeling a change of heart. I could be with Azalea, and I had Gannon. I love Gannon, but I also worried he would get bored of me since I am not even sure I can have sex or be with anyone that way. At least not yet anyway, but would he still want me as my broken, damaged self?

"Yes, I will let you change me, but do we have to-"

"No. We don't have to have sex, Abbie, but you know it would eventually send you into heat with me marking you. Azalea changing you won't, neither would Kyson because he has a mate, but I don't have a mate. So I wouldn't just be changing you. I would be claiming you."

I gulp at his words.

"I just want to be clear on that. You will go into heat eventually," Gannon says. I swallow and nod.

"I know, just, I want a little bit more time."

"And you have all the time you want, and we don't have to do it tomorrow. I just ask that if you are going to become a Lycan. When you choose that, I just hope you choose me to do it."

"Okay. But we can tomorrow, I just want to check on Azalea first. Do you think she is awake? I wouldn't mind ringing her too since it will be too late to see her by the time we get home."

"You can try her on my phone," Gannon says, handing his phone to me. I take it from him, and he tells me the pin to get in it.

"You know how to ring her?"

I nod. I had plenty of practice, but when I notice the time, I decide to send a voice text since I can't write. Usually Gannon types for me.

I open up the messages, only when I do I see a picture message from a thread he was in. I gasp at the mutilated body of a woman, and Gannon looks at me. He glances down at the screen before trying to snatch the phone.

"I thought you were ringing Azalea," he growls, trying to reach for his phone.

"Why is Blaire on your phone?" I ask, staring down, horrified at the screen. Why? I had no doubt it was her. I would recognize her face anywhere, it haunts my dreams, and I always wondered what happened to her. I hoped she got free of the pack, but here she is dead on his phone screen. Yet as I scroll through the photos, I begin to feel sick.

"Blaire?" Gannon asks.

"Pullover. I am going to be sick," I tell him, and he rips the car to the side of the road.

I toss the door open, throwing up. And empty my stomach. Seeing her mutilated body makes me sick, dry heaving until nothing but bile remains. Gannon races around the car, snatching the phone from my hand and pocketing it. He goes to grab me, but I take a step away and stand up.

"Did you kill her?" I ask, horrified, wondering why he would send that to Liam.

"What? No!" he says, stepping toward me, but I take another step back.

"Abbie?"

"Why is she on your phone?" I demand, and his brows pinch. Gannon pulls his phone out and looks at the screen.

"You know this girl?"

"Yes. Her name is Blaire. She was one of Kade's girls. Now answer me. Did you kill her?" I demand.

"No. Of course not. She was one of the bodies we found, I sent it to Liam so he could forward them to the packs so we could try to identify her. Wait ... she is from Kade's pack?" he asks.

"Yes, I just said that. She was one of the rogues there. She worked in the brothel," I tell him. Gannon looks at his screen again and flicks through the pictures. He takes a deep breath and shakes his head.

"What?" I ask him, feeling my legs shaking.

"We found a nurse not far from Blaire but in the opposite direction as the day after we got you back, she washed down the river at the back of the castle."

"You want me to look. You think they are linked?" I ask, taking a step forward.

"Just let me zoom in on her face. I don't want you seeing the rest," Gannon tells me. I nod, already wishing I could unsee Blaire's body.

He turns the screen to show me, and I stumble back, clutching my mouth, tears brim in my eyes. "You know her?" he asks.

"She is the nurse who helped me escape. She undid my handcuffs," I tell him, and I choke on a whimper. Gannon comes over, wrapping his arms around me, and he kisses my hair.

"I'm sorry, love," he whispers, and I clutch the front of his shirt. He rubs my arms before pulling away from me.

"We need to get back. I need to speak to the King and Damian about this," he says and I sniffle but climb back in the car, and he shuts my door.

He gets back in the driver's seat before reaching over and grabbing a blanket, a water bottle, and some mints. Gannon puts the blanket over me, and I shakily open the water bottle, gulping it down. He turns the heater up, which helps with my shaking against the cool night air. Or maybe it was my shock because he was still in a shirt and didn't look cold.

"Come on, let's get you home," Gannon whispers, pulling back onto the road.

CHAPTER THIRTEEN

AZALEA

I wake up to Kyson's leg draped across my waist, and I try to push him off. My bladder is screaming for me to get up and pee, and he is squashing it with his heavy leg. Instead, he rolls into me, crushing me further with his heavy weight. I push at his shoulders when I suddenly stop, everything coming back to me yet I feel no pain.

Kyson moves, lifting his head and yawning, covering his mouth with his hand before rubbing his eyes. I stare up at him, waiting for him to explain what happened after the council came here, but he clearly has other intentions as he leans down, kissing me.

His tongue invades my mouth and I push him away, making him growl, and he hits me with his calling, urging me to submit to him.

"Is Abbie back? What happened with the council? Cassandra? How long have I been asleep?" I ask around his lips which are assaulting mine. He doesn't answer, too preoccupied with mauling me.

"Kyson!" I growl, grabbing his head.

"Abbie is back, has been for a day now. Council sorted and

Cassandra is in the basement," he mutters nonchalantly, while collecting my wrists in one of his hands. He shoves them above my head awkwardly, his face dipping down to my naked chest.

"So Abbie is safe? What will happen with Kade's pack, or what's left of them? And why is Cassandra in the basement still, shouldn't she be dead?" Kyson doesn't bother answering, just nips at my flesh.

"That's it? That's all you have to say?" I ask angrily when I feel his tongue run over my nipple then sucks on it.

"Hm," is the only answer I receive which pisses me off.

"Kyson stop!" I snap at him as he pushes his knee between my legs. He growls, rolling off me and sitting up on his elbow while still holding my wrists in his hand.

"Everything is fine, I sorted it. We also have a lead on the rogues. Which is where I am going today," he tells me.

He palms my breast with his other hand before brushing his thumb over my nipple. I ignore the bond, not reacting to his touch. He sighs, his eyes moving to mine when he twists my nipple making me hiss. He chuckles and I glare at him.

"It is nothing you need to worry about," he tells me.

"Nothing to worry about? I just got whipped, and your men were knocked out, but I don't need to worry?" I ask incredulously.

"I said it is sorted, didn't I?" Kyson asks.

"That doesn't mean I don't have questions," I retort. I have so many questions, like where all the Landeena people came from and why I didn't know there were so many left from my parents' kingdom.

Why was the council freaked out at the mention of who I was, also why did Kyson never tell them who I am? It was clear that besides Cassandra, none of them knew I was Azalea the missing Landeena princess.

Kyson growls. leaning down to peck my lips. "I meant what I said, you don't have to worry," I growl at him trying to pull my hands from his grip. His grip tightens and he stares down at me.

"Well, aren't you in a lovely mood this morning," he says, leaning down and nipping at my lips. I wouldn't be in a bad mood if he would fucking answer instead of keeping secrets from me.

"Yes, because you aren't answering my questions! Instead, you are trying to fuck me, now stop it. And let me go! I need to pee," I snap at him.

Kyson presses his lips in a line and I can feel his anger at me denying him, but he reluctantly lets me go. I quickly rush off to the bathroom.

When I come back out, I find Kyson pulling on some clothes. He does the zip up on his jeans before pulling on a button-down shirt.

I grab some clothes, a black blouse and dark blue jeans. "You're not coming with me," he says, looking over at me while buttoning up his shirt.

"Of course not, I am supposed to be seen and not heard, right? Listen but don't ask questions. Sit and rot in the castle, waiting in the dark for you to feed me any minuscule piece of information," I snarl at him.

"Azalea, knock it off," he says, looking at me with darkened eyes.

"I'm coming with you," I tell him.

"No, you are staying here. Damian, Gannon, and I are only going for a few hours, so spend time with Abbie," he says, but I ignore him instead, pulling some socks on and reaching for my shoes.

He snatches them off me, suddenly becoming angry. "I said you're staying here!" Kyson snaps.

I purse my lips, fighting back tears. Why is it that every time I ask a question, he avoids answering or dismisses me? Kyson sighs when I sit back on the bed. He walks over and stops next to me, crouching down in front of me and placing his hands on my knees.

"I need to go check out Kade's pack for information regarding the missing rogues, those women we found, Abbie identified from her time there. When I get back you can ask your questions."

"But will you answer them?" I ask. He drops his head.

"There are some things that are safer if you don't know."

"Bullshit!" I tell him and his grip on my knees tightens. He clenches his jaw and presses his lips in a line.

"Why did the council freak out when they heard who I was?" I ask, and he looks at me.

"When I get back, not now. I am busy, and I don't want to argue. I nearly just lost you for goodness' sake, let me sort some things out, and then when it's safe, I will explain."

I shake my head and chew the inside of my lip.

"You're the King, you're always busy! Yet not too busy when you want something!" I snap at him.

"Azalea, enough. We will talk when I get back," he says, standing up and kissing my forehead. Kyson then walks out.

CHAPTER FOURTEEN

ABBIE

The weight of responsibility churns in my stomach like a storm as I watch Gannon stir from his makeshift bed. With each groan or snore that escapes his lips, the reality of Cassandra's precarious fate bears down on me. His body sits up from the couch with a series of pops and cracks as he stretches.

I'd offered many times to trade places with him, to take the couch so he could sleep in comfort, but Gannon is as stubborn as he is protective. He stretches, long limbs extending until his back issues a loud crack, the sound echoing off the walls and pricking at my conscience. Guilt gnaws at me, adding to the queasiness that refuses to abate.

Despite the turmoil inside me, my hands move with purpose, setting out his clothes on the bed. Meanwhile, I pull on my uniform when I notice him watching me.

My fingers brush over the fabric, smoothing out invisible creases, while my other senses remain acutely aware of his presence in the room, studying me.

As Gannon's gaze finally finds me, I feel the weight of his stare, heavy and searching, and brace myself for the conversation that would inevitably follow.

The fabric of the servant's uniform rustles softly as I adjust its fit, the black skivvy beneath it peeking through the gap at my neckline —a feeble attempt to conceal the jagged scars marring my shoulder and my old mate mark. My fingers linger for a moment, pressing down the material in a fruitless effort to make it cover the scars.

Gannon's voice cuts through the quiet like a blade, rough and edged with concern. "What are you doing?"

I glance at him, the intensity of his gaze making me straighten up.

"I can't sit in this room all day, Gannon. I want to work," I say, my voice steadier than I feel. To waste hours is to let anxiety consume me, and that is the last thing I want to do. My mind can be a dangerous place when left to ponder too long.

His approach is swift, a silent predator closing in. Before I can react, his hands are on me, fingers fumbling with the buttons of the dress I had carefully fastened. My heart races, a mix of alarm and irritation surging within me.

Instinctively, I slap his hands away, the sound is sharp in the air between us. His touch recedes but the tension remains, Gannon's brow furrows, his lips pulling back in a snarl that didn't completely reach the concern etched deep in his eyes. "You want to work? Fine, but not in this uniform. You aren't a servant," he growls, the words rumbling from him like distant thunder.

I square my shoulders, feeling the weight of the skivvy under the dress which makes my skin itch. "What does it matter if I am a servant or not? Clarice is a servant! Do you think so little of her too?" The challenge in my voice is as tangible as the tension that crackles in the air between us.

His reaction is immediate, a flash of surprise lighting up his features. Gannon's stance softens ever so slightly, the rigidity in his posture melting away as he grapples with the meaning of my words. Clearly, I had struck a chord, unearthed a sliver of guilt or an unconsidered bias he hadn't been aware of. When he suddenly becomes angry.

Gannon's fingers are quick and deft as they reach for the row of buttons on my dress, his movements driven by a blend of frustration and an impulse to protect. The fabric gives way under his touch, slipping free one button at a time as he works with a determination that is both infuriating and confusing for me.

"Gannon stop it! I am wearing it. Now leave me be!" My voice cuts through the mounting tension. The demand in my tone leaves no room for argument, even from someone as stubborn as Gannon.

For a moment, he pauses, his hands stilling mid-motion. His gaze locks onto mine, searching, perhaps for a sign of surrender that he won't find. Finally, his expression shifts into something like resignation, his lips pressing into a thin line of unhappiness. Slowly, his hands rise in a gesture of surrender, hovering uncertainly in the air between us before falling to his sides.

The room seems to exhale around us, the atmosphere relaxing ever so slightly. The chill of morning had not yet lifted when I turn from the mirror, abandoning my reflection dressed in the stiff fabric of the servant's uniform. Gannon's brooding presence fills the room like a brewing storm, his disapproval almost palpable as he watches me with an intensity that makes me want to apologize for snapping at him.

"You don't have to wear that," he says finally, his voice low and laced with an undercurrent of something I can't quite decipher—concern or command, perhaps both.

"I know I don't have to wear it," I tell him. My fingers brush against the crisp material of the dress, the texture foreign yet familiar as it grazes against my skin. "I know," I say, meeting his gaze head-on. I need him to understand that this is about more than clothing—it is about asserting some semblance of normalcy in a life that has become anything but.

Gannon holds my stare for a moment longer, his jaw set and lips in a hard line that speaks volumes of his internal struggle not to rip the dress from my body.

"Do you? You don't have to be a servant, you don't even have to work if you don't want to," he says, his voice threaded with a barely suppressed frustration.

My heart flutters against my ribs, yet I meet his gaze with steady resolve.

"Why are you so against this?" The question slips out, not accusatory but laced with genuine curiosity.

"Because I don't want you to think you are nothing more than a servant. I don't want you serving me like I am one of your chores," he says.

"I'm not," I respond, my voice a whisper of defiance. The defensive bite of my lip betrays my anxiety as his gaze sweeps over the room, taking in the room.

He turns abruptly, the muscles in his back rippling as he strides towards the bathroom. The door groans open under the force of his hand, and his growl vibrates through the air, mingling with the lingering scent of disinfectant I had left behind.

The sight of the pristine bathroom—scrubbed tiles glistening, the mirror free of water spots, and dirty laundry removed from sight—seem to ignite something within him.

Gannon's nostrils flare as he inhales deeply, the sharp tang of bleach cutting through the air. His eyes narrow as he turns to look at me.

"Really? Then why can I smell bleach?" he demands, his voice low and vibrating with an undercurrent of anger. The sound echoes off the bathroom tiles.

I try to maintain my composure, but his intense gaze is like a weight pressing down on me, demanding an answer.

"I want a mate, not a house cleaner," he says, pinning me in place with that intense look—a look that strips away any words I might want to say and sees right to the core of me.

I cross my arms across my chest. "And mates do that sort of thing. They clean up after each other. Geez, Gannon, my dirty washing was in there too, and I sure as hell don't want one of the other servants cleaning up after me." The words tumble out in a rush.

Gannon's brow furrows, the cogs in his mind visibly turning as he considers my argument. He had always been the type to think before he spoke, weighing each word with care like he was afraid of upsetting me, but not today. A deep breath fills his chest, and he runs a hand through his hair—a sign he is searching for a solution other than me being a maid.

"You could work in the library or the kitchens, or," he starts, halting mid-sentence. His suggestion hangs incomplete in the air.

I watch him closely, reading the conflict that dances across his features. He wants to support me, to see me happy, but the thought of me adopting the role of a servant seems to twist his insides. Yet, in his eyes, I glimpse a glimmer of understanding, acknowledgment that perhaps the lines we draw around each other are more confining than protective.

The thought of working in the library or the kitchens feels wrong —like trying to fit a square into a circle.

"The stables?" he offers, and I scoff, more to myself than to him.

My eyes dart across the room, skimming over the neatly made bed. "Gannon, I want to work as a servant. I know what I am doing." "Kitchens are full," I continue, each word punctuated by the ticking of the grandfather clock in the corner, "and the library? What use would I be when I can't read?"

Gannon's gaze softens, losing some of its earlier intensity. "Well, you can come with me," he finally says, his voice low and even.

"I am not following you around like a lost puppy. I need to have my own things to do. I don't see what the big deal is," I tell him, walking over and grabbing my flats and socks. I sit on the edge of the bed, bending down to pull my socks on when Gannon snatches them from my hand, kneeling in front of me.

"Let me," he says, not a command, but not quite a request either. His tone is gentle, but I sigh, allowing it.

He lifts my foot, resting it on his thigh. The sock slips over my heel, encasing my foot with a snugness that only his touch could bring. I expelled a heavy breath, a mix of exasperation and something far softer, watching him perform this simple act of care.

I bristle at the gesture, yet the warmth of his fingers as they graze my ankle is undeniably soothing. I let out an involuntary chuckle, the sound tinged with both warmth and a hint of irony as I watch him.

"You know I don't want a servant either, right?" I chuckle, the corners of my mouth lifting into a smile despite the fluttering nerves in my stomach.

"Huh?" Gannon pauses, his eyes meet mine with a curious glint as he processes the playful accusation in my tone.

"Is that why you think I do those things?" he chuckles, a low rumble that vibrates through the space between us. His head gives a slight shake, dismissing the idea even as his fingers resume their task, slipping the shoe onto my foot with ease.

"Here I thought chivalry wasn't dead. Apparently it is just non-existent," Gannon laughs, lifting my other foot to put the sock on. He kisses my foot.

I shrug.

"Abbie," Gannon begins, his voice taking on a softer note as he ties the laces. "I do those things because I like doing them for you," he says.

"And same with me setting your clothes out and cleaning the room, and making our bed. It's our room, I should be able to clean it," I insist.

A chuckle rumbles from his chest, the sound rich and warm. "Our bed and our room, huh?" His voice holds a playful note, my cheeks flush, the heat spreading across my skin as acutely as if he had traced the path with his fingertips. How easily the words had come, claiming his space as mine, intertwining our lives with the simplicity of a sentence.

His eyebrows arch in amused inquiry, his hands resuming their journey upwards until they encircled the curve of my hips. With a gentle tug, he drew me closer, the boundary between us blurring as our breaths mingled.

"If this is our bed, I should be able to sleep in it then, right?" The words hang between us, a grin tugging at his lips.

I find myself caught in the moment, my worries temporarily shelved. My teeth captured my lower lip, unsure of what to say.

"Maybe you could sleep in the bed?" My voice is barely a whisper.

"I'm playing, Abbie," he says, his voice softer now, closing the distance between us. A quick peck lands on my lips, a fleeting touch that sends an electric jolt through me, igniting my face with a warmth that surely matches the color of a tomato.

Gannon reaches for his shirt, pulling it over his head, muscles shifting beneath it. He replaces it with the crisp one I'd laid out.

Finished, he cuts through the stillness of the room with a playful twirl of his finger in the air, signaling for privacy. I avert my gaze.

The metallic rasp of Gannon's zipper breaks the hush that has settled in the room. I catch a glimpse of annoyance etching his brow as he fumbles with the fastening of his belt, a low groan escaping him—a sound laced with frustration that is uncharacteristic for the usually composed man.

"What's wrong?" I ask, curiosity piquing at his display of irritation.

"The King wants to leave early. He and Azalea had an argument," he says, each word heavy with a sigh.

He comes over and presses his lips to my forehead before gripping my chin, forcing me to look up at him.

"There is no rush to do anything. And if you want to clean the room, fine. I just don't want you thinking you have to, OK?"

I nod and he smiles, dipping his face closer to see if I would pull away.

When I don't, he presses his lips to mine, softly and my lips part invitingly. Gannon groans pulling me closer, his hand going to the back of my head as he tipped my head back, running his tongue across my bottom lip first before his tongue delved between my lips, brushing mine gently. I kiss him back, wanting to let him have this small victory because right now, that is all I could offer him.

CHAPTER FIFTEEN

ABBIE

The world crumbles around us, but in his arms, I feel untouchable. His hands, calloused from battles unknown to me, move with a tenderness that belies his warrior facade, tracing circles on the back of my neck. The intensity of his kiss speaks of promises and whispers secrets, sending a shiver down my spine as he gently tugs at my bottom lip, a playful nibble that coaxes laughter from deep within me. *Safe,* I think, the word resonating through every fiber of my being. It is an inexplicable trust, akin to the bond shared with Azalea, my confidant, my rock. Gannon's energy is a raging fire, yet around him, I feel nothing but warmth.

He pulls away ever so slightly, a smile playing on his lips, eyes reflecting a quiet storm behind the steel-gray irises. As our laughter subsides, he wraps me in a hug, pulling me into the solid comfort of his chest. I breathe him in; the scent is uniquely his—pine mixed with a hint of spice; an essence of strength and security. His arms are a vice around my petite frame—not constricting but protective; a silent vow of guardianship.

"I will be back in a few hours and-" His voice trails off as the rhythm of our moment together is interrupted by an insistent knock. My gaze lifts to meet his. I find his eyes now clouded with a distant fog rolling over the sharp glint I know so well. "Azalea is at the door," he murmurs, and a surge of euphoria overtakes me. I hadn't realized how much I needed this—needed her—until the possibility of her presence was just inches away.

The knock reverberates once more impatiently and my reaction is instinctual. With an energy that mirrors Gannon's own fiery spirit, I dart to the door; my hands barely cooperate as they fumble with the latch. The door swings open with a hasty creak, and before I can process the moment, I am enveloped in Azalea's embrace.

Her arms wrap around me and a sigh escapes her lips, carrying words that are a salve to my fraying nerves, "More than my life," she murmurs, her voice a soothing balm that seeps into the very marrow of my bones.

"More than my life," I whisper back, the echo of our sacred oath lingering in the charged silence that followed. My voice, a mere thread of sound, is as potent as any shout could ever be.

Hearing those words, to me, were the most soul soothing thing. Most don't understand our language, not like we do. Half the time we don't need to speak, just the subtle facial movements, the way we move, it speaks a language only we understand. We read each other's body language as if it were a spoken language. So the crack in her voice tells me she needed the hug just as much as I did.

As I reluctantly disentangle from Azalea, a shadow catches my eye. I glance up to find the King's imposing figure stationed against the wall, his presence filling the space. The air seems to grow denser around him, his watchful eyes not on me but fixed intently on Azalea.

"Ready?" His deep voice cuts through the silence, the question directed at Gannon.

But his gaze remains locked on Azalea. There is an intensity in his stare that sets my nerves on edge.

I watch Azalea's jaw tense, her lips press into a thin line before she attempts to soften the expression, the muscles around her mouth quivering ever so slightly. She draws in a breath through her nose, her chest rising and falling with controlled anger. And the way she sucks in her pursed lip as she tries to stop the action made me realize she is livid about something.

The moment stretches taut, the unsaid words hanging heavy between them. Azalea's eyes, usually so warm and open, now mirror the storm clouds gathering in her mind. It is clear that she's holding back what she wants to say.

Gannon's voice, a low rumble of assurance, cut through the tension coiling in the air. "Yeah, just need to grab my wallet," he says, his words pulling me from the electric stand-off between Azalea and the King.

Azalea leans her shoulder against me as she leads me away. Before she even gets two meters past Kyson, the harsh intake of breath she lets out tells me she is trying to keep her emotions in check.

"Azalea!" The King's voice is a whip-crack, laced with authority and frustration. His command snakes around us, demanding obedience, demanding acknowledgment.

But Azalea, with a will forged in defiance, gives him no attention. She moves past Kyson as if the very air around him holds no sway over her direction. "Where are you going now?" he demands.

Azalea's behavior is uncharacteristic; we had grown up in an environment where obedience to orders was central. Yet, there she is, defying expectations, perhaps even searching for the edges of the boundaries that bind her to him. It isn't just any command she is disregarding—it is the King's, her mate, his presence demanding attention and she refuses to give it, she looks like she is deliberately trying to push his buttons for some reason.

"Where are you working today? I will come work with you," she offers casually, her tone light as if the air isn't thick with tension from the growls that rumble behind us.

I glance over my shoulder, catching sight of the King, his brow furrowed and jaw set tight. It is clear he is not used to such blatant disregard.

The coolness of the stone stairs seep through the soles of my shoes as I descend alongside Azalea, our footsteps in sync. The air was thick with the scent of savory spices drifting from the kitchens below.

"You haven't answered Abbie, where are we working today?" Azalea asks.

"I'm not sure yet," I admit, matching her stride for stride, the uncertainty of my day oddly grounding in the face of her stormy defiance.

"Azalea, answer me!" The King's command booms from above us, echoing off the high walls and vaulted ceilings.

On the staircase landing, Dustin and Liam await us, their expressions a study in contrasts. Liam's smile is gentle, a subtle acknowledgment of the tension without adding to the unfolding drama. Beside him, Dustin's raised eyebrow speaks volumes—a silent observer cataloging every detail, perhaps even finding amusement in Azalea's rebellion.

Her steps never falter, her chin tilted ever so slightly upward in a silent display of her unshakeable will. Kyson's heavy footfalls grow louder as he descends behind us.

"For fuck' sake Azalea, answer me!" he bellows again, the undercurrents of power in his voice unable to sway her resolve. His frustration, a palpable force, surges forth before he reaches out and clasps Azalea's shoulder with a possessive grip. She halts abruptly, her body tensing beneath his touch.

Azalea's reaction is swift and feral; a low growl vibrates from her throat, resonating with a challenge that defied her outward calm. "I asked you a question?" Kyson's voice holds an edge of annoyance.

Without missing a beat, Azalea's retort slices through the tension. "I asked you one too! I got my answer. Here's yours," she declares, words laced with a mix of defiance and dismissal. She spins on her heel, the fabric of her dress whispering against the stone steps as she continues her descent, tugging me with her.

At the bottom of the staircase, she pauses just long enough to shoot Kyson a piercing look.

Liam's chuckle slices through the thickening silence, a sharp note of amusement that seems out of place against the backdrop of the King's anger. "Trouble in paradise, my King," he says, his voice carrying the smoothness of a smirk I can't see but could very well imagine.

I side-eye him briefly, wondering if madness was a trait that ran deep in his bloodline, or if he considered it more of a personal achievement. There is no doubt in my mind about his precarious grip on sanity.

"Shut up, Liam," Kyson snaps, his anger escalating as Azalea continues to ignore him. It's evident he craves her attention. Liam steps in front of Kyson, halting Azalea with an outstretched hand. Kyson growls, a display of the unspoken pact they share to prioritize her over the King. This loyalty extends even to interactions with Azalea—a fact that surprises me.

Gannon swiftly intervenes, placing a calming hand on Kyson's shoulder. Tension fills the air as Kyson glares at Gannon before relenting with a sigh. His gaze shifts to Azalea, who meets his stare with a raised eyebrow.

"It was a simple question, Azalea. I just wanted to know where you are going, so I can ensure you have proper guards," the King states wearily, pinching the bridge of his nose.

"Can't know all my secrets now, can you?" she retorts before striding away. I follow her closely, pondering if her words relate to Gannon's recent revelations.

"Where are you going?" I inquire as I catch up and link my arm through hers.

"Wherever you are going," she teases lightly. Her response puzzles me since she rarely ventures anywhere without his say so.

"Liam, you're with me and Trey. Gannon is now watching the

girls with Dustin," Kyson announces as he descends the steps. The King heads in the opposite direction while Liam grumbles and growls behind us, drawing our attention back.

Gannon approaches us with a mischievous grin. "Great! See what your defiance gets me, my Queen. I have to hang out all day with his grumpy ass and ferret face fucker," Liam taunts playfully as Dustin struggles to maintain his composure.

"Liam! Now!" The King's voice booms as he strides away.

"I'm coming! You royal pain in my fanny," Liam calls out before hurrying after him. Azalea shakes her head at Liam's antics while Dustin resumes his position by her side and Gannon trails along behind us.

CHAPTER SIXTEEN

ABBIE

The scent of fresh bread and the chorus of clattering utensils welcome us, a stark contrast to the tension I just witnessed between Azalea and Kyson. .

"So what's up with you and the King?" I venture, my voice barely rising above the domestic symphony as I glance sideways at her. Her gaze has a faraway quality, one that hints at inner turmoil and whispers conspiracies.

"Nothing." She flicks a dismissive hand, but her eyes, churning with unsaid emotions, tell a different story.

"I just think he is hiding stuff. No. I know he is hiding stuff." Her shrug tries to convey indifference, but it is a poor mask for the frustration lacing her tone.

"I asked him about the council and what happened the other day, and he never answered," she admits, her voice dipping into the well of secrets that seems to pool between them.

I watch her closely, noting how her fingers trail along the countertop, skimming over the cool marble as if searching for answers on its smooth surface. There is a determination set in the line of her jaw.

Whatever walls the King puts up, I know she will scale them, stone by unforgiving stone.

Oliver and Logan were sitting at the bench, chopping pancakes. I watch as Azalea affectionately messes up Oliver's hair before eating a berry he holds up for her.

"Clarice is hanging washing," Logan tells us. I smile down at them, while Gannon goes over to help Oliver use a butter knife to cut his pancakes up that he had been sawing at. Azalea looks in the fridge before pulling out some orange juice. She grabs some glasses when Dustin clears his throat. She looks at him over the fridge door.

"Your smoothie," Dustin says.

"I got juice," she says, holding it up and Dustin points to the blender. Azalea rolls her eyes, walking over to it. She grabs the jug before pouring the contents down the sink.

"My Queen, you know he commanded me to let him know what you are eating."

She pours her juice, uncaring.

"What he doesn't know won't hurt him. Tell him I am happily eating the lies he feeds me," she says holding up the juice to him before drinking it. She places some cups on the counter in front of the boys with juice and hands me one. She offers one to Gannon and Dustin but they both shake their heads just as Clarice walks in from out the back.

Gannon looks over at her from feeding Oliver some pancake on his little fork, before straightening up when she glares at him.

"He needs to learn to hold the fork properly himself, Gannon," Clarice says, she clicks her tongue before leaning down and kissing Oliver's little head.

"He was struggling ma, let me feed him," Gannon says, sending him a wink. Clarice swats Gannon's ass with her tea towel before flicking the kettle on.

"Have you girls had breakfast?" Clarice asks.

"Yep. I had some home truths for breakfast," Azalea says bitterly, and Clarice gives her a look.

"And how did they taste?" she asks.

"Bitter, like the King," Azalea mutters, sipping her juice. I snicker, she was indeed in a mood, making me wonder if it might be the pregnancy hormones. You could just make out the slightest bump if you looked hard enough. Her belly no longer looked sucked in from malnourishment, instead her belly was flat with the slightest hint of a bump. It is trippy to see how fast Lycan baby's grew.

"I heard you and the King had an argument," Clarice says.

"You did?" she asks skeptically.

"Pretty sure everyone heard you both fighting on the stairs before you went to get Abbie," Clarice chuckles. Azalea cheeks turn slightly pink.

"Well, if everyone stopped keeping things that involve me from me, we wouldn't be arguing," she says while looking around at everyone who averts their gaze as she says it.

Azalea looks around before biting the corner of her lip. "You all know what he is hiding," she states.

Clarice busies herself with cleaning the sink. Dustin, meanwhile, finds a spot on the roof to stare at, and Gannon starts shoveling food in Oliver's mouth so fast the kid soon looks like a cartoon chipmunk, cheeks full, chewing as fast as he can before swallowing and opening his mouth again.

Azalea growls. "Of course everyone knows but us!" she says, motioning toward me, and Gannon looks at me, giving a soft shake of his head. That movement does not go unnoticed by her either when her eyes go to mine.

I could never lie to her, and the knowing look on her face that I knew had me blurt it out like word vomit.

"Mr. Crux is your illegitimate cousin on your father's side. The council are suspected to be in with the hunters and your blood is special because you can change humans into Lycans" I blurt out loud before I can stop myself.

Gannon drops the fork he was holding and Dustin and Clarice gape at me while Azalea blinks at me clearly shocked. He then growls before pressing his lips in a line. I had never intentionally lied to her, and I wasn't about to start now.

"How hard was that? Geez!" Azalea says, sipping her juice. The room seems to let out a collective exhale.

"Wait! Crux is my cousin?" she asks like that is the most shocking information.

"Is that why he freaked out when he learned who I was?" she asks. But this time, I can't answer her, so I look at Gannon, who growls again.

"No. Because of your parents' gifts, they were probably worried you inherited them," Gannon answers and Clarice hangs her head.

"What sort of gifts?" Azalea asks.

"I am sorry, I can't tell you that. And Abbie wasn't even supposed to tell you what she did," he says, shooting me a look. Azalea looks at Dustin for an answer but not even he is willing to speak up about it. She puts her cup down and shakes her head, tears burning her eyes. I wish I knew so I could tell her.

"I am over this crap! They're supposed to be my family and no one tells me anything about them. Yet all of you had no issues telling me what a shit mother Marissa was to me!" she says storming off out the back door. Gannon and Dustin go after her but she spins around with a furious look on her face.

"Don't follow me! And don't come near me!" she snarls, and I nearly stagger back at the command. Gannon, too, rocks on his heels. She is gone before she even realizes what she had done. None of us thought we could move an inch to go after her.

"Bloody hell!" Dustin says.

"You bloody mindlink him! Because until she undoes it, neither of us can go bloody near her," Gannon growls, then rubs a hand down his face.

"Wait! Even me?" I ask, trying to go toward the door she walked out of. However, my feet won't let me go in that direction. At that same moment, Trey walks in completely oblivious to all us frozen. He is cupping his nose that seems to be bleeding and walks over to the sink.

"I thought you were with the King?" Dustin asks.

"I was. Until Liam called me a ferret face fucker, so I hit him," Trey mumbles.

"Idiot. You don't hit crazy," Gannon says, and Trey glares at him before looking around the room after cleaning his bloody face.

"Anyway, I was left behind," he says, shaking his head. "Where is the Queen?" he asks, his voice steady but bearing an edge of concern as his gaze darts from one corner of the room to the other, searching for Azalea. Gannon and Dustin exchange a silent communication that speaks volumes, their expressions a mix of resignation and unease.

"Did you get hold of the King?" Gannon's voice cuts through the quiet, tension wrapping around each word like barbed wire. Dustin's head gives a slow, deliberate shake, his hands clasped together as though in silent prayer or perhaps to stave off the urge to reach out and throttle something—or someone.

"He is blocking me out," he finally admits, the weight of those words settling heavily on his shoulders. The atmosphere thickens with implication, and the unspoken truth lies between them as palpable as the scent of iron and antiseptic still lingering on Trey's skin.

Trey's hand cuts through the air with an impatient flutter, his eyes seeking answers in the midst of the kitchen's sudden stillness. "Ah, hello? Where is the Queen?" There is a trace of frustration lacing his question this time, as if he expects Azalea to materialize from behind the cabinets or beneath the table.

Gannon, who had remained as rigid as the granite countertops, fixes his stormy eyes on a spot on the wall, avoiding Trey's probing gaze.

Dustin leans back against the fridge, arms crossed over his chest, the muscles in his jaw working silently. He finally breaks the silence.

"She commanded us, and none of us can follow her," he says, his voice flat.

Trey's hands drop to his sides, the gesture releasing some of his pent-up energy into the room. The surprise of Dustin's words seem to anchor him to the spot, and for a moment, the only sound is the faucet dripping steadily in the background—marking the passing seconds of tension within the kitchen walls.

Trey's next question hangs heavy in the charged air, his brow furrowed with sudden comprehension. "She figured it out?" His voice, a mix of awe and disbelief, echos my own thoughts—Azalea had indeed.

"Where did she go?" he demands, urgency sharpening his tone. The words are barely past his lips when he makes for the door, his movements quick and decisive, like a predator homing in on its escapee prey.

Gannon's reaction is visceral, a low growl rumbling from deep within as he turns to follow Trey's gaze, his own instincts flaring at the betrayal of secrets. He moved with a swift grace that belied his size, intercepting Trey just inches from the threshold. His hand clamps down on Trey's arm, halting him mid-stride, an unspoken command in the tension of his grip.

The muscles in Trey's arm tense beneath Gannon's hold, the air crackling with a current of challenge and restraint. Their eyes lock, two forces colliding without a word, each man's resolve clear in the stillness that follows.

Gannon's grip tightens on Trey's arm, his knuckles whitening with the force of his hold.

"You aren't trusted to be around her," Gannon states, his voice firm.

Trey's face twists into a snarl, shaking off the hold with a jerk of his shoulder. "I am the last person that would hurt her," he spits back at Gannon, defiance flaring bright in his eyes.

Trey's shove sends Gannon stumbling back a step, the force

behind it betraying the anger and frustration boiling under his skin. A vein throbs at Trey's temple, his jaw set in a hard line.

"Bullshit! You're not under the King's oath," Gannon snaps, regaining his balance with an ease. His eyes narrow on Trey, searching for any hint of deceit.

Trey stands his ground, his chest heaving slightly. "Yes, not under oath to the King. But to the Landeena's I am," he snarls, his voice a low growl that seems to resonate.

Dustin's hands clenched into fists, his knuckles going white with the effort to contain his fury. "Bullshit! You were a dick to her when Kyson chucked her to the stables! And always interfering with my shifts," he exclaims.

Trey's face hardens, his eyes flashing a shade darker with memories and regrets. "I thought she killed my charge is why. I didn't know she wasn't Marissa's daughter. The King said she was. I believed him." He pauses, his voice dropping to a pained whisper. "If someone killed your King, would you like them or their family?" His demand hangs in the air, as raw and sharp as an open wound.

Dustin turns towards Gannon, searching for some kind of guidance. Gannon only tilts his head to the side, his gaze locked onto Trey watching him carefully searching for any deceit. His silent scrutiny seems to probe at the truth of Trey's words, weighing them against every action, every choice they have observed him make.

The atmosphere hangs thick with unanswered questions and distrust.

"Whose charge were you?" Gannon finally demands.

Trey straightens, his shoulders squaring. His jaw clenches before he replies, his words carrying the gravity of confession. "Baby Azalea's. I was the one that reported Marissa. About her getting Azalea to call her mummy," he says, his voice barely above a whisper, yet it carries in the silent kitchen like a shout.

The revelation seems to hang in the air, a piece of a puzzle falling into place with an echoing click. Gannon's expression doesn't waver, but there is a flicker in his eyes, a spark of understanding—or perhaps it is the beginning of more doubt.

"Those reports didn't have your name on them," Gannon states.

Trey's face, already etched with lines of barely contained anger and frustration, contort further into a mask of indignation. His fists clench at his sides, knuckles whitening as he fights to control his rising fury.

"I had to fill out the same paperwork as everyone else did." Trey's voice is ragged, strained with the effort of holding back his emotions. He takes a step forward, his stance wide, ready to defend not just his actions but his loyalty. "You all know I come from the Landeena Kingdom! Fuck! I helped search for her for years!"

Without another word, Trey turns sharply on his heel. The door swings open with a bang, protesting against the abruptness of his exit, and then slams shut.

The door trembles in the aftershock of Trey's departure, the silence thickening around us as we try to figure out what just happened.

Gannon's jaw tightens as he turns toward Clarice, the lines etched on his brow deepening with concern. "Did you know that?" he asks, his voice barely above a whisper.

Clarice, her hands pause mid-wipe on the already spotless counter, meets Gannon's gaze. She shrugs.

"I knew he was from the Landeena Kingdom, and was in the castle. But I thought he was a guard," she says.

Her fingers resume their work, brushing invisible crumbs into her palm, each sweep a methodical attempt to order the chaos that had erupted in her kitchen.

Gannon's fists clench at his sides, the veins in his forearms standing out like cords as he turns sharply on his heel. With a purpose that silences any residual murmurs from the other staff present, he makes for the door, his steps heavy and deliberate.

"I'm finding his documents," he growls over his shoulder, not bothering to glance back at us.

He pauses, just before crossing the threshold into the foyer, his profile etched against the dim light filtering through the windows. "Mindlink the King and get him back here," he says to Dustin.

"What? Why?" I ask, my confusion knitting my brows together. I know Azalea will get in trouble with Kyson for commanding her guard.

"Because, if Trey is indeed pact oathed to the Landeenas," Gannon's voice echoes back to me, "that means someone else in the castle was poisoning her."

The severity of his words settles in my stomach like lead. All this time, their suspicions were misguided, pointing fingers at the wrong person while the true culprit lurked unnoticed. Which means Azalea is once again in danger.

"And we have been looking at the wrong person all this time," he finishes before walking out.

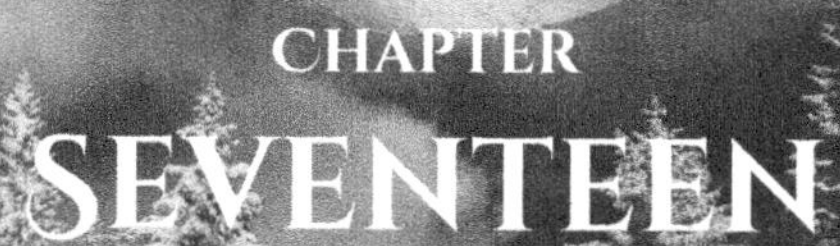

CHAPTER SEVENTEEN

AZALEA

The absence of footsteps trailing mine acts as both a balm and a burden, the silence calming me and allowing me to think clearly. But I also know my taking off will infuriate Kyson, which as worrisome as that is, I also don't care. Bursting through the heavy doors that lead to the castle gardens, the hinges groan in protest at my haste. A gust of air greets me, cool and crisp, carrying with it the rich scent of earth and blossoming life. It feels akin to taking that initial deep breath after breaking through the water's surface when having nearly drowned, the fresh air filling my lungs and dispelling the stifling atmosphere off. My pace slows as I wander down the gravel path, each stone softly crunching beneath my shoes.

I let my fingers trail along the velvety petals of roses as I pass, their blooms a burst of color against the forest backdrop that surrounds this place. Yet even their beauty can't distract from the frustration I feel. Secrets. They were trying to protect me, perhaps, but protection feels too much like caging.

Drawing in another deep breath, I exhale slowly, letting the tension seep out of my shoulders.

That's when I feel it—the intrusive touch of Kyson's thoughts brushing against my mind as he opens the mindlink.

'Kyson, not now,' I snap, clenching my fists as I push back against the mindlink.

To my surprise, his presence retreats as swiftly as a wave pulling back from the shore. It feels empowering, knowing I can shove him out with such ease when fueled by anger.

My gaze drifts across the expanse of green, settling on the fruit trees standing in neat rows, their branches heavy with ripe fruit. There is Peter, working alongside the gardener, reaching up to pluck fruits with practiced ease.

As if sensing my presence, Peter glances up, and his face lights up with an excited grin. He waves, his arm cutting through the air with boyish enthusiasm. I return the gesture, feeling a smile tugging at the corners of my mouth despite the turmoil that clouded my thoughts.

"Hey!" he greets, jogging over with an energy that seems to make the very ground beneath him come alive. In a few long strides, he closed the distance between us, enveloping me in a hug that is both unexpected and strangely comforting. "Hey, I haven't seen you in days," he says, pulling back just enough to look into my eyes with genuine concern.

"Want to help pick fruit with us?" he asks, and I look around. I want to get as far away from the castle grounds as I am allowed.

"Na. Do you want to go for a walk with me? I am hiding from my guards," I chuckle. Peter looks over at the gardener, who shrugs and waves him off.

"Where do you want to walk?"

"I don't know," I tell him. "We could walk by the river. It is pretty high at the moment from the floods upstream coming down it," he offers.

"Yeah, I am not fond of water," I tell him.

"Oh, well, we could go to the stables. I am supposed to clean out the stables today but got hauled up to help pick bloody fruit."

"Ah, I think I prefer the river walk to shoveling poop," I tell him, and he chuckles.

"It's a date then," he says, looping his arm through mine. We head toward the river. Peter is right. The river is quite high and flowing fast. We sit down on the bank for a bit.

"So, how did you start working here?" I ask him.

"I live with my grandparents, and they used to be servants here and got me the job."

"Where are your parents?"

"Dad, no idea. My mother dumped me with them when I was born. I see her every now then, but she doesn't really have much to do with me. She prefers to pretend I don't exist. I am her dirty little secret," he tells me.

Well, that sounds a bit harsh.

"And your father?"

He shrugs. "Mum didn't know his name, or so she claims."

"What does your mother do?" I ask him.

"Works at the grocery store in town. I usually pretend I don't have a mother. It's easier that way."

"I'm sorry Peter, that sucks," I tell him.

"All good. My grandparents are good enough for me," he says, getting to his feet. "I'll race you back?" he says, offering me his hand. I take it, and he pulls me to my feet.

"Ah, I probably shouldn't," I tell him. The last thing I need is to fall over or injure myself. Kyson would never let me leave the room and wrap me in bubble wrap if I did.

"Oh right, that probably isn't Queenly," Peter chuckles.

"No, it's not that," I tell him, my hand going instinctively to my barely there bump. Peter's eyes follow my hand and he gasps.

"Wait. Are you pregnant?" he asks, and my face heats and I nod.

"Well, come on. Had I known that, I wouldn't have made you trek through the forest," he chuckles.

Suddenly, a blur of movement catches my eye, and the crunching of underbrush signals someone nearby. Trey bursts onto the scene, his body propelled by urgency. He skids to a halt mere inches from us. He clutches his knees, panting heavily, as he raises his eyes to mine. There is a flicker of concern in his gaze that has me confused.

Trey straightens, his chest heaving from the exertion as he fixes his gaze on me, a blend of relief and mild irritation playing across his features. His eyes search mine for a second.

"There you are!" His voice carries a sharp edge, softened only by the undercurrent of worry that seems to thread through the words.

I shuffle my feet, acutely aware of the pulse of life within me, feeling the weight of his unspoken questions. I meet Trey's intense stare with an attempt at casual indifference.

"Why are you out here?" The query hangs between us.

"We went for a walk," says Peter, the corners of his eyes crinkling with excitement as he looks up at Trey.

Trey nods, though his expression remains unreadable, as he takes in Peter before looking back at me. "Go on, I will take her back," Trey says, almost daring me to tell him no. He returns his gaze back to Peter for a second. "Shouldn't you be in the stables?" His gaze holds Peter's just long enough to convey the unvoiced command that lingers beneath the surface.

With a playful roll of his eyes, Peter concedes to the silent authority in Trey's look and rushes off back toward the castle.

Falling into step beside me, Trey grips my elbow gently glancing around like he is worried someone or something will jump out at us and attack at any moment. Leaves crunch underfoot as we make our way along the path that will lead us back toward the looming structure that is both my sanctuary and my cage.

I can feel the weight of the castle's proximity pressing against me like the air before a storm—oppressive, electric.

Trey's voice cut through the silence. "You shouldn't wander so far from the castle, my Queen. What if something happened?"

His gaze holds mine, the furrow of his brow and the slight tension in his shoulders suggest he is all too aware of the dangers that lurk beyond the safety of stone walls and iron gates.

I halt, turning to face him fully, letting the seriousness of his question settle between us. “I have the mindlink,” I tell him, meeting his protective stance with quiet defiance. My voice is steady, betraying none of the frustration that had driven me to leave in the first place.

Trey’s expression hardens, the lines of his face etching a map of concern and urgency that makes me nervous. “The one you have been blocking for the past hour? The King is on his way home and he is not happy,” he says, parting a thick curtain of ferns to clear our path. He’s not exactly scolding me, but there is an edge to his voice—a sharpness that spoke of consequences I hadn’t fully considered in my bid for fresh air.

A heavy sigh escapes me. I follow Trey’s broad back as he navigates through the dense underbrush. I almost don’t see the fallen log until Trey reaches out, his fingers wrapping around my elbow with practiced care. Instinctively, I place my foot on the mossy wood, preparing to step over. But in that heartbeat—before sense could translate into action—the world shifts brutally beneath me.

There is no time to brace, no moment to comprehend. The log buckles, crumbling into decay. My foot plunges through the rotted trunk, and a jagged spike of pain lances up my leg as the air is punched from my lungs.

The scream that tears from my throat feels distant, disconnected from the agony blossoming across my ankle. Trey’s arms are suddenly there, steel bands hauling me up from the wreckage of wood and splinters. I scream again as darkness claws at my vision. .

“Fuck! Stay with me, Azalea!” Trey’s voice murmurs. But it is too late. Everything fades as I succumb to oblivion.

I have no idea how much time has passed. Eventually, consciousness returns with a rush of pain and disorientation. My back is pressed against something warm and solid — Trey’s chest, I realize, as my blurry vision focuses on his face above me. His jaw is set in grim determination as he works to dismantle the log that imprisons my foot, his hands moving deftly despite their size.

"Stay with me, help is on the way," Trey whispers close to my ear. The urgency in his voice is a sharp contrast to the gentle way he cradles me against him. I can feel the tremor of his efforts reverberate through my body as he pries away splintered wood.

A sudden snap echoes through the quiet forest, and a piece of the log comes free. Relief surges briefly, thinking it will all be over soon. But as Trey tugs at my leg, something holds fast. Panic flares in my chest, igniting every nerve ending with fire.

"Stop! Something is stabbing through my foot," I gasp. My fingers curl around my shin, an instinctive but futile attempt to soothe the sharp agony. Trey's hands stills against the wood, his body tensing when suddenly we hear a noise, thinking it is the guard.

The ominous crackle of a twig underfoot shatters the stillness, and with it comes a growl that claws its way through the air. My heart stutters at the sound, every beat a hammer against my ribs. Time warps, stretching each second into an eternity as fear claws at my throat.

Trey's form becomes a shield behind me, his warmth a contrast to the chill of dread that frosts my skin. His hand moves over my mouth, pressing firm yet gentle, silencing the scream that threatens to betray our presence. "Shh," he breathes, so close his lips graze my ear. The command simmers with a calm authority, but beneath it lies an undercurrent of tension that mirrors my own alarm.

"Forest, now!" Trey's command ripples through the mindlink, a forceful wave that crashes into the consciousness of every guard within reach. His voice full of urgency, I feel rather than see his muscles coil in preparation behind me, his instincts kicking into high gear even as his hand remains clamped over my mouth.

A rustle to our left—a softer sound, but no less menacing—whips Trey's head around, and I sense the sudden shift in his focus. The air thickens with tension, an electric charge that raises the fine hairs on the back of my neck. "What is it?" The words are muffled against his palm, my voice a mere vibration against the pressure of his skin.

Then, emerging from the underbrush, a bear cub ambles into view. Its innocent eyes scan the surroundings, unaware of the danger its presence signals. My pulse quickens, each thump echoing the dread welling up inside me. A cub? The implications send a shiver down my spine, a cold dread that seeps into my bones. Mothers are fiercely protective, and this cub's mother would be close—too close.

The moment of eerie silence breaks as another growl reverberates through the forest, this one closer, deeper, more terrifying. It's a sound that speaks of raw power and primal instinct. It originates from behind us.

Trey's curse slices through the tension like a blade, his body a rigid shield behind me. "Don't move!" The whisper is barely audible over my thundering heartbeat, a futile attempt to blend with the stillness of the forest.

A twig snaps, and my eyes dart to the source. From the corner of my vision, I catch the hulking form of the mother bear. Its massive paws, each one capable of crushing stone, press into the earth.

The cub, a little ball of fur with wide, curious eyes, sniffs at the air. It can't understand the danger; it just knows the scent of humans is something new, something interesting. My breath becomes shallow, trying not to stir the surrounding air any more than necessary. But my lungs yearn to gasp for more, my body betraying me with its need to prepare for flight.

I dare not move, yet the urge to flee is a living thing within me, clawing at my insides, begging for release. The mother bear, her dark eyes pools of midnight intelligence, continues her approach. She stops—a mere few heartbeats away—an imposing wall of muscle and fur. Her nostrils flare as she takes in our scents, and I can see the muscles under her thick coat ripple with restrained power. At least 600 pounds of raw, untamed force stands before us.

Time stretches, elongates, becomes an entity of its own as we wait, frozen, locked in a standoff . The silence is deafening, broken only by the distant rush of the river and the pounding of my heart—a desperate drumbeat signaling either survival or doom.

The bear's huff is the only warning before it charges, a freight train of animalistic rage barreling toward us. My scream pierces the stillness of the forest as I involuntarily crumple, arms over my head in a feeble attempt at protection. The weighty hand that had been stifling my cries vanishes, and I tumble backward, an awkward twist sending a jolt of agony through my ankle. Pain slivers up from my foot.

Pushing up on trembling hands, panic, and pain compete for dominance, I catch sight of Trey's transformation. His body expands, contours shifting into the ferocious form of his malt-colored Lycan. Fur bristles, muscles bulge, and eyes glow fiercely. He meets the bear's onslaught with a guttural roar, their bodies colliding with brute force.

Claws flash, drawing streams of crimson across Trey's face as the bear rears high on its hind legs, swiping at him. With teeth bared, Trey lunges, sinking his claws into the thick fur, the beast's roar vibrates through the air. It fights to regain footing, massive paws slamming down on Trey's chest with such power, I feel the impact in my own bones.

Blood mists the air, droplets catching the light. The bear drags Trey away from me, his body a streak of color against the brown and green of the woods. They crash into a tree, the sound a sickening crack that echoes through the forest.

As Trey staggers to rise, the bear lunges once more, jaws clamping onto his shoulder. The shaking of its head—merciless and violent—threaten to rend flesh from bone. Trey's groan of pain is almost human, filled with a strength born of both man and beast.

I want to help, to scream, to do anything but watch as they both fight their lives. But I am pinned, helpless, my own cry dying in my throat as I see the raw savagery unfold before me.

The earth trembles with the force, and I can feel each thunderous impact. My pulse hammers in my ears, nearly drowning the sound of snapping twigs and the hurried footfalls of the approaching guards. Yet despite my own distress, my scream for help is instinctive for Trey's safety as he lies pinned beneath the massive bear.

"Help him!" The cry tears from my throat, raw and desperate. A fleeting glance over my shoulder reveals figures moving through the trees—a blur of motion. But my attention snaps back to the scene before me as Trey issues a guttural groan.

Beneath the weight of the beast, Trey seems a figure of both despair and indomitable will. His legs, powerful and tense, draw up beneath the bear, finding leverage where none seemed possible. With a surge of strength, he kicks outwards. The motion sends the bear reeling backward, a hulk of fur and fury momentarily forced to retreat.

It lands with an earth-shaking thud, and in that heartbeat of opportunity, Trey pounces. His movements are a blur as he unleashes a barrage of strikes upon the stunned creature. The cub's return catches Trey's attention even mid-assault. His head swivels towards the small form.

My breath catches, heart aching for the cub wondering if Trey will be forced to kill it.

But Trey's hands do not seek the cub. Instead, they rain down upon the mother bear—once, twice, thrice—each hit punctuated by the thud. The fourth strike comes with a sound that is both sickening and merciful: the dull thud of unconsciousness overtaking the beast as it falls to the earth.

Trey stands then, blood paints him, the deep red of his wounds obvious against the malt hues of his Lycan form.

The guards arrive, bursting through the underbrush. Their eyes take in the scene: the fallen bear, the whimpering cub clawing at its mother and Trey, who looks like he bathed in blood. I search their ranks for Gannon and Dustin, but they are absent, their presence replaced by others whose faces blur through the shock and adrenaline.

"Quickly!" someone shouts, urgency laced in every syllable. They know as well as I do that we're running out of time. As for Trey, his gaze is on me again, assessing the damage done, ready to act despite his own grievous injuries.

Trey's growl is a guttural warning, reverberating through the clearing as he approaches. He moves with an urgency that contradicts his injuries, his form still imposing despite the blood drenching his fur. The other guards hurry to my side with equal speed.

Together, they attack the rotted log that encases my foot. Wood splinters under their combined strength, and the hollow log cracks, piece by piece. The air is thick with the scent of damp earth and the pungent odor of blood and the decay from the wood. Through my groans of pain, I hear a soft whine that cuts through the chaos.

The bear cub, innocent in its confusion, nudges its mother's unresponsive form. Its tiny nose working over her fur, seeking comfort or perhaps an explanation for the unnatural slumber that had claimed her. My gaze lingers on the small creature, so vulnerable without the protection of its parents.

"It's knocked out, not dead. We need to move quickly," Trey's voice comes to me, low but clear, pulling me back to the present danger.

"That's why we need to get you out of here before it wakes," he says, gripping my ankle. I swallow. His green eyes stare back at me and I know what he is about to do.

"Choose my Queen, or I will have to kill it," he says, and I look at the cub nuzzling its mother. The other guards are standing around in case it wakes.

"Do it!" I tell him, and he yanks my foot off the huge, thick nail that must have been in the tree when it fell and rotted away. My scream is silent before I pass out. My eyes roll into the back of my head and the last thing I see is Trey shifting back before grabbing me and the feel of the wind as he runs toward the castle. Then I saw nothing but darkness.

CHAPTER EIGHTEEN

KYSON

A growl escapes my lips as the driver spins the car around, heading back to the castle. Trey has been in my head the entire time, only for me to learn that Azalea commanded Gannon, Dustin, Clarice, and Abbie not to follow her. He keeps telling me that she isn't aware she commanded them. That much I believe. She isn't aware of her Alpha voice yet. But leaving the castle while carrying our child is just plain foolish. Liam and Damian stay quiet in the car, knowing anything would set me off.

The tires screech as the car pulls into the cobblestone driveway. I can't risk taking Azzy with me with hunters rearing their heads again, yet what we need to do is check out the packs. A letter or my word isn't good enough, and I can't send my men without the risk of endangering them or the pack refusing them entry. Which would either lead to my men killing them or them waiting for me to get there, which in turn would give them a chance to destroy any evidence. Neither is a suitable option and if the pack has something to hide, they would do anything necessary to hold my men off while they get rid of any damning evidence that could be used against them.

Jumping out of the car, the guards at the front door quickly open the doors before I even reach them, then step out of my way. She is one small girl, and she slipped away from them. Yet how is beyond me.

Clarice waits inside the door and scrambles to my side, apologizing as I stalk toward the stairs. Pain rattles through my ankle and foot, so much so that I know she is awake because I feel every time she passes out because the pain ends and her fear of me dissipates. She knows she is in trouble, and it irks me that she's more scared of me than she is of what she did to herself and our baby.

Clarice explains what happened, and I am pissed off that the gardener didn't deter her. Everyone here knows she wasn't supposed to step outside these castle doors. Coming to the steps leading to my quarters, Gannon and Dustin stand, they're staring toward the door but unable to move any further.

I shove past them, and they hang their heads as I growl. Despite trying to avoid it, I have no choice but to teach her how to use her command to remove them from her order. I can hear Azalea's screams for someone to stop doing whatever they are doing to her.

I shove the doors open, and they bounce off the walls with a crack, making the room fall silent. I see Trey leaning over her, and I see red. He only has a pair of shorts on and is covered in blood from head to toe. A furious growl tears out of me, and he moves, stepping aside with his hands up in the air.

My body trembles with the urge to shift moments before I do. Azalea throws her arm out. "He isn't hurting me!" she screams, making me halt. I turn my head to look at her only to see the huge nail protruding from her foot, and a piece of tree attached to it. Blood stains the sheets.

"Well, he kind of was, but not intentionally," she says. Her hands shake as she tries to grip the huge nail that speared through her foot.

"What the fuck happened? You told me she hurt her fucking foot! Not that she had a..." I kneel next to her and examine it.

"A 14-inch iron spike in her foot? Yes, I didn't tell you because she wanted me to rip it out before you got here," Trey answers. I look at her and she drops her head, her cheeks flushing. "I knew you would be mad," she blurts, her hands trembling where she tries to get a grip on it.

"How?" I ask, trying to figure this out.

"A fallen tree. She tried to climb over it, but it was hollowed out. She fell through it, and of all the trees, she had to fall into one of the old target trees," Trey answers, and I grip her ankle, examining it. Azalea hisses and grips my wrist feebly when I try to touch the flat end, holding the piece of bark to the bottom of her foot.

"Don't!" she cries.

"We had to break the tree to get her out. After I ripped her out, I noticed she took part of the tree with her," Trey says with a sigh.

I look him over. His mousy brown hair is a mess, and stuck to the skin on his blood-coated face. My eyes move over him, noticing the healing scratches and claw marks covering his body. He did say he got into a fight with a bear, and I purse my lips turning back to her foot.

"What do you want to do?" Trey asks her, and she looks at him, but turning my head, I see Trey is looking at me, waiting for an answer.

"I guess we're going to have to yank it out," I tell him. It's the only obvious answer. Azalea scrambles back as I pounce on her, and she shrieks.

"No! Get the doctor!" she says, but the doctor is delivering a baby. Trey told me earlier he had sent someone to find him.

"No! Kyson, I can wait! No! Trey, please don't let him!" she screams when I pin her to the bed. Suddenly, I'm thrown off with a roar and being flung into the dresser.

Shocked, I shake myself, trying to figure out what happened as I glance around. Dazed, I get to my feet to find Trey has shifted. "Fuck!" he curses, shocked, shifting back quickly.

He shakes his head and I can see he's shocked at his own actions as he looks at his hands. "I'm sorry. I didn't mean to..." He looks at Azalea while I observe him wondering what the fuck is going on.

"She screamed, I reacted. It's her blood... it's in my system... I'm covered in it... I." He stutters out while he shakes his head, looking at her. I growl at him, kneeling on the bed and ripping her back to me, then covering her eyes with my hand.

"Put some fucking pants on."

Azalea struggles against me, trying to escape, and I squeeze her even harder, holding her in place.

"Enough! Stop fighting me!" I command her, and she goes slack in my arms. Yet her tears, I can feel pooling in my hands. Trey retrieves some of my shorts and slips them on from the closet, and I remove my hand that was covering her eyes.

'Damian, get in here now!' I order through the mindlink before hearing feet on the floor outside. Damian sighs and clicks his tongue as he hurriedly enters, quickly assessing the situation.

Azalea whimpers as I position her on the bed, tucking her between my legs. I shrug my suit jacket off, tossing it aside before rolling my shirt sleeves all while she sits there stuck under my command. Damian looks at her rigidness and his eyes darken before he glares at me.

"Is she under command?" he asks. I nod once. The tone of his voice doesn't sit well with me, and the outrage behind it is getting on my nerves. "It's one thing commanding her normally, but she is fucking pregnant!" Damian snarls at me.

"She isn't in pain. I'm using the weight of it, and that is it," I tell him and he shakes his head.

"She was moving!" My actions are justified. What else could he have expected? Trey looks away and swallows, clearly also agreeing with Damian. It pisses me off how they always jump to her defense against me.

I pull her against me, waiting for them to move, but they don't. "Are you being serious right now?" I ask Damian when he doesn't move. He growls but kneels next to the bed.

"May I?" he asks. "Yes," she stutters out.

"See, she's fine," I tell them.

"She can't move, only speak!" he snaps back at me.

"She kept fighting me! What the fuck did you want me to do, have her thrash around while we yank it out?" I tell him.

"She is barely fucking eighteen, or did you forget that? She has a nail stuck in her foot, and a raging mate! I would be scared too," he snarls back at me. "Then, on top of that, you get mad at her for fearing you! What do you expect out of her when your reaction is always anger?" he snaps at me.

"She was fucking reckless," I shake my head. Why am I even bothering to explain myself?

"Reckless? She went for a walk in the forest. She took someone with her, she never went alone! Do you think she can predict a fucking bear attack? Or a rusty fucking nail going through her foot? You are pissed because she didn't stay in the castle. Locking her away like a caged bird isn't how you get obedience, Kyson! How many times do I need to argue this with you? She isn't going anywhere with your mark on her neck! So settle down! And drop your fucking aura off her! Now! Use the damn calling to calm her, not your fucking aura!"

I can feel her confusion at his words, and I sigh, dropping my aura and her body visibly relaxes and I let my calling slip out and she melts against me. "Azalea?" Trey whispers before leaning down to grab her ankle to hold it for Damian.

"Use the calling, close your eyes," he tells her softly and she turns her face, pressing her ear to the center of my chest, and he looks at me and swallows before looking at Damian. I cradle her head to my chest, stroking her hair and numbing her with the calling.

Yet as I watch Trey and Damian figure out the angle to rip it out at, I wonder what's up with him. He shoves me off her and we suspect him to be the one poisoning her, yet he saves her. He then defends her and I try to rack my brain for an answer. Something is off, and if he didn't poison her, then who did?

Damian taps my knee and nods to her foot and I clutch her tighter, my other arm going across her shoulders and I can hear her breathing. I see their lips counting down, and at three I flood her with the calling, almost knocking her out with it as they yank it from her foot.

Azalea jerks in my arms but doesn't scream out, and Damian holds it up to examine it. While Trey checks her foot to make sure it's all out.

'You and I will be having a chat,' I mindlink Trey. He nods in acknowledgment at my words but doesn't look up, instead retrieves a cloth from the bathroom.

So much doesn't add up, and once Azalea is sorted, I'm getting to the bottom of what's going on with Trey. And how he was able to attack me so easily, and also figure out what the heck is going on with all these rumors about him.

CHAPTER NINETEEN

KYSON

Azalea's voice, persistent and scared, finally ceases as she succumbs to exhaustion in my arms. Her breaths slow to a gentle rhythm beside me, and I feel the tension in my own body ebb, replaced by a silent vow—she won't be stepping foot outside these walls without me again.

However, the abrupt intrusion of Gannon's voice slices through the quiet of the room, jerking me to full alertness. "We finally found his files," he says, the words clear as crystal in my mind.

"Good," I respond softly, cautious not to disturb Azalea's slumber. Carefully, I extract my arm from underneath her, wincing at even the slightest shift that might wake her. Her face is serene at rest, making a stark contrast with the storm of questions that had raged from her lips just hours before. I watch her for a moment longer, the rise and fall of her chest a reassuring sight as it hits me how close we came to losing her today.

With deliberate movements, I slide out of bed and pad silently across the room. "You and Dustin can meet me at my office and wake up Damian. Tell him to meet me there too," I instruct Gannon, my thoughts already racing ahead.

Gannon and Dustin have been buried in musty texts and decrepit records for hours now, searching for any shred of information on Trey that might help us understand the mess we're in. The fact that they've unearthed something, anything, sparks an urgency in me that refuses to wait until morning.

I pull the door open with a soft click, finding Liam and Trey stationed outside. Liam's eyes flick to me, sharp and assessing, while Trey's stance remains firm—a living barrier between us and the unknown threats that lurk beyond these castle confines, making me question where all the unease came from surrounding him and my men.

"Trey, you're coming with me," I command, my voice low but laced with an authority that doesn't leave room for argument.

He peels away from the stone wall, every bit the disciplined guard he's trained to be. Liam gives a silent nod, stepping closer to the bedroom door.

Descending the staircase, the cool draft is like fingers of ice skirting across my skin, and I suppress a shiver. But it's not the chill that unsettles me - it's whatever I'm about to find out next.

Reaching the bottom, the familiar path to my office stretches out before us, the torches flickering along the walls casting elongated shadows that flicker on the stone floor. My footsteps echo, steady and purposeful, while Trey's fall silently behind me.

The door to my office ahead, the dark wood stark against the cold gray of the stone. Pushing it open, I step inside where the scent of leather and parchment fills my senses.

Motioning to the chair across from my desk, I take my seat. Trey slumps into the chair with a casual grace, his arms crossing over his chest as he stifles a yawn. He doesn't squirm or glance around nervously; instead, he sits there with an air of resignation, as if he's already accepted whatever judgment I might pass. His eyes, hooded with fatigue—or perhaps indifference—remain fixed on mine, steady and unflinching. I waste no time in questioning him.

"What did you mean earlier about her blood being in your system?" I ask, leaning forward slightly. The memory of his earlier words itches at my mind, and has all night. His claim had sounded absurd, impossible even, yet here he sits before me with an explanation seemingly at the ready, and I cannot ignore the genuineness that flickers in his gaze.

"I am sired to the Landeena bloodline," he states.

"Excuse me?" The words claw their way out of my throat, rough and edged with disbelief. Sired? As in the irreversible bond formed when one is turned? I push back from the desk, muscles coiled tight as I rise to my feet.

Instinct roars within me, a primal warning that he is a threat to my mate bond. My growl rumbles deep in my chest, a sound that fills the room with its threat. No one—absolutely no one—would claim any part of Azalea without facing my wrath. The very notion that someone could stake a claim on her, share in what is solely mine by right of our mate bond, ignites a fury that burns hot and unforgiving.

I tower over him now, ready to defend what is most precious to me.

"Wait, not in that way." Trey's words rush out like a dam breaking, his hands raised in a placating gesture. The moonlight streaming through the window glints off his anxious eyes as he tries to stem the tide of my fury. "I was born Lycan. King Garret didn't turn me. Landeena blood is different."

My growl subsides into a low hum of confusion. I hover over him, still a menacing presence, but curiosity now threads through the anger.

"Yes, King Garret sired me," Trey continues, urgency underpinning his tone, "but it works similar to an oath. I am loyal to not just King Garret but the entire Landeena bloodline!"

"Wait, how could you be sired to the entire bloodline?" The question slips from me. My stance softens fractionally as I process his words. A bond to a lineage, not merely an individual—this is unheard of, yet his conviction rings with an undeniable truth.

Trey's eyes lock onto mine, and I cannot ignore the earnestness that flickers in his gaze and I retake my seat.

I drum my fingers on the cold surface of my desk, my eyes narrowing as I take in Trey. The tension hangs heavy in the room, a palpable force that seems to press against the ancient walls of the castle.

"Landeena blood is special, you already know this," he says, his voice a mixture of frustration and exhaustion.

My thoughts mull over his statement. Landeena blood—revered, potent, the stuff of legends. I've seen its effects, the reverence it commands among our kind. Yet here stands Trey, his allegiance bound to it in ways that defy the norm.

"But you can only be sired to one person, not an entire bloodline," I retort, my skepticism obvious. The concept feels alien, like trying to grasp smoke with bare hands. Loyalty to one is tangible, measurable. But to a bloodline? Who would agree to that, how could someone blindly agree to that not knowing if the next King or Queen will be a good one.

Trey holds my gaze, unflinching, as if his very soul lays bare upon my scrutiny.

"Wrong!" Trey's voice slices through my doubt, sharp and certain. "Same as if I have children, they are automatically sired to the Landeena's as well," he continues, his arms unfolding as he leans into the explanation, a hint of desperation lacing his words.

I study him, trying to piece together this puzzle that doesn't fit into any frame I've known. The notion of blood ties extending beyond direct siring is uncharted territory beside pact oaths which are marginally different, yet the conviction in Trey's eyes is unmistakable.

"That bear ripped me to pieces, I was carrying her, she was also bleeding." His voice grows more fervent. "I only needed a drop of her blood to awaken the sire bond completely, though I could feel my sire awakening already."

"The stronger she gets, it does and eventually it will awaken any gifts she may have inherited from her parents." He presses on, urgency threading through his tone. "That is why I have been pestering for shifts as her guard."

I lean back in my chair, the leather creaking under my shifting weight. My mind races, grappling with the intricacies of Landeena lineage that now seem to expand before me like a complex puzzle. I can't shake off the feeling that there's more to Trey's story than mere loyalty.

"You wanted to awaken an old sire bond?" The question escapes my lips, and almost sounds accusing yet what I am accusing him of I am no longer sure.

Trey meets my gaze squarely, the weight of years etched into the lines of his face.

His chest rises and falls with a tremor that belies his usual calm. "It's more than that," he begins. His eyes are distant, lost in a sea of memory. "The sire doesn't just make us loyal, it... it makes us feel pained when we're not near our sired. Years, I felt my sire pulling. I never believed she was dead, not until years later when I could no longer feel the tugging of my sire blood thrumming in my veins." He pauses, the silence heavy with the weight of his confession.

"Then," he continues, voice barely above a whisper, "when her blood touched me while I was carrying her, it must have got in my system because I could feel my sire like an extra limb, an attachment. The stronger she gets, the stronger my sire bond gets."

I open my mouth to question the implications, but the click of the door announces new presences. Damian strides in first, his posture rigid with purpose, followed by Dustin's frame shadowed by Gannon's large silhouette.

"Kyson," Gannon nods and extends a folder worn at the edges with use. I take it. My fingers flip through the contents, images and texts blurring together until one name leaps out, snaring my attention.

"What's your link with Marissa Talbot?" The question is sharp, cutting through the air with the precision of a blade.

Trey's jaw tightens, the muscles working as he grapples with the question. The room holds its breath, the silence stretching taut between us.

"She was Azalea's nanny," he states. "I tried to warn the Queen about her."

Gannon's laugh is short and devoid of humor; it reverberates against the stone walls, a precursor to the storm brewing in his narrowed eyes. With a swift motion, he flings an aged diary onto my desk. It lands with a thud, which disrupts the balanced silence of the room.

"Bullshit," he bellows, his eyes full of anger.

Trey reacts instantly, snatching the diary up with hands that betray no tremor. His fingers skim over the worn pages, eyes darting back and forth as he searches for something, anything that could substantiate his claim.

Pages riffle under Trey's fingers, but I can see the tension coiling in his shoulders.

"It's a diary," he asserts, a note of defiance creeping into his voice as he looks up from Queen Tatiana's scrawled words.

Gannon leans forward, his presence like a boulder in the cramped space of my office. "Queen Tatiana's diary," he snarls with a sneer that could curdle blood, "not once does it mention you."

"Of course it doesn't." Trey's retort is a snarl to match Gannon's, and he flicks through the pages with a force that threatens to tear the delicate paper. "You think she would leave information about Azalea's guards for anyone to get their hands on?"

The question hangs between us, pointed and heavy. It's a valid argument; any Queen worth her crown would guard her secrets fiercely, especially when it came to the safety of her child. But I also understand her need to document everything in a diary, it makes me wonder if she kept notes for Azalea one day, yet she also left out crucial information that could have been used to help find her had I known.

Trey's finger stabs at a passage, his nail circling an entry. "See, a guard reported Marissa and that guard was me," he declares, thrusting the book towards me.

I reach out and take the diary. My eyes dart over the handwritten words, tracing the lines of ink that weave through the page.

"She didn't believe you?" I probe, incredulity lacing my tone as I look up from the text. The thought that someone could dismiss a guard's caution, particularly regarding a threat to her child shocks me.

Trey's gaze shifts to the cold stone floor, the muscles in his jaw clenching tight. "No, she did, it was Garret that refused to listen," he murmurs, almost too low for me to catch. The words hang between us, a confession that Queen Tatiana had, in fact, heeded his warning, yet an undercurrent of something unsaid flows beneath them.

I lean forward. "And why would he do that?"

Trey swallows hard, a man battling with memories that are clearly etched into his soul. His eyes, when they finally meet mine, are hardened and angry.

"Maybe because she was King Garret's mistress," Trey admits.

I reel back as if struck, the revelation sending a shockwave through me. My gaze snaps to Gannon, who stands rigid, his face a mask of disbelief.

"Impossible, Tatiana—" Gannon's begins.

With a swift motion, Trey raises his hand, asking for him to wait. His eyes lock onto mine, pleading to let him explain.

"She knew he was having affairs; she always knew. Yet she wanted to save her marriage and...." He trails off for a second becoming nervous.

"She knew?" I ask, shocked by this news. What Queen would allow that? Trey's voice breaks the silence, rough with emotion.

"Of course, she knew, but where would she have gone with

hunters killing off royal families, with the only other Lycan community being yours and with a baby that would be heir to both the Landeen and Azure name?" His eyes are wide, imploring me to understand the desperation of a cornered Queen, a mother protecting her pup.

I can't help but feel a pang of sympathy for Tatiana, imagining her plight, trapped between love for her daughter and duty to a marriage she never wanted. Trey sighs heavily and rubs his temples.

"The night of the attack then, where were you?" The command rolls off my tongue. It's not a question but an order for the truth, and Trey knows it. He meets my gaze, his own eyes shimmering with the threat of tears.

"With my brother. It was my night off." His voice falters, a single tear slipping down his face. "By the time we both got back to the castle, Azalea was gone. Tatiana was dead, and King Garret was barely alive."

"We tried to save him, but..." Trey's voice trails off, his body rigid with the memory. Then, with a sudden motion, he opens his shirt. There, on his chest, are three bullet holes.

I lean forward, my breath catching at the sight of the scars. Trey's chest rises and falls with shallow breaths.

"The hunters shot my brother in the head," he finally manages, the words hollow, as if spoken from a grave. Gannon stands motionless, the muscle in his jaw working silently as he listens.

The skin around the wounds is tight, pulled into pale circles that mark Trey's brush with death. He glances down at his chest. "A few millimeters closer, and I would have died," he murmurs, his voice steady—too steady. He touches the scar closest to his heart, a haunted look in his eyes. "This one collapsed my lung." His finger moves up slightly. "Another here, lodged in my sternum."

Then his hand hovers over where his heart beats beneath the flesh, a tremor betraying his stoic facade. "And this one," he says, his voice barely above a whisper, "only burned me when the bullet lodged into my Landeena crest pendant."

Damian shifts beside me, clearing his throat; he leans forward, resting his elbows on the desk, the weight of his gaze heavy on Trey. "What happened afterward?" His voice rumbles.

Trey straightens, the fabric of his shirt settling back over the scars, hiding them once again from view. "After the Landeena was taken down?" Trey asks, and Damian nods.

"I was beside myself with grief when Liam found me. I told him about Azalea. We searched the castle, and he left while we searched the river edge and the forest." Trey explains. "We came across some hunters. When I was shot, adrenaline kept me alive long enough to get back to Landeena when your men arrived."

"Then what?" Damian asks.

With a nod, Trey acknowledges Damian's question. The room feels smaller somehow, the walls closing in with the weight of his words as he continues. "Spent three months in your hospital with silver poisoning," he says, eyes locked on mine, compelling me to verify his claim later. "Check your records."

I make a mental note to do just that, but there's something about the way he says it—no hesitation, no falter in his voice—that makes me believe him without seeing the proof.

"Then, when I was released," Trey goes on, "I went hunting with a few other Landeena warriors." His gaze drifts past me, focusing on something distant and unseen. "We went looking for Azalea; we even thought we found her at one stage."

"But by the time we got to the camp by the river, it was empty." He presses his lips in a line.

"We picked up Jordan's scent by accident." Trey's hand absently moves to the Landeena pendant hidden beneath his shirt that was now a necklace—the crest that both marked him and saved him. "By the time we got there, there was no sign of them."

"That was years ago," he finishes his voice a soft echo of defeat.

"9 years ago?" The words taste like ash in my mouth as I voice the unspoken timeline we've all danced around.

Trey nods, his gaze holding a distant sorrow—a mirror to my

own heartache. "Yes, I got here just before your sister died." His fingers fidget with the hem of his shirt, a restless energy that speaks of unease and regret. "After Clai... she died, we gave up," he admits, and there's a tremor in his voice that doesn't escape me. A man haunted by his failures.

"Figured I would come to the trials and failed miserably for three years." Trey's eyes don't meet mine; they're fixed on Dustin. His jaw clenches tight, the muscle ticking with tension.

"I didn't want the last Royal family to die." There's defiance now in his voice.

"Tatiana wouldn't have wanted that," he finishes, and the weight of his loyalty—to a Queen long gone, to a lineage teetering on the brink—settles heavily in the room.

I narrow my eyes at him, pressing for an answer that makes sense. "And you didn't recognize Marissa when she was here, not even notice her scent around here?"

Trey shakes his head, the lines of frustration etching deeper into his face. "No, Marissa never had a scent, so I wouldn't have recognized her by scent anyway." He pauses, as if the next words are heavy on his tongue. "Tatiana and Garret were paranoid about security. She used to make everyone in the castle use a descenter, so our scents couldn't be tracked," he explains.

I lean forward, resting my elbows on the cold, hard surface of the desk, the weight of centuries-old wood bearing witness to the tension in the room. "Not even by sight?" I ask, my voice laced with incredulity.

"I wasn't here when she was here," he replies, a hint of defensiveness creeping into his tone. He shifts uncomfortably in his chair before continuing. "I failed the trials three years in a row. I worked at the mill in town before I made your guard; she was already gone by then."

The creak of parchment echoes softly as I sift through the stack of documents cluttering my desk, searching for corroborating evidence.

Trey watches me, his gaze never flinching as if daring me to challenge his words.

"The year you accused me of tampering with your trial was the year I was officially made a guard." The simplicity of his statement hangs between us, unadorned and raw. "I hardly entered the castle grounds except to drop wood off," he adds.

My fingers find the edge of a particular sheet, and I pull it closer, scanning the neat script that lists appointments and duties. Trey's name stands out; he was appointed guard two years after my sister's death, just as he said.

It clicks into place—after her death, I had created the blood oath for my men and selected staff.

"Your story checks out," I concede, my mind reeling from the implications. The pieces of the past settle into a new pattern, one where Trey's presence now makes a twisted kind of sense. His unwavering gaze tells me he knows it, too—that the truth has always been in his favor when Dustin speaks.

"Then why were you a jerk to her in the stables?" Dustin asks.

Dustin's question hangs in the air like a blade poised to strike, and Trey's jaw tightens visibly. For a moment, he simply stares at Dustin, his eyes dark pools of old pain and regret. Then he leans forward, gripping the edge of the desk.

"I told you," he starts, his voice rough, carrying the weight of years marred by a guilt that has never left him. "I thought she was Marissa Talbot's daughter." He pauses, swallows hard, and when he continues, there's a fierceness in his tone that wasn't there before. "Do you have any idea of the guilt I have lived with for not being there that night?"

"Azalea was my charge, and I left, and she vanished by the time I got back!" The words are like a confession, a plea for understanding from someone who has been living in the shadow of a single, haunting failure.

Trey's breath hitches, and he looks up, his eyes meeting mine with a raw honesty that is almost painful to witness. "I would never hurt her," he says, and there's no mistaking the sincerity in his voice.

"I just need to be around her now," Trey says, and his voice breaks slightly, revealing the cracks in his composure. "That is why I have been so desperate to stay on as her guard."

His admission lingers in the air, and I feel something shift—like a lock clicking into place that allows me to see the full picture of Trey's allegiance. It's no longer just about duty; it's personal and fiercely protective. And as much as I hate to admit it, I understand that desperation because I feel it too—every time I look at Azalea.

CHAPTER TWENTY

AZALEA

My eyes flutter open, and I'm met with a cold absence on the other side of the bed. Kyson is gone. A low growl vibrates in my throat, frustration simmering through me like a brewing storm. Of course, he would leave before dawn, evading the barrage of questions he knows all too well are perched on the tip of my tongue. I throw the blanket back with a huff, the air chill against my skin.

I snatch a robe from the end of the bed and draw it around me. The fabric clings to my body, offering a scant comfort as I stride across the room. My fingers grasp the door handle, turning it with more force than necessary.

I open the door to the corridor to find Liam, his feet moving in a rhythm known only to him, his voice lilting softly as he sings a tune under his breath. He twirls, a solitary dancer lost in his own performance, but halts mid-spin as our eyes lock. His dance ends abruptly as if he's just now aware of his audience.

"My Queen," he greets, the words rolling off his tongue.

"Good morning, Liam," I respond, my tone light despite my frustration. "Do you know where the King went?" My eyes search his, seeking an answer, but also gauging whether he'll be straightforward or send me on a merry goose chase for information.

Liam's eyebrows hitch upwards, his lips curving into a mischievous grin that doesn't quite reach the worry etched in the corners of his eyes. "He's with Trey," he says, almost casually, like he's commenting on the weather rather than the whereabouts of my missing husband. "Kyson's trying to untangle the mess you left with Gannon and Dustin."

My heart hitches as I process his words. "Huh?" escapes my lips. The command I had given in a moment of heated emotion now feels like a bomb I've inadvertently set off.

"Your command," Liam clarifies, gesturing with a slight roll of his wrist. "The one where you ordered them from following or touching you."

I bite the inside of my cheek, chastising myself.

"Right," I mutter, more to myself than to him, a reminder that my words carry more weight than I realize. "And Kyson thinks I can just... undo that?"

"Perhaps," Liam mumbles, his tone noncommittal, but the twinkle in his eye suggests he knows more than he's letting on.

"Great," I mutter, feeling the weight of my unintended consequences. "And why is Kyson talking to Trey?"

"Ah, matters of loyalty and trust, no doubt," Liam replies with a coy smile. He leans against the cool stone wall, arms folded across his chest, his casual stance belying the gravity of the situation at hand.

"To see if he's a traitor," he answers, catching the question in my eyes before it spills from my lips. The man who threw himself between me and death is now being doubted and is under suspicion.

Liam tilts his head, studying me, his light tone belying the tension in his posture. "What's wrong, Lass?" His gaze, sharp and probing, searches for cracks in my composure.

I shake my head, the frustration knotting in my stomach like a storm cloud ready to burst. "Nothing," I say, but my voice betrays the turmoil inside. Kyson's evasion is weighing on me. "He just doesn't answer my questions or runs from me when I have them, and now he's questioning one of my guards and hiding from me again!"

Liam's grin is all mischief as he leans in, his voice dropping to a conspiratorial whisper. "Stubborn man, the King, but you just have to think. There's a time he can't run." My brows furrow at his riddle, the answer skirting just beyond my grasp.

"Think about it, Azalea," he nudges gently, his eyes gleaming. But my patience is threadbare, and I'm not in the mood for games.

"Your cryptic advice does wonders for my mood, Liam," I retort, my sarcasm falling flat. His eyes dance with amusement, the kind that comes from knowing secrets the rest have yet to discover. "Was that supposed to help me?"

Liam's laughter rings out again, clear and untroubled, as if he's privy to a private joke between him and the universe. "I don't know, did it?" He stands there, still as a statue save for the twinkle of mischief in his gaze, watching me wrestle with the puzzle he's laid at my feet.

I shake my head, unable to stifle the chuckle escaping my lips. Liam flashes me his typical, mischievous grin, as if daring me to question his methods.

"You're an odd man, Liam," I laugh.

"That's why I'm so much fun," he replies.

"What about Abbie?" The question bursts from me, concern threading through the irritation in my voice as soon as I mention her name. She's been too quiet, too absent, and it doesn't sit right with me.

Liam straightens up, the smile never quite reaching his eyes as he responds. "She's with Clarice," he says, and the next part comes out almost reluctantly, "though I know the Ling wanted you to wait here until he returned." He watches me closely, gauging my reaction.

My eyebrow arches involuntarily at his words, a silent challenge against the notion of being caged by commands, even if they come from Kyson himself. Liam's lips twitch at the sight of my defiance.

"Did he now?" My tone is deceptively calm.

"And with that look, I don't think you intend to wait around for the King to return," he laughs.

"No, I want to find Kyson," I state, the words slicing through the thick air between us when his gaze roams over me before it flickers away.

"Probably be wise to put some clothes under your robe, My Queen," Liam's voice is light, but I can hear him holding back from laughing. At his words, a flush crawls up my cheeks as I glance downward, realizing I'm still naked beneath the thin silk.

"I don't mind the view, my Queen, but King Kyson may not approve of you sharing it," he laughs, and I snap the robe together.

"Right," I mutter, more to myself than to him. With a swift pivot, I return to the room, my mind racing with thoughts of Kyson. In moments, I'm slipping into a dress that clings to my form like a second skin.

Once properly dressed, I stride out, Liam's presence at my back. The murmurs of feuding leaking through the door of the King's office grow louder with each step, the voices sharp and jagged, cutting through the air.

Without hesitation, I push the door open. The space beyond the threshold feels charged, alive with tension. The arguing halts abruptly as if my entrance has snuffed out the flame of their conflict. Heads turn, eyes widen, and the room falls into a shocked hush.

"You're awake!" Kyson's voice slices through the silence, a mixture of surprise and something else—an emotion I can't quite place.

I nod, unwilling to offer more than necessary, and sit in his chair.

Kyson's posture is rigid, and the lines of his body are taut and straining as he stands over Trey. Gannon's hands are planted firmly on Trey's shoulders, holding him in place. I catch a glint of frustration in Trey's eyes.

"Please, continue," I say, my voice calm but carrying an edge that dares them to challenge my right to be here. "I believe I have an interest in the matters at hand."

"No, you need to leave," Kyson growls, and I ignore his words.

Dustin's presence is a storm cloud in the corner, his body rigid against the bookshelf, arms crossed over his chest. The lines etched into his forehead speak of a raw, simmering anger, and his eyes—sharp, calculating—remain fixed on nothing and everything at once. Damian, on the contrary, seems to wilt before us, with dark circles under his eyes resembling bruises from to be exhaustion.

"Kyson," I begin, but he cuts me off with a raised hand.

"You should go back to the room," he says, voice firm yet not an order.

I level my gaze at Kyson, my voice steady but edged with the authority that comes with my title, if I'm going to claim it, I should be allowed to use it. "Trey and Dustin are both my guards, aren't they? If you're speaking with them, I have a right to know about what," I tell him. The growl that rumbles from Kyson's throat is low and laced with frustration. Trey's shoulders shake ever so slightly, his lips pressed tight in an effort to hide a smile, while Dustin merely shifts his eyes toward Kyson, silent as stone.

"Oh, she has a point," Liam remarks, the light in his eyes dancing mischievously while the King glares at me.

"Wait, I thought you said I commanded Gannon and Dustin away?" My confusion sharpens into irritation, and I swivel to face Liam, who leans casually against the door frame.

"You did," Liam confirms with a nod, his expression serious for once.

"You commanded them not to follow or touch you. You came in here. They can't touch you or follow you if you leave, which you will have to fix." Kyson tilts his head, regarding me with eyes full of something akin to concern.

"I don't trust many with you as your guard, and until then, you are stuck with Liam or me permanently attached to you." Kyson shakes his head, the disapproval clear in his posture.

Kyson's gaze narrows. "And you were supposed to ensure she stayed in the room," he directs at Liam.

Liam tilts his head slightly, his voice laced with mock innocence.

"Was I now?" he quips, "Right my King. Well, for next time then, would you rather I pin her to the bed or tie her down?" The words slip from Liam's lips with a rogue's grin playing at the edges, but they land heavily in the thick air of the room, like stones into still water.

Kyson's growl rumbles through the silence, a low warning that vibrates against my skin. His eyes flicker with a fire not entirely meant for Liam but for the situation that has grown beyond his control.

"Enough," Kyson snarls. "We can continue this later."

Gannon's response is instinctual, protective—a growl emanating from deep within as he reluctantly loosens his grip on Trey, stepping back with a scowl etched onto his face. He folds his arms across his chest.

"Continue what later?" The words tumble from my lips. They're once again keeping me in the dark.

Trey straightens, his posture rigid, as if bracing against an invisible blow. His eyes, wide and earnest, seek mine. "The King thinks I'm the one who poisoned you." He pauses, swallowing hard, the Adam's apple in his throat bobbing with the effort. "I explained how it's impossible to harm you, even if I wanted to, not that I do, my Queen. It's all just a huge misunderstanding!"

A growl, low and menacing, cuts through Trey's defense—a sound that seems to originate from the very walls of the room. Kyson's warning to be quiet is clear.

I shift my gaze between Dustin and Liam, the weight of their previous accusations against Trey hanging heavy in the air. Dustin's shoulders are squared, his eyes a clear challenge as they lock with mine. With a nonchalant shrug that doesn't quite reach his storm-cloud eyes, he concedes, "It appears I was wrong." His words are clipped, edged with a reluctant admission as he glares at Trey.

"Really?" Liam quirks an eyebrow, skepticism lacing his tone. He leans forward slightly, arms crossed, his attention drilling into Trey. "He's suddenly off your creepometer?" The question is pointed, almost mocking.

I watch Liam's face harden, the cheerfulness that danced in his eyes moments before extinguished by a flicker of suspicion. "I still think there's something slimy about him," he accuses, his gaze narrowing to slits as he peers at Trey.

Trey's jaw clenches, and I can see the muscle tick beneath his skin, as if wrestling with himself. His hands, which rest on the table, form into fists so tight his knuckles bleach white. "Don't shove your prejudices against me, even if they aren't intentional," he snarls back, defiance raising the pitch of his voice. "We all know why you blame me. It's because I'm the only Royal Guard that was originally a Landeena, an outsider. I wasn't part of the Valkyrie Kingdom. That's what pisses you off. Just admit it!"

Liam's face reddens, and his words spit out like daggers thrown with precision at Trey. "You got in on a whim! You don't get to waltz on in and become part of the guard without working for it," he snaps, his finger jabbing the air toward Trey as if to pin him to his accusation.

"Enough!" Kyson growls, his eyes sweeping across everyone. "Everyone may enter the trials. He never cheated, and he was blood tested like everyone else."

"Wait! What's going on? What prejudices are you talking about?" I ask. Kyson's lips press into a thin line, his silence as telling as any confession. His eyes, dark pools of thought, avoid mine.

Dustin moves forward, his broad shoulders set in a way that tells me he's bracing for the weight of his next words. "When all the Kingdoms were alive, we all used to compete." His voice is steady, but underneath, there's an edge. "Landeena's were known for cheating.

The competitions had huge rewards. They liked remaining in control."

My head tilts, puzzlement etching my features as I struggle to piece together the fragmented history that Dustin lays bare. "Huh?"

Kyson finally breaks his silence. He rubs at the stubble on his jaw, a gesture of frustration that's become all too familiar. "The King ones were separate from that of the Guard ones. We competed, but not like that. The game trials were just for added effect to amp up the Kingdom's," he says, his head shaking as if to dispel the memories.

"What would you win?" I ask curiously.

My question hangs in the air for a moment when Kyson's gaze locks with mine.

"Pure bloodlines," he starts, his voice a low rumble of distant thunder. "Reign over the council for that year." The air thickens as he continues, "My father bet was Landeena's first daughter."

I feel my breath catch, a silent gasp that fails to break the surface. "You," he adds, and it feels as though the world tilts on its axis, "you were the bet between our fathers."

"Not that he ever won that one. However, I did. For years before, though, it was tradition for the kingdoms to compete." Kyson explains. Meanwhile, a low growl escapes from Liam, making me glance at him.

"Wait, slow down. How many Royal families were there? I'm so confused right now. They would bet on bloodlines?"

Kyson exhales a heavy sound. He strides from behind the desk, and as he approaches, I rise instinctively from his chair, the leather still warm from his presence.

Kyson lowers himself into the seat. His demeanor is noticeably calmer as he reaches for me. His hands, strong enough to kill, are tender as he guides me onto his lap, wrapping me in an embrace that feels like both shelter and captivity.

Damian moves, taking a seat next to Trey, whose eyes flicker. Gannon sprawls on the couch, his posture relaxed but eyes sharp, missing nothing.

"Oh yes, story time!" Liam declares, voice slicing through the tension with the ease of a blade through silk. His excitement is infectious enough to draw a chuckle from Dustin, whose demeanor cracks just a bit at Liam's antics.

Liam nudges Gannon, forcing him to scoot over on the couch, making room for him. The movement leaves Dustin as the sole figure standing; his arms crossed over his chest when Liam speaks again.

"I have a knee, good sir. You may use it," Liam offers, each word dripping with mischief as his eyebrow wiggles in a gesture that's borderline scandalous.

Dustin's reaction is immediate, his usual composure splintering under the weight of embarrassment. His cheeks flush a deep shade of crimson, a different contrast to the mask he usually wears. He growls, low and dangerous, a sound that might've sent anyone else scattering. But not Liam. He thrives on this; I can tell by the glint in his eyes.

"Will you stop with that filth talk? We fucked. Get over it and stop mentioning it," Dustin hisses, voice barely controlled as he levels a glare at Liam, one that could curdle milk.

"Correction, we *are* fucking. I never said I was done with you. Now sit," Liam growls. His grip wraps around Dustin's wrist. With an unexpected yank, he deposits Dustin onto his lap, a move so swift it leaves no room for Dustin to fight him.

A chuckle rumbles behind me, warm and deep from Kyson as we all watch Dustin struggle in Liam's lap. "Stop squirming, or I will spank your tight ass," Liam warns and Dustin growls.

Dustin's eyes flash dangerously, his jaw setting in a hard line when Gannon speaks up.

"I told you not to go there, and I warned you that he's clingy as fuck!" Gannon's voice cuts in with a laugh.

Liam's retort is instant. "I'm not!" His eyes flash menacingly.

Dustin's chest heaves in a silent huff, his irritation palpable, yet restrained.

"You're so cute when angry, like a savage chihuahua," Liam

chuckles as he reaches out, fingers aiming to tweak Dustin's reddening cheek.

Dustin's hand shoots up to intercept Liam's, slapping it away with a swift motion.

But their banter lightens the tension in the room.

CHAPTER TWENTY-ONE

AZALEA

"So, the trials?" I ask, looking around at everyone. Damian sighs, and Kyson leans forward and opens a drawer, his hand on my belly, stopping me from slipping off his lap as he moves. He pulls out a scroll and hands it to Damian, who unrolls it on the desk. I lean forward. Trey then grabs a paperweight and places it on the end to hold it out while Damian does the other side. I lean forward to see it's a map. It looks ancient, the paper yellowing around the edges.

Trey points to a vast Kingdom by the river, which I know has to be this one or the Landeena's. "There are four Kingdoms. This one is the Valkyrie Kingdom, Kyson's Kingdom," Trey says, pointing to Kyson behind me.

"Your last name is Valkyrie?" I ask, looking at Kyson over my shoulder.

"Yes," Kyson chuckles. Trey looks at me like I'm absurd and should have known that.

"She didn't even know her own Kingdom. How could you expect her to know his last name? She can't read," Damian defends me.

"Plus, I never bothered to ask which I probably should have," I answer, my cheeks burning.

"Kyson Keller Valkyrie, Valkyrie Kingdom," Kyson whispers next to my ear. He kisses my shoulder, and I nod, turning back to Trey.

"This is your Kingdom, the Landeena Kingdom," Trey says while pointing to another along the river but high in the mountains.

"So all the Kingdoms are named after the reigning King?" I ask, and Trey nods.

"Now, this one in the mountains. This was the Azure Kingdom. Which was your mother's original Kingdom. It was also the first Kingdom to fall when she married into the Landeena Kingdom. About six months later, the Kingdom was raided. Not a single person survived. The Azure Kingdom was the largest of all."

"Azure was my mother's maiden name?" I ask, and Trey nods sadly.

"Your mother was one of twelve daughters and the only one that survived that bloodline and only because she married your father," Damian explains.

"But how does that lead to the trials?" I ask.

"Because your parents weren't mates. Their marriage was part of a treaty. The Landeena and Azures were constantly at war, a treaty between the oldest daughter and the oldest son. Your parents brought the two Lycan packs together. They wanted to strengthen the bloodlines. Both the Azures and Landeenas were said to have certain gifts," Trey says, and Kyson growls at him.

"She has a right to know!" Trey exclaims.

"Not that, and not now," Kyson snarls, and Trey curses but turns back to the map.

"Azures owned the council. They were the founding family of it after all, but when the Kingdom fell, none of the three remaining kingdoms could decide who to run it. So they made the trials, but then it turned into some sort of Olympics every year, and since it brought the kingdoms together, they ended up making it annually."

"When I was a teenager, your father competed. My father

wanted an alliance with the Landeenas. The only way to guarantee an alliance was through marriage. So when my father won, he asked for the hand of any Landeena daughter they had in the future," Kyson explains. "Which he refused, so Valkyrie took hold of the council for years until your father won it back."

"So, who were the other two kingdoms?"

"The Cyprus Kingdom, which was my mother's family Kingdom, they fell a few decades after the Azure Kingdom. They weren't far apart and also part of an alliance with my Kingdom. Though a few survived and are within my pack now, however, none of the royals survived," Kyson tells me.

"And your parents had an arranged marriage, too?" I ask him.

"Yes, it is rare for royals to find their mates. Most of us are promised before we even exist, just like you were promised to me many years before you were ever a thought in your parent's minds."

"And what of this Kingdom?" I ask, looking at a fifth one that was crossed out with what looked like charcoal.

"That was the Credence Kingdom. They were as old as the Landeena Kingdom," Kyson tells me.

"So Landeena's and Azures are the two oldest kingdoms?"

"Yes. The Azure Kingdom. The first royal was a woman, and Landeena was a man. Legend says they were basically like the Adam and Eve of Lycan bloodlines. They argued for centuries over who the real OG Lycan was, hence the treaty being made. So many people were killed over such a foolish argument," Kyson says, shaking his head.

"So what about your Kingdom?" I ask him.

"My Kingdom was the second largest."

"And the Credence Kingdom?"

"They weren't Lycan. They were a human Kingdom. The four Lycan Kingdoms took them down, or so we thought, but they rebuilt and remained in the shadows and slowly, one Kingdom at a time, they started taking us out."

"So, what is there now?" I ask.

"That is where the council is," Kyson tells me.

"So what is with the trials?"

"Well, when Kyson's father beat yours, your parents refused to have children and refused his request. Your father competed every year after that, trying to win the council back. Then there were claims your father cheated, which he did. Once Kyson came of age he then started competing against your father and that is when it got really out of hand because your father made a stupid bet and lost, in turn Kyson won your hand," Trey admits.

"How did he cheat?" I ask.

"Your father put silver in the water fountains, making all Kyson's men sick," Damian says.

"And me, Valkyrie still won that year," Kyson chuckles.

"So you agreed to the marriage, you wanted it?" I ask Kyson, and he shrugs.

"Yes, I wanted the marriage. But I also wanted to maintain control over the council. Once I won your hand though, your father cheated four years in a row, then once Cyprus fell, your family went into hiding, but even after all the kingdoms fell, I kept up with the trials for the men; instead, they competed for a position on my personal guard."

"So, only four kingdoms and a human kingdom initially existed here?"

"No, there were others, but they were minor players. These four, plus the human ones, were the most powerful kingdoms in the era, but now mine is the only one left. The entire Lycan population now lives in my Kingdom, including those left from Cyprus and Landeena."

I nod.

Dustin sighs. "So you thought Trey was a cheat, like my father?" I ask, and Trey sits back and smiles smugly.

"He never cheated," Kyson says behind me.

"No, I won my place fair and square. Also, they are wrong in thinking I would poison my sire," Trey snarls, and my brows furrow.

"Sire?"

"Like a blood oath, only stronger. When you were a baby, I was your personal guard, but there is one way to be a hundred percent sure to clear this up," Trey says.

"No!" Kyson snarls behind me, making me jump.

"You want proof that what I claim is true. That will prove my innocence," Trey growls.

"She is pregnant, definitely not! I won't have my unborn child or mate put at risk!" Kyson spits at him.

"My blood is clean, I am not tainted, she can't sire me when I am already sired to her, and it will only strengthen my sire to her, not affect her, or your bond," Trey argues.

"Wait, what is he talking about?" I ask, but Kyson shakes with rage, and Trey glares at him.

"Meeting dismissed, everyone out, now!" Kyson orders, and they jump to their feet to leave.

"What? No!" I growl, twisting in his arms.

"Enough, we can talk about it later," Kyson snarls.

"What are you so fucking afraid of me finding out?" I yell at him.

"I'm not afraid of anything, so stop causing a scene. As I said, we can talk about this later!" Kyson growls.

A scene? I was causing a scene?! I could show him a scene if that's what he wants.

"Yeah, you keep saying that but later never comes, does it Kyson!" I snap and try to climb off his lap, but he refuses to let go and nips at my mark in warning, which only angers me further. My claws slip out and I stab them in his thighs.

"Let me go!" I snarl.

CHAPTER TWENTY-TWO

AZALEA

As I struggle to get out of his grip, Liam pauses by the door, waiting to see if I am leaving, seeing as he is the only one besides Trey that can follow me. Kyson's grip around my waist tightens, and he grips my wrist with his hand, prying my claws from his leg.

"Let me go," I repeat.

"You would have to drink his blood!" Kyson snarls at me. He yanks my hand off his thigh, which is now dripping blood on the floor.

"Do that again, and I will put you to sleep!" he snarls in warning.

"Drink Trey's blood?"

"Yes, and you're not. His DNA would be in your system! So no, it isn't happening!"

I scrunch my face up at the thought of drinking someone's blood. I never would have agreed to that anyway.

"Wait! Why not just say that? You make no sense!" I ponder, looking at Liam, and he shakes his head and shrugs.

"Because I am not smelling his scent on you, is WHY! And risking you bonding to him."

"I am marked and mated!" I growl. Not that I wanted to drink Trey's blood. I believe him, he had so many chances to kill me and didn't. He also could have walked off with the bear and it would have looked like a freak accident, but he stayed instead, getting ripped apart trying to save me.

"You're Landeena!" Kyson growls.

"Huh?"

"It doesn't matter. Come on," he says, tapping my leg for me to hop up. But now I want to know why the heck being Landeena is so important.

"No, what do you mean?"

Kyson sighs. I twist in his lap, but he glares at the ceiling, refusing to answer when Trey steps just inside the door. His voice makes me turn to look at him.

"Landeena's aren't tied to anyone, neither are Azures," Trey says. As soon as the words leave his mouth, Kyson roars. The growl that rips out of him sounds almost painful, his aura hitting all of us like a shock wave, which makes me feel queasy. He moves so quickly I fall off his lap onto the floor just as he reaches over and grabs Trey. He slams him against the door and Liam jumps back just as startled.

"Kyson!" I shriek, watching Trey's face turn purple. I get to my feet and grab his arm.

"Let him go," I demand. Kyson's eyes are wild with rage and his nostrils flare, and hair spreads across his body as he fights the urge to shift. Trey tries to speak, his mouth opening as he tries to breathe, yet Kyson doesn't let him go. I look at Liam for help, who moves the moment I do and grips Kyson's shoulder.

Damian also steps back in next to him from outside the corridor. "Kyson, you don't want to kill him; he isn't lying. I know you know that and a sire bond is stronger than an oath! Think about this!"

Kyson's grip tightens more and Trey makes a gasping noise when Damian speaks again.

"You kill him and you kill her biggest protection," Damian mutters. Kyson growls, but his grip loosens and Trey gasps loudly, yet Kyson doesn't let go completely.

"Please!" I whisper, looking at Trey, who is trying to catch his breath. Kyson shoves him, but steps back. Trey clutches his throat and hunches over. I rub his back, glaring at Kyson. Trey clutches my arms and I help him sit in the chair. He looks like he's been through the ringer, though the fingerprints around his neck are already starting to heal.

"What did you mean?" I ask Trey. Kyson growls and glares at him. "If you won't tell me, I will get answers from others," I snap at him.

"Landeenas are not tied to anyone. They can sever a bond and live afterward, though it would kill Kyson. You would survive. That is what your mate is worried about. You could leave him and it would kill him, but not you," Trey answers, glancing nervously at Kyson.

"That's what you are worried about? That I would leave my own mate?" I ask Kyson.

"Yes, because your father did, his mate was a human woman. First time a Lycan ever had a human mate. He changed her and made her Lycan. Then a treaty agreement was offered. So he rejected his mate for your mother, which in turn killed the girl and that started the war with the Credence Kingdom. The Kingdoms took them out, or so we thought," Kyson answers.

"So you think I would do the same thing?" I ask him, remembering the pain of being without him even briefly. I could only imagine the pain of a severed bond.

"No.. Well, yes.. Maybe. But also no, because it is nearly impossible to do. Plus, I have actually marked and mated you, making us destined mates. Lycan souls are tied once, marked and mated. For you to do that would not only kill me, but kill a part of you."

"But my father did it?" I ask and Trey nods beside me.

"Yes, he was also having an affair with Marissa Talbot. Unfaithfulness is nearly impossible with actual mate bonds, but arranged marriages and forced bonds, they can still do those things. It causes pain to the mate. But for some reason, when your father rejected his mate, he lived and remarked another. We believed it was a backup plan for when the moon goddess created Lycans so we could procreate," Trey answers.

I am horrified by the things my father did, it disgusts me to know my mother not only was forced to marry the man responsible for killing most of her family, but also forced to suffer through a forced mate bond.

"Yes, but you said the Azures were the first females?"

"They were, but there would be no guarantee they would be compatible. So everyone believed that it was the creator's backup plan that the original Landeena could reject his mate and take another. All four royal bloodlines were created at once, but Azures and Landeena were the first and considered blessed," Trey answers. My eyebrows raise at his words. I think I could be told this over and over and still not fully understand. Comprehending this news is like trying to read a book.

"Then after generations and Lycans breeding with humans, it created werewolves, then eventually it was generations of the bloodlines dying out, so that is also why the royals never found mates. They were deemed to be marked and mated through alliance to keep the bloodlines strong and pure, or some crap if you believe in all the Goddess mumbo jumbo," Trey continues, his voice becoming clearer, and by the time he finished, I knew his throat was healed.

"Ok, is the history lesson done?" Kyson snaps, and Trey swallows and nods. Yet I have more questions, but with the way Kyson's aura is rippling out, I figure it would be best not to push him.

Liam grabs Trey and hauls him out of the room quickly before Kyson goes on another strangling spree. Kyson wanders over to his bar area and pours himself a glass of whiskey and then another. Three glasses later and his aura settles some even though his anger is still buzzing beneath the surface. I wait for him to speak, but he doesn't. After 30 minutes, he simply walks out of the room. I race to catch up to him, I slip my hand in his and he stops. He looks down at my hand and sighs, lifting it to his lips and giving it a kiss.

"I'm sorry," he whispers.

"I'm not leaving you Kyson, I am just curious about who I am. What I am. You don't need to feel threatened by any of it," I tell him. He nods but doesn't say anything else, yet I know he is hiding something.

When we are nearly back to the room, we run into Peter carrying a cloth and bucket of soapy water up the steps. Kyson takes the bucket from him, and Peter sighs.

"Since when are you on cleaning duty?" Kyson asks as Peter follows us up the steps.

"Since Clarice asked me to clean the steps as punishment," Peter answers.

"What did you do?" Kyson asks.

"I forgot to feed the horses. So Clarice said since she had to do one of my chores, I had to do one of hers," Peter says, and Kyson chuckles.

"Well, get scrubbing," Kyson tells him, putting the bucket on the top step. Peter groans, but tosses his cloth into the bucket and gets to work.

"I am going to visit your old pack today. You're coming with me," Kyson says, leaving no room for argument. He pushes the door open.

"Warm clothes; it is supposed to rain today. Get dressed," Kyson says, wandering off to the bathroom.

CHAPTER TWENTY-THREE

ABBIE

Gannon is off doing an errand for the King. He had been nagging me about Cassandra and what I wanted to do about her, but I still have no idea. I don't like the idea of having someone's life in my hands, especially when I've hardly had any control over my own. Yet, when Gannon goes off with the King, I wander around the castle. I explore the wine cellars and am getting ready to clean them when I hear a familiar voice calling out from the cells down the corridor.

The wine cellar runs what appears to be the entire length of the castle, with different underground corridors leading off in different directions, and the one to my left I know goes to the dungeons. Guards stand on either side of the arched tunnel leading to them, and I glance at them. They pay her no attention while she continues screaming out for them to set her free.

Finding the cobweb brush, I head back toward the stairs leading into the kitchen's huge pantry. Only once I am halfway up do I stop. Cassandra has three children, which has been nagging at me. As much as I want the woman dead, I don't want to punish her children for her crimes. Her husband and their father are dead, and her life is now resting in my hands.

Leaning the cobweb brush against the stairs, I walk back down the steps, over to the corridor, and stop in front of the guards.

"Miss Abbie?" one asks, and I chew my lip, glancing toward the dark dungeons.

"Can I see her?" I ask, looking at the man. He has a mustache and light blue eyes that are almost white they are that light. He glances at the other guard, who has a full beard, dark eyes, and long hair that cascades almost to his waist and is tied in two braids.

"One of us will come with you," the other man says, and I nod. I start walking down the corridor when I hear her screaming out again, and I stop. Her voice grating in my head as memories of the same voice teased and taunted me while she would hold my head to stop me from trying to pull away from him. She is just as sick as him to do that to another woman. I hadn't realized I had stopped moving until the guard's hand falls on my shoulder. Only then do I realize I am shaking like a leaf.

"I'm right here. She can't hurt you, Miss; I have mindlinked Gannon," he says, and I swallow.

"Maybe this was a bad idea," I murmur.

"It's up to you. No one will force you to go in there, Miss Abbie," he whispers.

I look at the man, and his dark eyes look black under the dim lighting. I should feel embarrassed that he knows what she did to me, yet his gentle voice holds no contempt.I nod but force myself to keep going until I am stopped outside her barred cell. She sits in the cell's corner sobbing, her head in her hands and knees to her chest.

Cassandra looks up, and I can tell she is about to scream out again, but her words die out when she notices me standing there.

"I suppose you're here to gloat?" she says, resting her head back on the brickwork. She turns her face away from me. She looks like crap, her nails all chipped, her hair a mess, her clothes wrinkled, and she has no shoes on.

Turning to the guard, I hold my hands out for the keys, and he looks at me. "Abbie," he asks questionably.

"Keys, please," I tell him, and he pulls them off the key chain and hands them to me.

Cassandra looks at me and jumps to her feet as I put the key in, but I don't turn it. Instead, I notice the bottled water just outside the cell door and pre-packaged sandwiches. I move to the small table and grab two of the triangle packages and a water bottle before tucking them under my arm. My hands shake as I open the cell, and my eyes move to her when I notice the chain around her ankle that is attached to the wall.

Cassandra watches me warily as I enter, closing the door behind me. This isn't the same scornful, confident, and entitled woman I knew. This woman is helpless and looks petrified of me. She knows her life is in my hands. Gannon told her that much.

I take a step toward her, and she takes one back, her back hitting the wall. I hold the water bottle out to her, and she looks at me funny, tilting her head to the side. She reaches forward and grabs it like she thinks I will toss it at her.

She opens the cap and starts gulping it down thirstily. When she is done, I hand her the sandwiches, which she takes, and I watch her for a second before taking a few steps back and sitting next to the cell door. She eyes me suspiciously before also sitting.

"Eat. You look hungry. I am not here to hurt you, Cassandra," I tell her, and her lip quivers. She seems shocked by my words.

"Why not?" she asks, but peels the wrapper back on her sandwich and moans as she takes a bite.

"Because I am not you, I am not a monster," I tell her, and she stops mid-bite and looks at me. She chews slowly and swallows, picking at her sandwich with her fingers. I observe her, and she can't be much older than me. Without all the makeup staining her face, she looks very youthful, making me curious about who she really is.

"How old are you?" I ask her.

"Twenty," she answers with a sigh.

"Twenty!" I ask, knowing her oldest child was six years old.

"But Micheal is six," I tell her, and she chews slowly and nods her head.

"I had him two days before my fourteenth birthday," she answers, and I swallow. How different our lives have been, though that must have been tough to have a baby that young.

"I thought you and Kade were high school sweethearts?"

She laughs and shakes her head.

"No, that's what he tells everyone. He is eight years older, although he doesn't look like it. I was one of his working girls," she says with a shrug.

"But you just said you were fourteen when you had Michael?"

"Yeah, I was also a rogue. Kade took me in when he met me at another pack, I was placed in when I was thirteen. He saved me."

My eyebrows raise at that. *Saved* her? Knocking a fourteen-year-old up is saving her?

"I know it sounds bad because of the age difference, but he saved me. I was to be sold off to another Alpha regardless."

"He bought you?" I ask.

"Yes, and I worked at his brothel for a couple of weeks."

"That is not saving you," I tell her, and she looks down at her hands.

"I know, but it's better than who Alpha Dean would sell me to," she says.

"Pardon, did you say Alpha Dean?" she nods.

"Yeah, my family was picked up outside his borders. He said I was old enough to be sold off, and he needed the money. He killed my parents right in front of me and handed me over to his son," she says with a growl and shakes her head. A lone tear slips down her cheek.

"Then what happened?"

"His son was done with me, and Kade was visiting. He offered me to Kade, but then Kade said he would buy me off him under the table, that no one had to know. They have been dealing in sales of the flesh ever since."

"You mean trafficking?" I ask, and she swallows.

"I know what I did was fucked up, but," she stops.

"When he brought me back, you figured I would replace you," I tell her.

"I didn't want to go back to work, and I have children now. What would become of them?" she asks before stopping, hearing footsteps coming down the corridor, she glances behind me and gets to her feet, and I hear a thunderous growl echo off the walls and I stand quickly. Gannon steps up next to the guard.

"Why is she in there with her?" he demands, and the man steps away from him.

"I'm fine, Gannon," I tell him, and he looks at me, tearing his eyes from the guard. He sighs and twists the key in the lock, and opens it. Cassandra whimpers and presses into the corner further.

I put my hand on his chest when he moves toward her. "Back off," I tell him, and he looks at me.

"You're not touching her," I tell him.

"She helped him. How can you say that?" Gannon snaps at me.

"And she will have to live with what she did, she is a monster, but even monsters have a story. Even monsters can feel, but I am not a monster, and I won't be responsible for her children being orphaned," I tell him as my eyes move in her direction.

"She is just as much a victim as I am," I say, tears burning my eyes. Gannon growls.

"No!" he snarls.

"It's my choice. You said it's my choice," I whisper, and he looks at me.

"She needs to be punished for what she did. She doesn't deserve to live after that," he snarls, stepping toward her, and she whimpers, cowering away from him and I grip his shirt in my fist, making him stop.

"My choice, what she did was wrong, but-" I look at Cassandra.

"Fear makes people do foolish things. That is something I do understand," I tell him.

"No, I am not letting her go," Gannon says, shaking his head.

"You said I got to choose what happened to her, so mindlink the King."

"Abbie!"

"No, Gannon, either you get the King, or I go see Azalea. I won't allow you to kill her. She has kids, and I am not leaving them orphaned to suffer the same fate I did," I tell him and he snarls angrily. Gannon walks out of the cell, slamming the door. Cassandra whimpers before she collapses, her body shaking as she sobs.

"Thank you, thank you," she cries.

"Go home to your children and forget about me Cassandra, I was never a threat to you, but if you come back, I will let him skin you alive like he wants to do, and I will hand him the tools while he does it," I tell her.

She nods, glancing at him and her face pales.

"Don't ruin your second chance. I won't give you a third," I tell her, walking out of the cell. Gannon growls and looks away from me and I stop beside him and place my hand on his chest. "Don't be mad," I tell him.

"I'm not mad at you."

"Yes, you are, but that's ok. I don't expect you to understand my request," I tell him and he sighs but cups my face in hands, pulling me closer. He kisses my forehead, hugging me tight, and I wrap my arms around his waist and look up at him.

"Kyson and Azalea are on their way down," Gannon whispers.

"Thank you."

CHAPTER TWENTY-FOUR

AZALEA

When Kyson gets out of the shower, he seems to be in a better mood. He wears nothing but a towel draped low on his hips while I pull my socks on. I have put on a loose-fitting off-shoulder top and jeans I only just managed to squeeze into.

Yet my skin itches and burns, the fabric irritating my skin. The clothes feels constricting, and I can't stop scratching. Kyson eyes me, clearly happy to see me doing what he asked instead of arguing with him. The truth is, I am excited to leave the castle grounds. I don't care where we are going, I just want out of this place.

Kyson walks into the closet before returning with some black suit pants and an undone gray button-down shirt. He tosses a jacket beside me on the bed. "It's going to rain. Put it on," he says, pulling his belt through the belt loops.

"Where are we going?" I ask him.

"Well, we were going to Kade's pack, but now we are going to your old one," he says, and I look up at him, tugging down my shirt, the seam rubbing against my skin.

"Why the change?" I ask.

"Cassandra told Abbie she was bought off Alpha Dean's son by Kade."

"So?" I ask.

"She was thirteen when she was sold to Kade, so I want to find out what deals they had on the side. With Kade now dead, only Alpha Dean will be able to answer those questions. Cassandra is apparently helpful now Abbie has decided to let her go."

"What?" I ask, sitting up, my tone coming out harsher than intended. "You're not letting her go," I tell him. My skin feels tight under my clothes, and I scratch at my bump and sigh.

"It is what Abbie requested. We decided she could choose Cassandra's fate," he says, and I shake my head but still don't agree that she should just get off so easily.

"Did Clarice change washing powder?" I mutter. My skin is now burning fiercely.

"Hurry, I want to leave, and we need to stop by the dungeons on the way," Kyson says, ignoring my question.

I pull my shoes on, but my feet ache the moment I pull them on. My toes feel squished, and my feet feel puffy. Kyson watches me before bending down, tugging my shoe off, and looking at my feet. He presses his thumb down on it, and my skin indents. His brows furrow.

Kyson scratches his chest, raking his nails over his skin before his eyes widen, and he grips the front of my shirt and yanks me to him. He sniffs it before I am shoved back on the bed, and my clothes are shredded to pieces instantly. I shriek, wondering what he is doing, but I don't have time to ask when he scoops me up and pushes me into the shower. The rush of cold water steals my breath when he starts scrubbing my skin furiously. Yet the cold water soothes my burning skin so I don't fight him.

Trey and Liam rush in moments later, and I squeal, hiding behind Kyson's body, using him as a shield.

"Find out who brought the laundry up yesterday!" Kyson growls, not even looking at them, solely focused on scrubbing my flesh raw.

"Ah, I did," Liam answers.

"Who gave it to you?" Kyson asks.

"Clarice, why?" he asks, looking frantically at me.

"Her clothes are washed in wolfsbane," Kyson snarls, and I gasp. Trey rushes off and returns with a handful of my clothes and sniffs them. He holds it out to Liam, who sniffs it too.

"I can't smell it," Trey whispers, and Liam agrees.

"It's faint, but it's wolfsbane," Kyson growls, and I look down at my reddened skin, and Kyson's hands are just as red from my scrubbing soap on my skin. My thighs and stomach are red and angry, looking swollen, and I try hard not to panic from the pain.

"Get me the laundry roster," Liam snaps at Trey, who rushes off.

"Liam, go to my sister's storage room and find her some clothes and ask Clarice to wash Azalea's clothes by hand, and someone needs to sit by the dryer," Kyson snarls furiously.

Liam rushes off, and I shake my head, and tears burn my eyes. Why does someone keep doing this? What did I do that someone keeps trying to kill me?

"Shh, Azzy, it's alright. We will figure out who it is. I promise, even if I have to kick every person out of the castle until we do," Kyson murmurs, and I look down at him.

Goosebumps cover my flesh as the cold water is rinsed over me. He kisses my thigh before turning me to scrub the rest of me. Kyson's fresh clothes are now ruined and sopping wet and my teeth chatter from the cold.

Once done, we hop out, and Kyson goes through the drawers and rips all my clothes out, chucking them by the door and checking his own, but his clothes are fine. He pulls on new clothes when Liam knocks on the door. I tuck the towel tighter around me when he cracks the door but doesn't enter.

"I found some of her maternity clothes. They might be comfier," Liam tells him, handing them to Kyson. Kyson shuts the door and comes over to me.

"You kept her clothes?" I ask, and he nods.

"Yes, everything was suctioned down and packed away. I couldn't bring myself to throw them out, and neither could..." he says, but trails off handing me some tights. He sniffs the shirts.

"They smell clean. Put those on," he says, pecking my cheek. Once dressed, Kyson gives me an antihistamine to bring the reaction down. Though my skin is no longer burning, I think washing it off quickly has saved me from any permanent reaction.

"Come on," he says, offering me his hand. I take it, and we walk out of the room.

"Liam, have the cleaners come pick up the laundry and strip the linens, even the drapes. Anything fabric needs to be cleaned while I'm gone. Check every person in and out as they come into this room. And don't let anyone in by themselves. Gannon is to remain with them once we are done in the dungeons. No one in or out of my room without Gannon knowing," Kyson tells him, and Liam nods. His cheeky mood is gone, and one of Kyson's loyal soldiers is in its place.

"Find out who had access to her clothes, and I want every staff member questioned and have someone check the cameras," Kyson adds and before giving Liam a list of things to organize before we leave.

Kyson leads me downstairs, and we pass Trey with a notepad in his hand. "Give it to Clarice to give Dustin, and you're on guard with Liam Damian and me today. Meet us in the dungeons," Kyson tells him.

"Yep, I will be down soon. Clarice washed the clothes and hung them on the line. Says they were on clothesline for most of the day," Trey says, showing him.

"Are the outside cameras installed yet?" Kyson asks while flicking through the notepad.

"Yes, but not hooked up on that side, but we have the far garden ones and front ones working. We should be able to see who went up that way," Trey answers.

"Have someone watch them while we are gone," Trey nods,

"Also, Clarice wants to know if you want her to pack you food and drinks."

"No, I will buy anything we need on the way. I don't trust anyone right now handling anything to do with Azalea."

"Understood. I will let her know," Trey says, rushing up the steps. We make our way to the dungeons. We had to go through the kitchens, and I can see Clarice busy going over sign-off sheet pages.

"My Queen, I am sorry. I will figure out who had access, I promise. I will wash everything myself and sit by the dryer," Clarice says.

"Thank you, Clarice," I tell her, and she nods, and goes to hug me but freezes, not her too. Stepping forward, I hug her. Kyson watches her warily. In fact, he watches everyone present in the kitchen warily, and his aura is deadly, making them cringe when we pass them, heading toward the colossal pantry that is nearly as large as the kitchen.

Kyson leads me to the back, where an enormous set of stairs lead underground. Kyson keeps a firm grip on my arm as we descend them because it is dark, and they are pretty steep. Once at the bottom, I look around and see this part is a vast wine cellar, filled with rows and rows of wine and spirits.

Kyson leads me around like he can walk this with his eyes closed and brings me to a dark tunnel. I see Abbie, who rushes toward me before freezing like she has hit a brick wall and becomes stunned. It is dark down here and cold, and I groan realizing I commanded her too.

"You can go to her, but when we get home, we are going to have to work on you removing the command over them," Kyson tells me.

"You will teach me?" I ask him.

"I don't have a choice," he grumbles, and I get the impression he doesn't like me being able to command anyone, making me wonder if I can command him, and that is why. Repeatedly, I have heard that Landeena's blood is special. They have gifts, but after the way he said it and the feeling through the bond, it makes me wonder if my command would be stronger than his.

I reach for Abbie, who stands frozen, so I rush to her and huge her. Abbie explains about Cassandra and everything that she and Gannon found out. I wish she could come with us, but when I look over at Kyson to ask, he is in the cells with Cassandra, his entire body tense, and I can feel he wants to kill the woman but is respecting Abbie's wishes. Yet he is angered because she didn't just affect Abbie, but I was punished for it, and I know she won't get off so easily.

"You will endure the same punishment," I hear Kyson tell her.

"Kyson!" I call out to him. After hearing about Cassandra and Kyson commanding her to double-check what she said was true and confirming it, I feel the same as Abbie.

It is clear Kade brainwashed her. To her, he was a hero, yet she was entirely aware of her wrongdoings and apologized countless times. She just wanted to go home to her boys, and I agreed with Abbie she was as much a victim as we were in all this.

Kyson looks at me. "Let her go; I am fine. Enough blood has been spilled. Leave it be," I plead with him. Kyson growls and glares at her, and she backs away from him when he bends down, gripping the chain off the ground that is wrapped around her ankle. He yanks it, ripping it clean off the wall. Cassandra shrieks, and my heart beats quicker. I think he is about to whip her with the chain when he growls and drops it, instead grabbing her face.

"You come anywhere near my mate or Abbie, or I hear even a whisper of their names coming from you, I will have my guard hunt you down and string you up, then I will make your boys watch as I kill you for it, understood?"

She nods and whimpers, tears rolling down her dirt covered face.

I feel his aura rush out, and she gasps like she is choking. "You will come nowhere near Azalea or Abbie. You will never speak or utter their names again," he says, his voice so calm it chills me to the bone. She nods, and he shoves her away before turning to the guards, and his eyes fall on Dustin.

"Dustin, run her back to her pack and get back here and help Gannon," Kyson orders, and Dustin steps into the cell and grabs her arm, dragging her out when Abbie runs over to a small card table and snatches some sandwiches off it and bottled water before chasing after them.

Dustin stops, and she hands them to Cassandra before shocking me and hugging her. Cassandra stands frozen and looks pained, probably because of Kyson's command not to come near either of us.

"Thank you," I hear Cassandra murmur, and Abbie lets her go just as I wander back over to her.

"That didn't feel right," Gannon says, glaring after Cassandra.

"It wouldn't have been right either to punish her," Abbie says to him before groaning when she tries to step closer to me.

"I wish you could come with me. I don't want to go back there by myself," I tell her, walking to Abbie since she can't come to me.

"And play this tug of war. I can't move to you. Only you can come to me, that would be an issue, but it's ok. I don't think I could go back there, anyway. I never want to see that place again," Abbie says and smiles sadly.

I feel the same way, but Kyson would not change his mind, and much as I was not too fond of going back there, it may also be a good way to put that place behind me.

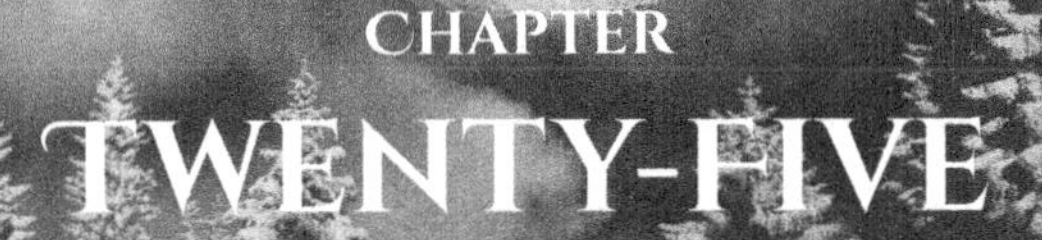

CHAPTER TWENTY-FIVE

KYSON

Azalea was in a strange mood. She was scared, not that she would admit it. I was kind of glad to get out of the castle with her. At least she would be safe with me. Or so I hope. I hope bringing her back to this place doesn't dredge up unwanted memories for her or haunt her, especially after this morning. She knows I am keeping stuff from her, but I am only doing it to protect her, though I can't lie, some of it is for selfish reasons. Trey blurted that one out.

"Are you worried about returning here?" I ask her, but she shakes her head. Which only confirms my original thoughts. She's more scared about being at the castle. I am struggling to figure out who I could trust myself.

Every lead we have is a dead-end, and I knew this one would be too. They always were, yet still, we investigated.

"What are you worried about, then?"

"Everything," she murmurs. I can feel the weight and pressure on her. In the blink of an eye, she's been thrust into a world she knows nothing about. Laws, kingdoms, and her own family history are a mystery to her. Then, on top of that, she is worried about Abbie. She is always worried about Abbie. Concerned about who is trying to kill her and why. But most of all, she is curious to know who she is, and as determined as I am to keep it from her, I know she also needs to know. So I will start teaching her to use her Alpha voice even if it means hers would one-day overthrow mine.

Yet feeling her through the bond, her nervousness and anxiety worsen the closer we get, and the overwhelming urge to comfort her grows stronger. I want to touch her, put her mind at ease, and let her know she is safe with me.

"Come here." I can't stop the edge of a growl escaping me, but she turns her head to look at me, pulling her attention away from the window.

"Seatbelt, Azalea. Sit up, Azalea. And now, you want me to remove my seatbelt to come to you?" she spits at me sarcastically while shaking her head. My little mate is growing more cunning. I always find her attitude amusing until it's used against me.

I growl and unclip my seatbelt before moving toward her, sliding onto the seat beside her and undoing her seatbelt before looping my arm around her waist and dragging her onto my lap. She growls, and I purr back at her. She will not escape me so easily. My hand sneaks under her shirt to rest on her lower belly. The bump is quite prominent already, and I smooth my hands over it. She sighs and relaxes against me as I caress it. I can't wait to watch her belly grow with our child, I can't wait to see what sort of mother she will be. I want a big family, and I wonder whether she shares the same thoughts.

To me, her scent is like a balm, soothing yet also teasing, making my mouth water. She smells sweet, cherry, and vanilla, and I can't explain the strange urges her scent entices. I have never liked sweets, yet her scent is addictive and inviting. It's delicious

So I can't help the purr that slips out and vibrates against her back. My calling works every time, and I love how she melts under it. At least, that is one thing I will always have that she can't resist. I bury my face in the crook of her neck, inhaling deeply.

My cock grows hard beneath her, and I am glad Abbie didn't

come. I feel like I hardly get time with her alone anymore, so having her so close and all mine, I can't resist the temptation her flesh is offering. My fingertips draw circles on her skin before teasing the waistband of her tights. My purr grows louder, and I can feel the effect I am having on her. Her arousal through the bond is intense and perfumes the small space in the limousine. Her scent becomes overwhelming. I am supposed to be distracting her and calming her, and all I manage to do is work myself up.

"Kyson! Damian, Liam and Trey are in the front!" she hisses, gripping my wrist and trying to stop it from slipping lower. Ignoring her, I slip my hand beneath the waistband and cup her warm pussy with my hand.

"Kyson!" she squeaks, while squirming on my lap. I groan as her ass brushes against my erection. Stroking the seam of her wet lower lips, she can deny me all she wants, but she can't hide the feeling I am enticing out of her.

Azalea squirms as my fingers tease her folds, drawing out moisture with each brush across her slit. "Hmm," I hum, shoving my finger inside her.

Any words of protest she has, die off as my thumb gently rubs against her swollen clit. Her legs open wider for me, and I chuckle, kissing her shoulder and withdrawing my finger that is slick with her arousal before sliding it back in and curling it deep within her. Her inner walls clench around my finger, and she moans softly, her head rolling back against my shoulder as she gives in to the feeling I am building up with the friction.

However, it is short-lived when I hear the screech of tires, and the limo slows. I growl, peering out my window, and Azalea scrambles off my lap. My hand slides out of her pants, and an angered growl leaves me as the car comes to an abrupt stop. We are stopped by the side of the road, just outside the pack borders and men surround the vehicle.

Snarling, I hear Damian get out of the car and listen to him talking to Alpha Dean's men, who are trying to refuse us entry.

Reaching for the door handle, I toss it open and climb out. Six werewolves are arguing with him about there not being any announcement of our arrival. My aura slips out as I stare at the man with his gun pointed at Damian's chest. Damian snarls, unflinching, and daring the man to pull the trigger.

"Issue?" I ask, shutting the door behind me. The other men are smart enough to back up, but one sniff of the air, and I can tell this man is the Beta. His scent is more substantial than the others.

"I would have thought after your Alpha's experience with stepping out of line and giving my men orders, that the rest of you would have more sense. Apparently not!" I tell the man while coming up behind Damian. His mud brown eyes flick to me over Damian's shoulder and he swallows. The other five have scampered off, leaving the Beta to fend for himself when they realized they are dealing with Lycans and not random fleabag werewolves with no authority or rights.

The man glances around, his curly brown hair blowing in his face when he realizes his pack members had abandoned him.

"No issue, my King. I didn't recognize you," he stammers. Lie, the flags on the front of the limo show our immunity.

"Did you have trouble recognizing my Beta too?" I ask. He pales, glancing at Damian, who holds his signature smirk.

"I um... The Alpha, he..." the man babbles like an idiot.

"Your Alpha what? Told you to ignore hierarchy? To hold a gun to a Lycan's chest?" I ask the man.

"He said not to let anyone in without notifying him first," the man stammers. Damian glances at me.

"Even the King's guard?" I ask. The man nods his head.

"Yes. Said that we must be prepared after last time. Two of your men killed the butcher and Mrs. Daley and kidnapped two rogue children," he says.

"You mean the pedophile I sent them here to kill? And the headmistress that mistreated your Queen?" I ask the man. The man shakes his head.

"They were good people," he claims, and my eyebrows rise into my hairline.

"Good people don't rape and sell little girls!" I sneer, and he opens his mouth and closes it quickly. His hand trembles and I snatch the gun from his grip before he accidentally sets it off. I tuck it down the back of my pants before punching him. Damian whistles and leans against the hood. Nothing angered me more than this twit thinking he can deny my men from entering pack lands that are under my rule.

He grunts, clutching his nose as blood sprays out everywhere. "Do not forget your place, Mutt! And it will always be beneath a Lycan's feet! You dare tell my men they can't enter on the ground I own again and I will have you tossed out and made rogue. Then you will see how your Alpha treats rogues," I tell him. He nods, his eyes darting to Damian, he mutters an apology, and I turn, shaking my head, climbing back in the car.

Now, why are Alpha Dean and Alpha Brock so worried about my men and me coming here? Maybe this trip won't be so pointless after all.

I slide across the seat to catch Azalea's nervous glance. My fingers clench and unclench, trying futilely to release the building tension. The leather creaks under me, echoing the mutters that escape through my gritted teeth. My aura flares invisibly around me, a storm of simmering rage that I struggle to keep contained.

My earlier mood dissolves and reforms into something sharper, more dangerous. Anger, pure and undiluted, courses through me for their Alpha. To think he has the gall, the sheer arrogance, to dictate terms to me? To suggest I cannot enter his territory without his express permission?

"What's wrong?" Azalea asks.

"Just border controls," I reply, the words sharp and clipped as if biting them off could sever my annoyance. "Forgetting who they are speaking with."

She nods, and the SUV lurches forward, continuing toward the town square. But Azalea becomes more anxious the deeper we drive through this middle-of-nowhere ghost of a town. Her hands twist together in her lap, knuckles whitening. She is nervous, and her fear reaches me through the bond.

I flick my gaze toward Azalea as she shifts in her seat, when she says. "Abbie told me Katrina took over the orphanage?" Her voice trembles slightly, betraying the turmoil beneath her calm exterior.

"Uh-huh," I confirm, my words clipped, not wanting to delve into the gruesome details that lurk behind Mrs. Daley's demise. The memory of what Gannon did – the savagery of his actions – coils in my gut. I can still see the images he sent me, sickening and vulgar, etched into the backs of my eyelids. I suppress a shudder, forcing my attention back to Azalea, who nibbles her lower lip between her teeth.

"What are you thinking right now?" I probe gently, unable to shake the feeling that I made a mistake by bringing her back here.

Her hand moves instinctively, almost protectively, to her belly. She brushes the fabric of her shirt over the subtle curve, an unconscious gesture that speaks volumes. I catch the corners of my lips twitching upward, amused by the act she's oblivious to performing.

"I wondered if the children would still remember me," she murmurs softly.

"Do you want to go back there... to see them?" My voice betrays my shock, a slight crack in the facade of calm I try to maintain.

Her eyes, once lost in the distance, now shift back to me, carrying an uncertainty that mirrors the tremble in her hands.

"I think I do," she answers, her voice barely above a whisper.

"If we have time on the way home, we will stop in there," I tell her, watching for a reaction.

"So we are just here to see the Alpha?" Azalea asks.

"Yes. And once we are done, I will take you to see the children if you like."

She nods, her eyes becoming a little glassy. I am not sure if she's upset because she missed the children who lived there. Or because she's coming back to the place that caused her so much pain.

I know this place haunts both her and Abbie. And after the tortures they endure at this place, I am once again second-guessing bringing her here.

It takes another ten minutes before we pull up out the front of the Pack house. Alpha Dean and Alpha Brock stand waiting out the front on the porch. However, when Azalea glances out her window and looks at them, her mood shifts through the bond. Her eyes burning brighter, flickering, and almost glowed, her jaw clenched as she glared past me and out the window.

The car rolls to a stop, and the silence that has enveloped us is now pierced by Azalea's soft intake of breath. I reach over, my fingers brushing against hers. She glances at me before returning her gaze back out the window.

As I watch her struggle to compose herself, I feel a surge of regret, wishing I had left her at home. The tortures they endured at this place were unspeakable, and though she stands unbroken beside me, the scars run deep, invisible and haunting.

Yet, the sight of the two Alphas has struck something within her, kindling a fire that I can almost feel licking at my own skin.

With a sigh, I push the door open and step out into the cool air, expecting to leave Azalea in the safety of the car with Trey and Liam. But then there's the click and creak of her door swinging open, shattering that plan into fragments. She steps out, and closes her door.

Behind us, our convoy disperses, as my men fan out and create a perimeter. Trey exits quickly behind her, I can see the confusion on his face, Azalea said she never wanted to see Alpha Brock again, yet she climbs out of the car. Liam's hand meets the door, shutting it also watching Azalea. Damian sends me a questioning look, one eyebrow arching, and all I can offer is a shrug. None of us expected her to get out of the car.

Her mood—volatile and fierce—wraps around me. It's a swift change from the uncertainty that clouded her before, sharpened now into something potent. The sight of Alpha Dean and Alpha Brock has stirred a response in Azalea yet I can't figure out what. Besides her clear anger, something else lays beneath the surface. They've unknowingly flipped a switch, and the current running through her is electric, demanding attention.

I watch, an observer, as she strides forward with a determination that has me shocked. There's a grace to her anger, a beauty to the wrath that unfurls from her. Trey stays close, his presence both shield and support, while Liam scans the area with the focus of a hawk.

"Kyson," Damian murmurs, a subtle tilt of his head toward Azalea, seeking guidance on this unplanned variable. I shake my head slightly, a silent message to let this play out, I am curious to see what she will do.

She moves past me to the Pack house, and I follow. Not as her King now, but as the partner to a Queen stepping into her power, and the feeling through the bond tells me she is about to show them her title.

The gravel crunches under my boots as I approach Alpha Brock, who descends the steps with a hand outstretched. His greeting hangs in the air, but my senses are tuned to Azalea's movements.

Alpha Brock's practiced smile falters, his gaze sliding past my shoulder to where Azalea stands. "What a pleasant surprise," he says, though his voice betrays him, a tremor of unease beneath the sly smile on his face.

Silence stretches for a heartbeat as Azalea's presence commands attention. Her aura is magnificent, invisible and yet palpable, rushes out around us. His lips part, and Alpha Dean also pauses to stare at her. She stops beside me, and Alpha Dean's hand shakes as he offers it to her.

"Alpha Dean," Azalea's voice slices through the tension, sharp and clear. Her hand dismisses his attempt at familiarity with a brisk wave, as though swatting away a bothersome insect. I hear Damian huff when she doesn't take it and just stares at it like it is diseased.

"Lovely to see you again, Ivy," he says, caution lacing his tone. The man is clearly shocked she isn't the broken girl she once was.

A cold smile plays on Azalea's lips. "That's Queen Azalea, to you, Alpha. Now move," she commands, her words leaving no room for argument. They trip over themselves trying to get out of her way as she brushes past the stunned Alphas, climbing the steps as if she owns them—and perhaps in this moment, she does.

They are left, mouths agape like fish out of water, their authority slipping through their fingers like sand. Liam, quick to react, darts up the steps, his hands deftly turning the knob and pulling open the front door.

I trail behind, my curiosity piqued by this new side of Azalea—this commanding presence that has seemingly emerged from the depths of her being. I am content to let this play out, to see how far she will take it. The Alphas, desperate to regain some semblance of control, stumble over themselves in their eagerness to please her.

"Would you care for some coffee or tea, my Queen?" Alpha Brock stammers, his voice betraying the uncertainty that swirls around us.

Azalea doesn't respond verbally; her disdain is clear in the sharp tilt of her head, the curl of her lip.

"No," Azalea's voice is a whip-crack, decisive and cold. "I wouldn't trust you not to spit in it!" she sneers.

"And we aren't here to chat, we are here for..." She pauses, eyes flicking to me, and in that split second, I see a flicker of confusion.

'Looking for all the rogue reports. And to go through their archives,' I supply through the mindlink, my voice steady in her head. She absorbs the information, nodding slightly—barely perceptible, but enough for me to know she understands.

The sudden fear that washes over the Alphas' faces is almost palpable, I can't help but revel in the way Azalea's aura has them off-balance, the way her mere presence suddenly scares them like they used to scare her.

"I'm here to inspect the rogue reports and your archives," she asserts, each word laced with the kind of authority that cannot be questioned.

Alpha Dean's response is immediate. "We don't keep such files, Iv...My Queen," he stammers, the slip of the tongue betraying his nerves before he hastily corrects himself.

Azalea's brow lifts ever so slightly, and I can't help but feel a surge of pride at her poise, the way she embodies her role as my Queen.

From behind her, Trey's lips pull into a knowing smirk. He leans closer, whispering a breath against her ear that only she can hear. I watch the exchange, curiosity nipping at me. Whatever he says draws her attention, and she gives him a quick nod, acknowledging his words while keeping her eyes fixed on the Alphas before her. They gape at her, and I can't believe they had the audacity to lie when they have no issue trying to label her as a traitor.

"Your archives are kept in your basement. And you should have reports of every rogue that steps over your borders. If not, that is an infringement on your behalf, and if it is simply you refusing to hand them over that is punishable by death. Beheading sounds good?" she says, looking at me.

"As you wish, my Queen," I answer.

"So which is it, you don't have the archives I have requested, or you don't want to hand them over? Either way, Alpha, you seem to find yourself in a direct violation of Lycan law and your next answer determines the severity of your punishment," she says, staring at them both. I have no doubt Trey is feeding her laws through the mindlink. Both Alphas stumble over themselves to answer.

Alpha Dean's hands twitch nervously, his eyes darting from Azalea to me and back again as he grapples for a semblance of control in the face of her unyielding demand. The air between us crackles with tension, each second stretching into an eternity as he formulates his response under the weight of Azalea's piercing gaze.

"What we meant is that we haven't dug them out," Alpha Dean finally musters, his voice carrying the strain of one walking on the blade's edge. "We weren't aware of your arrival or the King's. If you come back in a few days, we can have them ready."

My lips press into a thin line, the scent of their anxiety palpable in the stillness of the room. Their ignorance of our presence doesn't sit well with me; it's a convenient excuse at best. I feel the anger simmering beneath my skin, but it's Azalea's cold composure that holds my focus.

Her eyes narrow ever so slightly, the silver flecks in her irises catching the light like shards of moonlight. Her stance remains statuesque, embodying the very essence of regal authority that seems to reach into the depths of the earth itself and command its obedience.

"If I wanted you to dig them out and remove any incriminating evidence, we would have called prior," she retorts sharply, her voice cutting through their excuses like a knife through shadow. "But seeing as your pack is under investigation for the mistreatment of rogues, I don't want you handling any such evidence or giving you a chance to get rid of it completely."

The Alphas stand before us, their bravado peeled away to reveal the vulnerability they had hoped to conceal. In this moment, the power dynamics have shifted irrevocably. Azalea, once a victim, now dictates the rules of engagement, and they know it.

"Mistreatment of rogues, my Queen. Whatever happened with Mrs. Daley, I assure you, your King has seen to her punishment," he murmurs, his voice threading through the tension-charged silence.

Azalea's gaze doesn't waver, her eyes like frosted steel, unyielding and cold. She seems not to hear him, or perhaps she chooses not to acknowledge the excuse that falls so pathetically short of genuine remorse. The air around her crackles with her disregard for his pitiful defense.

"I would also like to see my files and Abbie's. So if you can point me in the direction of your basement, that will be very helpful," she commands, her voice resonant with authority that leaves no room for argument.

I feel the shift in the room, a palpable change as the power firmly roots itself in Azalea's grasp. Alpha Brock's face tautens, his eyes narrowing ever so slightly. The telltale sign of a man unaccustomed to being cornered, especially not by someone he once deemed beneath him. With a stiff nod, almost imperceptible, he motions down the hall, conceding to her demand with a visible twitch of irritation.

Azalea's footsteps echo in the hall, each step measured yet still, she manages to look graceful. The tension coils around us as we approach the door next to the staircase.

Alpha Brock's fingers curl around the handle, a muscle twitching in his jaw as he swings the door open with a reluctance that seeps into the stale air beyond. His gaze flickers to his father, seeking silent counsel or perhaps drawing from a well of shared unease.

"May we ask what you are looking for exactly?" Alpha Brock's voice is a strained thread of composure. "Most of the files down here are outdated and are of no use to anybody."

A cold draft snakes out from the darkness behind the door. Azalea doesn't flinch. She looks back at me, like she is asking permission, and I nod subtly. This is her show; I am merely the witness to her command.

"Outdated or not, they hold relevance to us," she adds, her voice resonant with the power that has shifted so visibly in her favor.

Alpha Brock swallows hard, his Adam's apple bobbing. He seems to shrink ever so slightly under her scrutiny. Damian watches him closely, an unspoken warning clear in his stance.

"Step aside," Damian commands, his voice brooking no argument, and for a moment, Alpha Brock hesitates.

"We can show you down. It will be easier if we help, and ..." Alpha Brock begins, but his offer dies in his throat as Azalea growls—a low, guttural sound that reverberates off the narrow walls and chills the air. Her aura surges forward, invisible yet palpable, a wave of suppressed fury that crashes against him.

I watch as he falters, his back pressing into the wall, his authority crumpling like paper caught in the wind. Azalea's voice slices through the tension, sharp and commanding. "You heard my Beta. Now step aside, Alpha." Her sneer is a thing of terrifying beauty, laced with a venom that leaves no room for challenge. The Alpha before us, a man of power in his own right, looks as if he's swallowed a stone. His Adam's apple bobs in a nervous gulp, his authority dissolving under her gaze.

Compliance is swift; the Alpha retreats, stepping away with haste. Liam descends into the darkness first to check if it's safe. A signal from below lets us know it's all clear.

Azalea's eyes find mine, the connection between us pulsing like a living entity. I sense her request before the words form in my mind, her will pressing against my consciousness. *'Go on. If you want to take over, I won't stop you,'* I say through our bond, granting her the freedom to as she pleases, and she starts moving into the basement.

I stroll past the Alphas when Alpha Dean stops me.

"Are we in trouble, my King?" he asks.

"That's for her to decide," I respond curtly, the words slicing through any hope he harbors, and I can't help but smirk at the fear emanating off them as I follow my mate.

CHAPTER TWENTY-SIX

AZALEA

The basement is stacked to the ceiling with boxes of files, no order, nothing, just boxed and stacked. I do not know what I am looking for, and I have no clue where to even start. Damian comes up behind me, leading me to a table in the center and flicking a small lamp on.

"I'm sorry, I stuck my nose in. It made me mad when I saw them," I admit to him. I am unsure where my bravado came from. Probably from seeing my old Alphas ticked off, returned the favor for all the times they made me feel less than dirt.

"No, you did well," Damian says when Kyson comes down the steps. I wait to see if he is mad that I kind of just took over when I was supposed to remain in the car with Trey. I wasn't supposed to step foot in here at all. Yet when he comes down the last step, he has a silly smile on his face as he strolls over to me.

"Ah, this will take forever," Liam growls, rifling through boxes. Kyson comes over, places his hands on my hips, and buries his face in my neck. But Liam is right. This will take days to go through.

"So, what do you want to do now?" Kyson asks, and I look up at him.

"Pardon?" I whisper.

"You're in charge, boss. So what now?" he asks, brushing his nose across my cheek. I gasp, looking around. Kyson purrs behind me then taps my hip with his hand and wanders about the huge basement before stopping.

I try to figure out what to do because Liam is right, this will take days.

"Can we take them?" I ask Kyson, and he nods.

"For real, my Queen? You want me to cart all these boxes up?" Liam whines, jutting out his bottom lip and pointing to Trey, "He wants to do it," Liam whispers, and I chuckle.

"No, I..." I press my lips in a line. There are hundreds of boxes down here. I look up at Kyson, and he shrugs, not offering any help.

"You're in charge, so I'm not helping. So what are you going to do, my Queen?" Kyson says, and I peer back around the room. They wouldn't fit in the cars. There are too many. I glance at the steps leading up before walking past Kyson and back up the steps to the main house. Alpha Dean and Alpha Brock stand by the doors, looking terrified at the two guards beside them. Seeing them grinds my gears, the humiliation of being put on that podium in front of the entire town square while they threw stuff at us makes my blood boil as I remember the last time I saw them.

"Have you got a trailer?" I ask them. They both shake their heads.

"Find one," I tell them.

"You want us to find a trailer?" Alpha Brock asks, looking at his father.

"Don't look at him. Find a trailer, I said," I snap, and he growls, the noise cutting off when I growl back at him. Only mine is a lot louder, and the power behind it almost makes me gasp and jump before I contain those urges of shock. I feel the power ooze out of me, my aura coming out like a shield and suffocating the Alphas.

"You will find a trailer and attach it to the car. Then you will come back here, and you and your father will cart every box and piece of paper from that basement and stack them in it," I tell them.

"Every box?" Alpha Dean says.

"Are you hard of hearing, Alpha Dean? Do I need to repeat myself?" I ask him, and he shakes his head. Turning to the guards beside them, I drop my aura and speak to them.

"Make sure they bring every box up. And if they miss one, Kill Alpha Brock,"

"Yes, my Queen," they nod, and one smiles like he would enjoy that job. I go to leave when I pause to see Kyson leaning against the wall.

"Oh, and once they have attached the trailer, they have 18 minutes to cart them up," I tell the guards.

"18 MINUTES!" Alpha Brock exclaims.

"Yes. Because 18 years is a wonderful age to kill innocent rogues, so I give 18 minutes to cart those boxes up," I tell him.

"And if we don't complete it in that timeframe?" Alpha Dean asks.

"I suggest you get it done, and you won't have to find out," I tell him, turning on my heel and walking out.

Stepping outside, I let out a breath. It is exhilarating holding the control, yet also petrifying. Adrenaline makes my heart rate quicken and flutter in my chest.

"Now what?" Kyson asks me. I bite the inside of my lip and look around only to see Alpha Brock rush off to his neighbor's house.

"Will the guards make sure they retrieve everything?" I ask, and Kyson nods his head.

"Then can we go to the orphanage?"

"Are you asking?" Kyson says with a devious smile on lips. I swallow, glancing at Trey, who raises an eyebrow at me and nods toward Kyson. I shake my head and cringe, looking up at my mate.

"No. I want to go to the orphanage, so we are going," I tell him. I am turning away from him when he grabs my arm. My heart lurches in my chest, thinking I pushed him too far, demanding him. Yet he only turns me to face him before his hand slips to the back of my neck. He leans down while tilting my head back. His lips crash against mine, his tongue demanding as it invades my mouth, forcing my lips to part. He kisses me hungrily, his tongue tasting every inch of my mouth before he pulls away and smiles.

"I like it when you're bossy," he purrs.

"You say that now," I tell him.

He responds with a grin, one that crinkles the corners of his eyes. "For now," he agrees, the words rich with amusement as he drapes an arm around my shoulders, drawing me closer.

We walk to the orphanage since it isn't that far from the pack-house. It is odd walking through the streets; this place no longer gives me the same fear it used to. It looks different, run down. People stare as we head toward the orphanage, and I pay them no mind, ignoring their curious gazes.

CHAPTER TWENTY-SEVEN

AZALEA

Once there at the orphanage, I stop, staring up at the building I once called home. Heart pounding, I pause at the sight of the dilapidated building looming before me. Paint peeling, windows like hollow eyes, and yet it tugs sharply at my heartstrings. Children play out the front, and for a second, I watch them. This place dredged up so many memories, yet I can't seem to conjure up one good one.

As if sensing my presence, the noise of play momentarily hushes. The place should be condemned, yet the kids all stop as I step over the little brick fence.

Tiny feet patter against the cracked pavement, and then they're upon me—a tide of small bodies with bright eyes and eager hands. They swarm around me, their little fingers plucking at the hem of my shirt, warm smiles and giggles piercing the air.

"She's back, Ivy is back!" They screech out excitedly.

"Ivy! Ivy!" bubble up from the lips of children, their calls threading through the air like a lifeline back to my past. I feel their small hands tugging at my sleeves, their unspoken pleas for attention wrapping around me with an intensity that is both heart-warming and heartbreaking.

Katrina bursts out the front door, her expression one of concern and surprise.

"Katrina!" I gasp, my voice catching on the wave of emotions that crashes into me. I navigate through the throng of tiny bodies, their energy buzzing like electricity in the air, until I collide with the familiar warmth of her embrace.

"Oh, sweet girl," she breathes out, her arms enveloping me. She steps back, her eyes scanning me with a nurturing scrutiny reserved for those who have known your darkest moments.

Her fingertips ghost over my shoulder, where fabric has slipped to reveal more than it should—more than I want. The lash marks, remnants of my time here, peeking out. She meets my gaze, a sorrowful smile gracing her lips as tears pool in her eyes, threatening to spill over. She stifles a sniffle.

In her eyes, there's an apology, one that needs no words, for the kindness she gave could never undo the hurt we endured—but oh, how it helped.

The warmth of Katrina's embrace lingers as she holds me just far enough to search my expression, her concern palpable. "How's Abbie?" she asks, the words carrying more than a question—a hope that the world hasn't been too cruel to us.

"She is okay," I tell her. She nods, relief softening the creases of worry that had etched themselves into her features.

Katrina's arms encircle me once more. "You look good, sweetie," she murmurs, and I feel the genuine warmth in her voice washing over me like a gentle tide.

As she releases me, a small, insistent pull at the hem of my shirt draws my attention downward. A pair of wide eyes, brimming with innocent curiosity, gaze up at me. It's Jack, his youthful energy irrepressible despite the harshness that surrounds us. With a practiced ease borne from years of looking after the younger ones, I scoop him into my arms. He is lighter than I remember, a reminder of the scarcity that still plagues this place.

"Hey, Jack," I greet him, my smile broadening at the sight of his joy. His fingers find a strand of my hair, playing with it, tugging gently.

"Where is Abbie? She didn't come to visit us?" Jack's voice wobbles, making my heart clench. He pouts, a gap evident where his two front teeth used to be, making his words lisp slightly.

I set him down and kneels to his level, my gaze softening. "No, she couldn't come," I say. He nods sadly.

Katrina then ushers us inside. She strides towards the kitchen, and I hear the familiar click and hiss as she turns the kettle on.

I slip into the kitchen, my hands instinctively reaching for the mugs hanging on their hooks, chipped and mismatched from years of use. They clink softly as I set them out. Kyson's gaze weighs on me, silent, yet his concern screams at me through the bond, but I push aside the discomfort it brings, focusing instead on the task at hand. "Let me," Katrina says, but I slap her hands away, knowing my way around this place like the back of my hand.

"It's fine, just sit down."

She resists only for a moment before acquiescing with a weary exhale, the fight seeping out of her as she collapses into a chair. Her fingers trace the grain of the wooden table, worn smooth by countless meals and meetings.

"Kyson mentioned you're looking after the children now," I continue, filling the silence that threatens to consume us. A nod is her only reply, the gesture heavy with the burden she carries, one I'm all too familiar with.

"Yep." Katrina's voice cracks. "But the Alpha cut back rations again. This place is falling apart, and Dad is sick, so I am back and forth." Her eyes, dull with fatigue, flicker to mine.

I hand her a steaming cup of tea. Her fingers wrap around it, Kyson accepts his own mug with a nod.

"No one to help?"

"Margaret comes over when I ask," Katrina replies, her voice laden with contempt. "But you know how she is."

I nod, understanding all too well the type of woman she is. Margaret was one of Mrs. Daley's friends, and she hated children, even her own. Just hearing her name has memories clawing its way to the forefront of my mind.

"Careful, you!" Margaret's voice had been sharp as a blade, slicing through the air. But it was too late; my small, trembling hands fumbled and tea splashed onto the floor. Her hand cracked across my cheek, a stinging punishment for a simple accident. My skin burned with the impact, tears welling but never falling. I had learned early that showing weakness only invited more pain.

"Sorry, sorry," I had whispered, the words barely escaping as I scrambled to clean the mess.

Shaking off the memories of the past, I focus on Katrina's furrowed brow and weary eyes. "Margaret..." I trail off, unable to mask the distaste in my voice. Her presence would offer Katrina no relief, only adding to the weight she already carried.

"Anyway, don't worry about it," Katrina forces a smile, though it doesn't quite reach her eyes. Her fingers trace the rim of her mug absently, as if finding solace in the familiar circular motion.

"Margaret's help isn't the kind you need," I say softly, setting down my own cup.

"I've asked the Alpha to employ someone but he said no. I swear I could run this pack better than that twat, he keeps saying he hasn't got the money to put in this place." She takes a sip of tea to moisten her lips before continuing. "I checked his finances for him the other week again and he has gambled everything. So with Dad getting worse, I have no choice but to ask her."

With the weight of her burdens etched into the lines of her face, Katrina gazes out the window at the overgrown yard, a small sigh escaping her lips. Her hands, which have known the roughness of relentless work, tremble slightly as she clutches the mug.

"What's wrong with your father?" The question slips from my mouth, my voice barely above a whisper.

She turns back to me. "Dementia," Katrina confesses, the word falling heavily in the space between us. It paints an all-too-clear picture of the struggle that lies behind her tired gaze. "He needs a full-time carer now, but I can't with this place, and mum is just as bad, so she is no help." She pauses, her shoulders slumping as if the admission siphons the last bit of strength she has. "And I haven't got the funds to pay for one." She smiles sadly.

"I don't know how you girls kept up with all the chores here either," she says, shaking her head. The motion sends a few strands of her hair, the color of faded autumn leaves, drifting across her tired eyes. Her gaze sweeps over the mess as if seeing it for the first time.

"We didn't have a choice," I tell her. She nods, understanding etched into the lines of her face as she stares at me.

"I'm sorry, Ivy," she murmurs.

"Azalea," Kyson corrects her gently from where he stands.

Katrina's brow furrows for a moment before smoothing out as she nods in acknowledgment, her lips curving into a sad smile. It doesn't matter what name she uses. She had tried to be a buffer between us and Mrs. Daley's cruelty. And despite her Beta heritage, Katrina's hands were tied, her good intentions constantly thwarted by the Alpha's blind eye.

"Don't be, and it's not your fault," I reassure Katrina, my voice steadier than I feel.

"I could have done more," she murmurs, her gaze drifting to the floor.

Before I can say anything else, movement at the periphery snatches my attention. A small form detaches itself from the fray of children—a little boy with wide, searching eyes that seem too ancient for his youth.

"Tyson?" The name slips from me, a whisper that carries the weight of a thousand unshed tears and I nearly break down at the sight of him. He has some disability that was never diagnosed because Mrs. Daley believed you could beat disobedience out of a child and saw his speech impediment as disobedience.

He motions toward his mouth, trying to speak, but it comes out in grunts and growling. Abbie and I believed Mrs. Daley would have killed him by now. I kiss his cheek and squish him too, which makes Kyson glance at me funny; I shake my head. He has no idea who this boy is to Abbie.

Grunts and growls spill from his lips, his small face contorting in frustration. My heart clenches as I reach for him, lifting his shaking body into my arms. He nestles against me, his babbling softening into quiet whimpers.

"Shh, it's okay," I murmur, pressing my lips to his forehead. Memories surge unbidden, a torrent that rips me back to a night seared into my soul.

The shrill cries of an infant wrench me from sleep. Abbie is already on her feet, fear etched across her features as she bolts down the attic steps with me right behind her. Tyson's wails pierced the air loudly. While Mrs. Daley's voice is a venomous hiss, commanding silence. "Shut up! Just shut up!" The threat in her tone is palpable.

Abbie reaches Tyson first, throwing herself protectively over his makeshift crib, which was a fruit box, just as Mrs. Daley raises her cane. The thwack of wood against flesh echoes through the room, each blow meant for Tyson absorbed by Abbie's quivering frame.

I lunge forward in panic and shove her with all my might. Her attention snaps to me, rage contorting her features. She strikes—again and again—until darkness claims me. Only later would I understand the cost of that intervention; my back was raw from the whip, but Tyson and Abbie managed to get out of the room safely. After that, Tyson slept in our bed with us until he started sleeping through the night. I still remember Abbie begging Mrs. Daley to let her keep him with us, but she refused.

"Azzy?" Kyson pulls me out of the memory as his voice flits through my head and blink the images away to see Katrina staring at Tyson.

"I never know what he is trying to say," Katrina says as he squeezes his fists, shaking as he becomes frustrated, and gurgling loudly.

My fingers dance through the fruit bowl, bypassing fruit that's seen better days, until they close around a firm apple. I briskly wipe it against my shirt, polishing its surface. "Apple," I say gently, holding it out to Tyson. Memories of deciphering his sounds, his own form of communication, flood back—a language only Abbie and I seemed fluent in.

His eyes light up with recognition, and he snatches the apple, his small hands enveloping it. Excitement bubbles out of him in a string of babbles as he scampers away, the apple now a prized possession.

"Apple," Katrina echoes, her voice carrying a trace of weariness. She's been trying; I can tell. I nod and take a sip of my tea.

"He likes the crunching noise they make, and he hates cornflakes, so don't give him those. He will have a meltdown, Tyson doesn't like the texture once the milk is added," I tell her, and she quickly jumps up and grabs a notepad from the fridge. She jots it down, and I tell her a few more noises he makes and what they mean.

"Man, I wish you and Abbie could stay here a while to show me," she says. Kyson shakes his head instantly, and I don't think I could even if he let me. Too many bad memories here, and I know this place would give me nightmares when I go home.

"I have to take dad for brain scans next week. I am hoping the Alpha will come over like he said. He said he would watch them for me," she sighs.

"Brock? What did you have to give him to convince him to do that?" I ask, and she blushes, not looking happy about that. I click my tongue, already knowing the answer.

"No one else?" I ask her, and I can only imagine what she had to do for her to get him over to watch all these kids.

"We can try to help you find some help?" Kyson offers, and she looks at him, hopefully.

"Please. No one is willing to help, and I have my exams coming back up."

"You're back studying accounting?" I ask her.

"Trying. When I get a chance, that is, it's online," she says. I smile sadly before I place my cup in the sink and nod, knowing we will have to leave soon.

"Do you mind if I look around?" I ask her, and she shakes her head.

"Of course not, but upstairs is a little messy," she says. Walking back to the main hall and into the living room, I see the kids huddled around the tiny box TV in the corner.

"How many kids are here now?" I ask her.

"111," Katrina answers. I sigh, looking around. The place is falling apart, and I suddenly wish I could take them with me. Katrina can't look after them by herself, and this place has seen better days. I swallow, taking the set of stairs, while Katrina tries to settle the kids who are becoming rowdy with afternoon tea approaching.

Ascending the staircase, the heavy air grips my lungs. Each door I pass reveals a room steeped in dust and disarray. Beds unmade, personal belongings strewn without care—a stark contrast to the order imposed on us during our time here. It's as if the rooms are holding their breath, waiting for someone to care enough to breathe life into them once more.

Kyson's footsteps echo behind me. "What are you doing?" he asks, his tone laced with confusion—or is it concern?

I find it hard to answer, the sights before me dragging me back through time. Memories flash before my eyes: Abbie and I tiptoe through the hallways, avoiding the squeaky floorboards and carrying piles of laundry that threatened to topple over. The same corridors now lay silent, save for the ghosts of our whispered voices trying to evade Mrs. Daley's wrath.

"Remembering," I reply finally, my voice distant even to my own ears.

Reaching the end of the hallway, I pause before the attic stairs, my heart thundering against my ribs. That was mine and Abbie's room. How often were we forced to crawl those stairs after our lashings or our chores? It felt like a lifetime ago, yet also yesterday, everything is still so fresh.

Kyson touches my arm, and I jump, stuck in my memories. "Are you alright?" he asks before turning to Liam and Trey. He nods toward the stairs and they go back down them.

"I'm fine," I tell him, blinking back tears. He looked like he wanted to say something, but I grip the broken banister and force myself to climb the steps to the attic. The door handle jiggles in my hand as I push it open.

CHAPTER TWENTY-EIGHT

AZALEA

"Why did you want to come up here?" Kyson asks, his voice echoing off the bare walls. He looks around at the small space, taking in the dirt-covered window, the single mattress we shared, and the bedside dresser. It all looks exactly as it did when we were here, untouched by time.

I walk over to the dresser and open the top drawer, revealing a stack of tattered clothes. Among them is a spaghetti necklace, its colors faded but still recognizable. I pick it up and hold it in my hand, memories flooding back to me.

"We hated these dresses," I say, holding up an old tunic. "And the stupid peasant skirts she would make us wear." I can still feel the itch of the rough fabric against my skin, the way it would cling to my sweat in the hot summers.

"Azalea?" Kyson whispers behind me.

"It's mine and Abbie's room," I tell him. My voice sounds distant to even my own ears.

Kyson's eyes widen as he takes in the room. "This is where you slept?" he asks, his voice full of disbelief.

I nod, unable to speak as my emotions threaten to overwhelm me. I walk over to the cupboard and run my hand along its wooden surface, remembering the countless times I was locked inside, unable to escape until Mrs. Daley deemed it was time for me to come out.

"Are you alright, Azalea?" Kyson's concerned voice breaks through the haze, and I tear my gaze away from him to glance at the wooden chair he's turning in the corner. Suppressed memories flood back, crashing against the walls of my mind, reminding me of why that chair is up here. It's a painful reminder of the time we broke a similar one while trying to retrieve Christmas decorations from storage. Mrs. Daley, always one for dramatic lessons, made us bear the weight of that damn chair above our heads, claiming it would teach us about the burden she carried in looking after us.

To most people, it's just a chair. But for us, holding two legs each above our heads for what felt like an eternity, we learned firsthand how even the lightest things become unbearably heavy after hours. Each time our strength faltered and we dropped it, Mrs. Daley's cane would strike the back of our legs, leaving stinging reminders of her displeasure.

As I watch Kyson move the chair now, its screeching sound along the floor ignites an inferno of rage within me. I growl, snatching the chair from his hands, causing him to jump back startled. Without a second thought, I hurl it at the shitty little window. Shards of glass shatter everywhere, raining down around me as I stalk towards the chair. My sole focus is on obliterating it, as if by destroying this physical object, I could somehow erase the haunting memory it represents. Erase the echoes of Abbie's cries as her knees buckled from each merciless strike of Mrs. Daley's cane.

I pick up the chair once more and begin smashing it into the unforgiving floor. With each crash, wood splinters off, filling the air with the sound of destruction and releasing pent-up frustration that had been festering within me. The floor quakes beneath my feet, mirroring the turmoil in my soul, until Kyson grabs hold of my arms.

"Hey, shh, shh," he murmurs gently, his eyes flicking down to the chair leg still clutched tightly in my hand. He reaches out and takes it from me. "Give it to me, Love," he says softly, his touch calming. My hands tremble as I struggle to catch my breath, and Kyson cups my face in his hands, forcing me to meet his gaze. His eyes are filled with concern and understanding, watching my face intently as I attempt to regain control of my emotions. But this place, this wretched place... it feels like I never left. Some part of me will always be trapped within these walls.

"I hate this place! I hate her! I hate what she did to us!" The words burst forth from me, accompanied by a sudden burst of tears. I despise this place with every fiber of my being, loathing everything it represents. It's as if this single location has imprinted itself onto my heart and soul, screaming out that it will forever hold me captive. That escape is an illusion. The floodgates open wide, releasing all the pain and anguish I've been suppressing for far too long.

"She ruined us," I sob.

"No, love. She ruined nothing. And you're safe now. She is dead, she can't hurt you no more, this place is just a place," he says, hugging me.

"You don't have to be strong all the time, Azalea," he says softly. "It's okay to let yourself feel."

Tears fill my eyes as I lean into his embrace. For so long, I had pushed down my emotions, burying them deep inside of me in order to survive.

"I hate this place," I say, my voice muffled against Kyson's chest. "I hate what it represents."

"I know," Kyson whispers, rubbing soothing circles on my back.

We stand there for a few minutes before finally pulling away from each other. I wipe at my tears and take a deep breath, trying to compose myself. It was just a chair. I broke a perfectly good chair. I inhale his scent, letting it calm me before I chuckle, knowing how many whippings I would have got if Mrs. Daley heard me crying. Kyson probably thinks I lost my damn mind, and even I question that possibility. I sniffle, feeling stupid and childish.

"You okay?" he asks, and I nod, wiping my face and glancing around the small space and the broken chair. I need to leave. I can't stay here any longer. It hurts too much, and I want out. Suddenly feeling claustrophobic, I rush down the steps needing air, feeling like the walls are closing in around me and that I am going to wake up at any moment and everything has been a dream, and I am really stuck here still. Kyson chases after me, and I rush through the kitchen and burst into the living room, heading for the front door. But the faces of the children make my feet halt. Trey and Liam look over at us, alarmed, and Kyson nearly runs into the back of me as I stop.

Little eyes, filled with innocence and curiosity, peer back at me, reflecting the shock mirrored in Katrina's gaze. Her startled expression mirrors my own as I try to gather my thoughts amidst the chaos that surrounds us. "Azalea, dear, are you okay?" she asks, concern lacing her words. But this place, this dilapidated dump of a building, no longer holds me captive. Yet, my heart sinks as I realize that all these children still remain trapped within its crumbling walls. Desperation tugs at my soul as I turn to Kyson, hoping he can decipher the unspoken plea in my eyes.

"No!" he exclaims, his eyes widening in alarm. Confusion furrows my brow as I tilt my head to the side. But he folds his arms protectively across his chest and shakes his head vehemently.

"I'm not asking!" I assert, frustration seeping into my voice. His lips part as he glances around at the frightened faces surrounding us.

"No! What am I going to do with all these kids?" he hisses at me, his disbelief palpable. Ignoring his resistance, I pivot towards Katrina, determination etched on my features.

"Ring the bus depot and find a driver," I instruct her, urgency coating each word. Confusion flickers across her face as she processes my request.

"You want a bus?" she questions, her voice tinged with uncertainty.

"Yes. Maybe two. I am taking them with me," I declare firmly. She gasps, rushing towards me in a flurry of movement.

"You want to take all the children?" she asks incredulously, stealing a quick glance at Kyson who stands behind me, simmering with anger.

"Yes. So ring the bus depot. I want a bus here now," I command, my gaze unwavering as I turn to face Kyson. He growls, frustration emanating from him.

"Are you insane?" he questions, his voice laced with worry. I shift my focus back to the young faces before me.

"Either I stay, or they come," I retort, my eyes locking with him in a silent challenge.

"What are we going to do with all of them?" he asks, throwing his hands in the air.

"Some of the Lycan families might be willing to take them in," Trey interjects. I nod, seeing the possibilities unfold before me. We'll figure it out.

"And where do you think I am going to put them?" Kyson counters, his frustration palpable.

"The castle is big enough," I state, refusing to take no for an answer.

"Azalea!" he growls, his anger flaring.

"No! You said I am running things here, and I say they are coming. Now get on board, my King, or get out of my way," I declare, my voice firm and unwavering. He growls in response.

"Yes, I said that, but I didn't think you were going to bring an entire orphanage back with us!"

"Fine. You tell them then. Say no to them, Kyson," I say, motioning toward the kids. He swallows and glances at their little faces and I smirk, knowing very well he won't or can't utter those words. He presses his lips in a tight line.

"Fine!" he growls, and Liam chuckles.

"Come on, kids. Uncle Liam is helping you bust out of this crap box! Come on, let's go!" Liam says, waving to all the kids to follow him. They glance around at each other and look at Kyson, unsure. He sighs and shakes his head.

"Come on then. Follow Uncle Liam!" Kyson says, motioning them to follow him. The kids don't need to be told twice and rush after an excitable Liam and Trey. I laugh, following them.

"Where to, my Queen?" Liam calls.

"The town square. There is a bus stop," I tell him. Katrina races out on the phone, telling the driver to come to the town square.

"You're lucky I love you," Kyson growls, grabbing my hand. I laugh before racing after the kids and tugging Kyson along with me.

CHAPTER TWENTY-NINE

AZALEA

When we arrive back at the town square, I can see the Alpha is still loading the trailer. Alpha Brock glances over, noticing the children. He snarls and stomps over to them.

"What are you all doing here?" he snarls, and Liam growls at him, making him jump, having not seen him. Alpha Brock backs up with his hands up while the children all stand frozen in fear. It angers me that they fear him.

"Seeing as you are still stacking boxes, I am assuming you didn't make the 18 minute time frame?" I ask him, walking through the crowd of children.

He backs up further. "No. Um... we got delayed," he mutters. "See, the last box. Everything is there," he says, pointing to his father, who is placing a tarp over the trailer.

"That wasn't what I asked. I asked if you did it in 18 minutes?"

His lips part, and he glances at his father when one of the guards steps forward.

"That is the last box, my Queen. But no, they didn't get it done in the timeframe," he answers, and I nod, turning to look at Alpha Brock.

"Hmm... On the stage, both of you!" I order, my voice coming out strong along with my aura, which I am finding more effortless and easier to use. They both rush up the steps and stand at the top of them.

"My King, is this really necessary? We did what she asked," Alpha Dean says.

"But you didn't. Your Queen gave you 18 minutes, and you didn't complete the task in that time frame," Kyson answers him as I wander over to the fruit stall that is just closing its shutters.

"How much for all of it?" I ask the elderly woman. She jumps, not seeing me come up behind her.

"You!" she sneers, pointing her withered old finger at me.

"Excuse me?" I ask her.

"You! The rogue girl!"

"My name is Azalea Landeena! You will address me as such unless you want to join your Alpha!" I snarl. She stutters out an apology.

"Now I asked you a question. How much for all of it?"

"You want the entire shop?" she asks. I shake my head.

"No, just the fruit and vegetables."

"I um... just take what you want."

"I don't want to send you broke, ma'am. Despite your lack of manners."

Kyson comes up behind me and touches my shoulder. "We have fruit at home," he whispers, and I nod, picking up a tomato.

"I know, but pay her, I am taking the lot," I tell him, turning around, tossing it in the air, and catching it as I walk and stop in front of the stage.

"Kids," I call out, and they all turn to face me.

"Grab some fruit," they rush off, taking fruit from the shelves.

They all return as the buses pull up. "Now, to show you the same dignity you showed me, Alpha," I tell them. Some of the children are eating their fruit while I chuck my tomato at the Alphas. My tomato hits Alpha Brock square in the face, splatting with an audible sound and covering him in tomato juices. Alpha Brock growls when Trey laughs before screaming out. “Food fight!”

Like a mini-army, the kids turn. Their eyes light up with mischief as they toss their fruit and vegetables at the Alphas. Who try to dodge their attacks but can’t step off the small stage. When they are finished, I tell the children to grab more fruit to eat as a snack on the way before helping load them onto the buses. Once that is done, I wander back over to the Alphas covered in bits of fruits and vegetables and juices.

“You will both step down as Alpha until a new one is appointed. And I...” I look at Kyson, needing his help. I’m not quite sure how to actually strip someone of their title.

Kyson’s aura rushes out, bringing them both to their knees. “I King Kyson of the Valkyrie Kingdom, hereby strip you Alpha Dean and Alpha Brock of your Alpha titles! I declare you both the very thing you despise. I declare you both rogue until you are accepted into another pack or your new Alpha declares you a pack!” Kyson says, stripping both of them of their titles.

“Wait! Wait! I will do better!” Brock begs, wanting to step off the stage, but he is stuck under my command.

“You may approach,” I tell him, and he jumps down and falls to his knees in front of me.

“Please! Please! I will do as you ask! Anything! Without an Alpha, this place will go to ruin” he begs, and I look at Kyson, who shrugs and tells me it is up to me. I bite my lip. Yet he has a point. They need an Alpha, or things could be even worse off than with the Alpha. I glance around to see Katrina hold up her hand behind Liam. She is technically Beta blood, and she is studying accounting. I smirk, knowing there is nothing Alpha Brock would hate more than having to answer to a woman.

“You answer to Katrina now. And until she deems you fit, you remain as rogues. You will also make sure she has time to finish her course and help her anyway she asks," I tell him.

"She is a woman!" Alpha Brock snaps at me.

"Yes! But she is so much more than that. Now she is your Alpha!" I tell him, and Katrina smirks and folds her arms, and I look at Kyson, knowing he was the only one right now that could make this happen. He would have to teach me to give someone their titles because I had a funny feeling it wasn't the same as stripping them of their mate bond. And I am right.

Kyson waves Katrina forward and gets her to kneel, and he slices his palm, letting his claws slip out on his other hand.

"Open your mouth open," Kyson tells her, and she obeys.

He squeezes his fist, letting his blood drip into her mouth. Before he says a pledge, she repeats it before declaring her as Alpha. She gasps, clutching her chest, and falls backward on her bottom, and I could feel her aura slip out stronger than before, showing she was now in charge.

Alpha Brock roars, getting to his feet, and he charges at her, and she glares at him, rising to her feet calmly.

"Sit!" she orders, and he freezes, falling on his ass. Alpha Dean hangs his head, looking ashamed of his son's behavior. While I am shocked at how easy it is for Katrina to command him. I hope it gets easy for me like that, and I would be able to have complete control of my aura and command as she does.

CHAPTER THIRTY

AZALEA

Once Kyson is sure Katrina has both Alphas under control, he escorts me back to the Limo, and I climb in the back and slide across the seat. My hands shake with adrenaline, and I feel a little giddy. The feeling wears off as the car starts. I glance out the window at the bus and the cars follow, however the bus heads down a different street, as the orphanage street is too narrow for the bus, with its low-hanging trees to fit. We slow a little as the orphanage comes into view out my window.

That place will never hurt anymore children. I unclip my seatbelt and tap on the window. Trey winds the glass window down and I tell them to stop. The car does and one of the other cars follows after the bus, while the other three stop behind us.

I open my door when Kyson grips the back of my pants. "You don't need to go back in there. There is nothing there for you anymore," he whispers, but I want no remnants left of this place.

"I know," I tell him and he lets me go and sighs. I climb out as do the guards, taking positions around the cars. Trey comes over to me.

"What's wrong?" he asks. I shake my head, moving toward Liam as he steps out of the car.

"Have you got a lighter?" I ask knowing he smokes. He lifts an eyebrow at me.

"Terrible habit. Shouldn't smoke when up the duff," he tells me, and I roll my eyes and hold my hand out for the lighter.

"I'm not smoking." I tell him, and he pulls a packet out before lighting a smoke.

"Since we have stopped," he says, he lights his smoke then hands me the lighter. I step over the little brick gate, and Kyson grips my arm.

"What are you doing?"

"Making sure no more kids ever come back here." I tell him, shaking his arm off. Guards rush ahead of me as I walk around the outside of the building to the small garden shed out the back. Kyson follows but just watches me as I reach above to the low hanging tin roof for the padlock key. I feel around before pulling it down and unlocking the padlock.

Ducking my head, I step inside and see a red jerrycan. I grab it off the small shelf and shake it to find it had a bit of fuel left in it for the mower. I crack the lid and the fumes confirm it is indeed petrol. Stepping out of the garden shed. Kyson gasps, coming over and snatching it from me.

"You are not playing with petrol!" he growls.

"Give it to me," I tell him, holding my hand out. But he refuses.

"Give me the lighter. I will do it," he says, holding his hand out. I don't care who does it, as long as the place is reduced to nothing but soot and ash. I hand him the lighter when Liam bounces on the balls of his feet like an excited kid in a candy store.

"Oh pick me! Pick me! Can I help? Liam likes playing with fire," he says, his eyes sparkling mischievously.

I glance inside the small shed when Liam clears his throat behind me.

"No fuel needed. I always have lighter fluid," he says and I look at him over my shoulder to see him rummage inside his jacket.

"Here, hold this," he says, passing me a knife. "Ah, and this," he says, dropping a pistol in my hand. Kyson growls, snatching it from me.

"Liam!" he scolds.

"It's in here somewhere," Liam mutters, pulling out an apron covered in blood. He sniffs it and pulls a face. "I was wondering where that smell was coming from!" Liam mutters, chucking the apron over his shoulder and rummaging around some more. "Ah, found it!" he announces, holding up a bottle of lighter fluid. He then turns to Trey, who is watching him, like Liam is a madman.

"Here ferret face fuck, hold my shit!" Liam says, dumping his apron and taking the knife from me and his pistol from Kyson. He loads up Trey's arms, before removing his jacket.

"Genuine leather. Can't ruin that," Liam says, dumping it in Trey's arms. Kyson growls as Liam skips like a kid to the back door. He gives a ninja cry, before kicking in the back door, "Honey, I'm home!" Liam sings out and Kyson shakes his head.

"Can't take that idiot anywhere," Kyson curses, stalking after Liam with the jerry can in hand. Trey nods for me to follow him back to the cars.

"I think that man needs a psych evaluation," Trey mutters, nudging me with his elbow. I laugh, following Trey back out the front with the guards surrounding us.

"Call the fire brigade. I don't want it getting out of control," Trey tells one of the guard's, who pulls his phone out. Leaning against the hood of the limo, I listen to Liam singing at the top of his lungs inside the house. I also hear glass shattering before he comes to the front window on the top floor. He waves and I laugh, waving back.

"That man is unhinged," I tell Trey as Kyson comes out, shaking his head. He reeked of petrol fumes. Kyson stops beside me.

"The fool is going to kill himself one day," Kyson says, when Liam suddenly sets the curtains of the room on fire, with the lighter he stole from Kyson. He starts catcalling out the window and dancing.

"Liam, get out of there! The room is on fire, you twat!" Kyson calls out, and Liam stops the weird ass fire dance he is doing. The entire room goes up and he yanks the curtain rod of the window.

"You smell smoke?" he asks, smiling, and showing all his teeth. Kyson shakes his head again, as Liam climbs out the window, dancing on the roof and chanting about fire gods, or some crap. The room beside him catches on fire and Liam rubs his hands together, getting ready to jump off the small porch roof, when he suddenly vanishes. I blink before hearing a crash, as he falls through the porch roof. He groans sitting up, while Trey erupts in laughter.

Liam holds his hand up. "I'm okay!" he announces before rolling on his side. A tile falls off and hits his shoulder, shattering on the ground.

"That hurt my fanny!" he says, rubbing his butt and skipping down the steps when the entire porch collapses behind him.

"Wow! Talk about in the nick of time!" Liam says.

"I swear, you have nine lives!" Kyson tells him with a shake of his head. We watch the place burn, the roof caving in and the air fills with black smoke. Once we hear the sirens on the way, we climb in the limo, knowing they would contain what is left of the burning rubble. But as the wind carries the smoke away I feel myself relax, as if it is also carrying my past with it.

Ivy is no more. Mrs. Daley is no more. I know my past and what we endured would always remain, but the sense of relief that comes with watching that place burn gives me hope that maybe the memories would one day fade. Maybe they won't hurt as much. Kyson reaches over and squeezes my hand, and I look at him.

"Ready to go home?" he asks, and I nod.

I am ready to go home, and for once the castle feels like home, as much as I am terrified of going back knowing there is someone there trying to sabotage everything, and ruin me. It still doesn't bring the fear this place did. And for once I feel free. Free of everything and this place. Free to try to move on. Because one thing I know is if I could survive eight harrowing years here, I could survive anything.

Nothing breaks a soul more than being suppressed. Nothing breaks someone more than being shackled and trapped in a repetitive loop of torture. Kyson and I have our differences, different beliefs that came with different upbringings, different views of how we should be. Kyson was raised with a silver spoon, while I was raised with whips and canes, we are complete opposites, yet the same both having suffered at the hands of our upbringings, both having suffered losing ourselves at the hands of someone else.

Both of us have our own struggles to contend with, and I know what Kyson struggles with most is insecurity. While what I struggled with most was beaten into me, engrained. Making me meek and fearful of everything, something I am trying to work on, yet you can't beat a dog every day and expect it not to flinch when you pat it. Everything takes time, but I know Kyson will be patient. I just need to remember I have to be patient with him, too.

I know little about who I am, but I trust Kyson will eventually teach me. As much as he angers me, I do trust him. And after today and him letting me have control, I trust he will also one day let me find my voice. The one that was squashed and was suppressed living here. So with those thoughts in mind, yes, I am ready to go home. Home is something I never thought I would have, but now I realize home is anywhere Kyson is.

We meet up with the bus at the first service station on the way out of town, which waits parked on the side of the road for our convoy. The bus is following us back to the castle. I feel terrible for all the children being cooped up on the bus for so long. Although we do stop twice to let them burn off some energy, and at the last stop, the children become too rowdy, so Liam climbs on the bus with them. When we finally reach the castle, it's early morning.

We've arrived and are pulling into the castle when Kyson shakes my arm to wake me.

"We're home, Love," Kyson whispers, and I yawn. It's still dark outside, but the castle is lit up like a Christmas tree.

"Clarice and everyone have set up the ballroom as a sleeping quarters for the children," Kyson tells me, and I'm glad he thought ahead. I was too busy sleeping and forgot they would need somewhere to sleep. Kyson, however, seems to think of everything.

I climb out of the limo, and Kyson grips my arm to steady me since I'm still half asleep. The bus door opens, and Liam stumbles out, nearly getting knocked over as the kids rush out behind him. He stumbles past us. "I need a fucking drink," he growls, looking worse for wear as he makes his way inside.

Clarice comes out the front doors, and I cover my ears at all the noise, trying to wake up as kids rush around everywhere. Moments later, I hear Abbie's voice reach my ears.

"What the heck is going on out here?" she yells out. The kids, not hearing her, continue to rush around, and the castle staff look overwhelmed when Abbie sticks her fingers in her mouth and whistles loudly.

The kids freeze and glance in her direction, taking in the woman who stands before them, their eyes light up with excitement and then they are suddenly rushing toward her. Abbie smiles and is nearly knocked over when they spot her, all trying to hug and touch her. She beams, reaching for them, grabbing them, and hugging them. I stand back and watch as Tyson squeezes through the bodies, and tugs on her dress, she looks down and I watch every possible emotion cross over her features. "Tyson," she almost whimpers, her eyes glistening with tears of relief before picking up Tyson. She buries her face in his hair with tears in her eyes while I make my way over to her.

"I missed you, mister," she says, and he makes his grunting noises, bouncing in her arms. Gannon comes out behind her and leans in the doorway, watching her as she says hello to all the kids.

Abbie, finally noticing me, pulls me into a hug with one arm.

"You got them out," she whispers, wiping her tears. I nod sadly but now we have to find homes for them all.

"Katrina?" she asks.

"Now, Alpha," I tell her, and her green eyes widen. She glances at Kyson behind me. He places his hand on my hip and pecks my cheek. The heat of his body seeps into my back before he reaches over and messes with Tyson's hair. Tyson stares up at him before sucking on his thumb. I chuckle as the small boy who stares at him like he is a giant.

"They never have to go back?" Abbie asks worriedly as she glances at all the kids rushing around.

"Nothing to go back to," I tell her, looking at the kids. Abbie looks at me, confused, and I answer her questioning look.

"I made them burn it to the ground. It's gone, Abbie. All of it," I assure her, and she sucks in a shaky breath and nods.

"We are never going back," she chokes on emotion, tears slipping down her cheeks.

"Never, we are home now," I tell her, and she clutches me, pulling me into a hug with one arm.

"More than my life," she whispers.

"Forever more than my life. We have a home now, and we have set them free."

"We are free," she chokes on the word that for so long meant death to us, only now freedom holds a different meaning now.

"Free," I repeat, and she sniffles and lets me go. She wipes her face before clearing her throat. She glances at the children who Clarice is trying to get their attention. Abbie and I both stick our fingers in our mouths simultaneously and whistle. They stop all freezing.

"Line up and settle down. You will wake the entire town," I yell out at them. They all immediately line up into four rows. Abbie shakes her head and sighs, yet the kids listen and when Clarice claps her hands loudly, they straighten up.

"Now we have breakfast cooked and ready for you in your new

room, but everyone has to be quiet and use your inside voices," Clarice says. The kids all remain quiet before she turns on her heel.

"Now follow me, quietly!" she calls out to the kids, and they file in after her. Abbie and I follow behind them, and Gannon stops Abbie as she goes to pass him with a hand on her arm.

"Who is this?" he asks, shucking Tyson under the chin to look up at him. Tyson sniffs the air, and he must be able to smell Abbie's scent on Gannon because he then waves and grins at him.

"This is Tyson, and Tyson, this is Gannon," Abbie says, smiling fondly down at Tyson. Tyson makes one of his noises, and Gannon smirks.

"Hello, Tyson," Gannon tells him softly, placing his hand on Abbie's lower back. Abbie starts to follow after Clarice when she looks at Gannon before looking ahead, a strange look crosses her features, one I recognize to be fear. However, instead of heading toward the ballroom. I stop at the stairs because I am heading toward our quarters when Abbie stops also and I know immediately why she hesitates, she doesn't want Tyson going into a new home, and I know she won't lose him again.

She looks at me. "Az..." she doesn't finish, but I know what she wants and I nod once letting her know it's okay, he is hers, before turning to wait for Kyson to catch up, but he is talking to a guard.

"Abbie?" Gannon asks as she climbs the stairs. She doesn't answer. She just keeps climbing the stairs, and I follow up behind her. At first I think Abbie is coming to my room, knowing she'll need to be assigned elsewhere if Gannon doesn't allow her to keep Tyson, when I remember she cant follow me, so I wait allowing her a chance to navigate the command over her when she stops looking back at Gannon before rushing off toward the guard quarters.

"Where is she going?" Gannon states stomping up the steps. Yet if he thinks he can take Tyson from her he has another thing coming. That is not an argument Gannon will win with her, she would choose Tyson, that I have no doubt about. I wait, but she turns down the opposite corridor toward hers and Gannon's rooms. Gannon races up the steps behind her and passes me. He stops, staring after her before calling out to her.

"Abbie, where are you going?" he calls out.

"Tyson is mine. I want him," is all she says, not bothering to turn around or ask permission from him. Gannon scoffs and looks at me.

"Is she being serious?" he whispers.

"Now she got him back, she won't let him go, and if you make her choose, you won't win," I tell him, and his lips part. Gannon glances down the corridor where she disappeared.

"What do you mean now she has him back?"

"Abbie was his primary carer. She raised him since he was newborn," I tell Gannon. "Don't make her choose," I warn him. Gannon sighs, and Kyson comes up the steps while I worry Tyson would be a deal breaker for Gannon.

"What's wrong?" Kyson asks him, and Gannon looks at him.

"Looks like I have a son," Gannon says, turning on his heel and jogging after her.

"Abbie is pregnant?" Kyson asks, and I roll my eyes and click my tongue at his silliness.

"No, Tyson!" I tell him.

"Ah... Wait. You both know we can't keep them all, right? Clarice has the two boys already, and now Abbie has Tyson. You're pregnant. I am not running boarding school here," Kyson tells me.

"I know that, but they stay until they all have homes, but you won't take Tyson from Abbie," I tell him, grabbing his hand and tugging him back to our room.

"I need a bath," I groan, and Kyson growls.

"Am I invited to this bath?" he asks.

"Only if you wash my back," I laugh, and he growls.

"I'll wash more than your back," he says, tugging me closer and purring.

CHAPTER THIRTY-ONE

GANNON

I rush to my room and open the door, but she isn't there. My brows furrow as I check the bathroom, wondering where she went when I hear a babbling noise from out in the hallway.

Turning around, I follow the noise to her old room. Knocking on the door, the room falls quiet, and I grip the handle pushing the door open to find her sitting on the bed.

Tyson is still attached to her hip and eating a candy cloud she has pinched between her fingers, his little lips sucking the sugar off while she holds it, watching him.

"I am keeping him. And I understand if you don't want kids. And I know he is a special needs child, so if you aren't comfortable with it, I understand. I will ask Azalea to move me elsewhere if it bothers you," she says dismissively as if she thinks I will toss her away over him.

"It would have been nice to be asked," I tell her.

"I'm done asking. I'm done begging. It gets me nothing, Gannon. I won't lose him, and I won't give him up," she tells me, hugging him tighter. She sniffs his hair and kisses his cheek.

"What do you mean? I've never denied you anything, Abbie, nor would I," I tell her, and she looks up at me before looking down at him.

"Kade promised. He promised, so I stayed. I stayed quiet. I stayed on the promise I would get Tyson back. Everything was going to be okay when I got him back," Abbie says before whispering, "Only he never kept that promise." Tears slip down her face and her lips quiver, making me realize then a lot of what she was willing to endure was based on the promise of having this boy returned to her. She held out hope the mate bond would not only make Kade love her but also return her to the boy she raised. Tyson is why she never said anything, why she remained. It wasn't just the bond, she wanted Tyson, and Kade dangled him on a string in front of her.

"Tyson you get no say over, just like Azzy, Gannon, I would die for both. Don't make me choose. You won't like the answer," she whispers.

"Like Azzy?" I ask her, and she nods, her eyes softening as she stares at him through her tears.

"More than my life," she whispers. Tyson babbles, leaning down to gnaw at the candy cloud between her fingers as I step into the room. I lean down, brushing his hair with my fingers.

"And you're more than mine," I whisper, and she lifts her head. "More than my life and if he is part of yours. Then he is now mine also," I tell her, and she blinks at me before swallowing. Her lips part, and she stares at me as if wondering if she heard me right.

"Come on, he needs a bath and he is clearly hungry," I tell her, holding my hands out for him. She looks at my hands like she is wondering if it is some trick. I can see her hesitation written on her face.

"No one will ever take him from you, and I will kill anyone who dares try to take our son," I tell her. She blinks back tears.

"You're not leaving me," she breathes out.

"Never!" I tell her, taking Tyson from her. I set him on my hip, offering my other hand to her. She slips hers in mine, and I pull her to her feet. Tugging her closer, I press my lips to her temple before walking out of the room with her and Tyson when I spot Liam smirking as he stands near the door of his room as we pass.

"I hear I am an Uncle brother?" he says, and I smile down at Tyson.

"That would be correct."

"I will go make him some food while you get him settled then," Liam says, and I nod, watching as Abbie pushes our door open and walks to the bathroom to run him a bath.

CHAPTER THIRTY-TWO

KYSON

As we step into the room, Azalea growls as the fresh linen scent overwhelms her. Trey rushes into the room behind me, looking alert despite having not slept in two days.

"What is it?" Trey says behind me. I watch as Azalea moves toward the bed, sniffing the air.

"Nothing. Liam had Clarice clean everything in here. It smells wrong to her," I tell him. Trey sighs. The only lingering scents are Gannon, Dustin's, and Peter's, who must have helped oversee everything because I forgot Gannon couldn't come with us because of her command over him.

"Okay, as long as everything is alright."

"Go to bed, Trey. Try to sleep before the sun comes up. She is safe with me," I tell him. He nods and reluctantly leaves. I find his bond to her odd, but now trust him because I am seeing what an advantage we have with him being able to sense her so clearly.

Azalea growls, fixing her den as she destroys the sheets. She raids the closet, trying to find clothes with my scent, and I step inside behind her as she snatches stuff off the hangers.

Tears trek down her face as she sniffs each piece. They aren't supposed to touch my stuff. I hoped they would have left a few pieces, knowing how savage she may become once her den was ruined. She tosses them down in frustration and rips more off the hanger, sniffing each one when I grab her arms.

"Hush, you don't need my scent when you have me. We can fix it," I tell her when she spins around, her eyes glowing, and she looks crazed. Her eyes run over me as she sniffs me and licks her lips. I groan in frustration. I like this suit too! When she looks me over from head to toe, I back away from her.

"Wait, Azzy. I will take them off, and I will climb in your den with you. Please don't—" she pounces on me, cutting my words off as her claws slip out. I catch her, my arms slipping around her waist as her legs lock around my hips. I sigh.

Damn it.

Her claws rip at my clothes, and I purr, trying to calm her frantic instincts as I turn around and move toward the bed. My suit jacket she has claimed and my shirt as buttons go flying as she tears it to shreds. I love and hate seeing her like this. Hate how vulnerable she becomes in this state, all instinct, yet love seeing her go crazy over my scent, knowing that is what she seeks.

"I really liked that suit," I mutter, placing her on the bed as her teeth sink into my chest. She licks me, and sparks explode across my skin. I press her into the clean linens earning a snarl as she lets me go and rolls, taking my clothes with her. She rearranges them in her den, duck feathers going everywhere as she rips a pillow apart.

"No, you have my shirt and jacket," I tell her or what is left of them. She whimpers, the sound crushing as she stares at my pants.

"I will lie in your den until you're satisfied, but the pants I am keeping," I tell her, determined to keep them. She just shredded a suit that cost me a damn fortune. Her bottom lip quivers. Damn pregnancy hormones are making her wild. I pull my belt out of the loops while cursing, slipping them down my legs and stepping out of them. I grab and hold them out to her, and she snatches them, rolling them into her den.

She won't be satisfied. I know that. My scent is still faint in the sheets, why is my scent so faint still? I hate seeing her so distraught with instincts she barely understands.

She growls at me when I press my hands onto the bed. "Where do you want me, then?" I ask, not wanting to ruin her den until she has it the way she prefers. Her breathing becomes harsher. It is dangerous to go into a Lycan den or near a frantic pregnant Lycans den. You don't touch or change it, especially scents not belonging to the mate. It's their cocoon of safety, and other scents are intruders.

Azalea grips her hair in frustration. The moment I kneel into her den, instant regret hits me when I realize how not a speck of our scent is in here. Whoever polished and cleaned this room would hear about it. They know better, and this is now becoming a problem as she suddenly starts clawing and ripping at her clothes, her hair, the lack of our mingled scents and cloying scent of bleach I can smell radiating out of the bathroom is sending her mad.

I open the mindlink, searching for Dustin, Gannon, and Clarice. They all answer simultaneously, *'Yes, my King.'*

'Who the fuck cleaned the room and bleached the bathroom?' I demand.

Clarice gasps, and I know it wouldn't be her. She wouldn't be stupid enough.

'We changed the sheets and removed her clothes and the curtains like you asked,' Dustin answers.

'Then why would you wash all of my clothes?' I growl. They could have at least left some of those.

'We replaced them with the ones from your office. They are covered in your scent, and we used gloves,' Gannon answers.

'Who else was in this room?'

'No one, just us and Peter when he came up to drop food off.'

'So no one else has been in here?' I ask, gripping Azalea's hands as she pulls her hair out.

'I have some of your clothes here that I haven't washed yet. I will bring them up,' Clarice says, slipping from the link.

'No one else should have been up there. We shut the doors to your quarters after we were done,' Dustin answers.

'Well, someone has been because all I can smell is chemicals and bleach, and all my clothes in the closet smell fresh out of the press,' I tell them.

'Is she alright?' they ask.

'What do you think? Someone stripped her entire den. Even the mattress smells like chemicals,' I snarl, pushing into her den when she claws her face. I cut the link off abruptly as I press my knee between her thighs, forcing her onto her back. I press my body against hers. My calling slips out instantly as I bear my weight on my arms so I don't crush her belly. Her breathing evens out, and she licks my chest, answering my call.

"Shh, love. I will fix it," I purr, nuzzling her neck, and she moans. My teeth nip at her mark, and her legs fall open more, allowing me to press between her thighs. Her body is languid beneath me as she gives in to the calling. I run my tongue over her neck and jaw, across her cheek, where she cut her face with her claws, healing it.

She lifts her hips, brushing against my boxers, and my cock strains in my pants when her desire perfumes the room, an aroma so sweet it has pre-cum leaking out of me and ruining the silk of my boxers as I become hard. Azalea groans when I hear the door.

'Leave them just inside, don't enter,' I tell Clarice through the link, and I hear the door open and quickly close. Azalea mewls and rolls her hips against me while my lips travel down her neck, and I remove what is left of her clothes while using the calling to subdue her enough that she doesn't harm herself. Soon enough, her den will smell the same, tamping down her anger and instincts.

Azalea pants and gazes up at me as I slip her pants down her milky thighs before removing them and tossing them aside. I growl when her knees close; the sound vibrates through her, and her legs fall open as she watches me with her lust-filled gaze, breathing heavily.

I run my hands up her thighs, spreading her wider before settling myself between them. Watching her face, I suck on the inside of her thigh, and her back arches off the bed as I lick and nip my way to the apex of her thighs. Her sweet arousal makes my cock throb in my boxer shorts. I watch as she shivers when my breath sweeps over her glistening wet lips, slick spilling from her, and she moans loudly when I flatten my tongue and run it across her wet pussy.

A moan escapes me as I taste her sweet nectar on my tongue. My tongue delves between her folds as I part them and lick my way to her clit. It pulses against my tongue as I suck it into my mouth, making her cry out.

Her skin flushes, and I love how she moves her hips against my mouth, seeking her release. I pin her thighs to the bed, relishing and tasting every inch of her, giving her no reprieve as she comes apart on my tongue. I know what she needs and wants and know she won't calm until our scents mingled through every piece of fabric on the bed, making her den complete. Azalea whines, clawing at my shoulders and tugging on my hair.

I growl as she lets go, and her whines turn to cries as I bring her to the edge again, only to make her crash over it. The sheets beneath became soaked as I sit up between her legs.

The heat of her gaze makes my cock twitch as I slip out of my boxers and toss them aside. Her breathing is harsh as she watches me. Gripping her hips, I tug her down the bed then line my cock up at her entrance.

Her hands reach for me and I lean down, kissing her, and her arms lock around my neck, kissing me deeper while her tongue invades my mouth hungrily. I thrust into her with one swift motion, making her bounce on the bed. She gasps into my mouth as her warm, smooth insides squeeze around me.

I growl, dragging my cock out and thrusting back into her while gripping her hip to hold her in place. Azalea turns to a puddle of writhing moans and cries as I pick up my rhythm and pound into her hot core, her inner walls quivering, coating my cock in her slick.

"Harder," she rasps while rocking her hips trying to meet my thrusts and growling when she can't. My grip on her hip is pinning her beneath me and forcing her to take what I give her. Her skin glistens with sweat as I pound into her, my lips moving to her mark and her lips going to my jaw, her warm tongue rolls down my neck and makes me shiver as she sucks on it. Her teeth graze my skin, and I feel my knot swelling, stretching her further. Her head falls back as I work it inside her tight confines.

Her walls grip me, her breathing heavy when I feel it push through the barrier. I groan when I feel her cum, her walls clenching down on me and locking me inside her. And I explode, my cum coating her womb as she moans, her pussy milking my cock as her walls spasm around me, her body arches and I kiss her, pushing her back down and invading her mouth with my tongue.

Her heart rate settles as I become locked inside her, and I roll, dragging her on top of me. Azalea buries her face in my chest, licking my pectoral muscle, and I purr for her until she falls flat against me, pressing her ear to the center of my chest while I catch my breath.

I smooth her hair down as she relaxes on top of me. The room smells of sex and our mingled scents seem to soothe and calm her. Lulling her out of her panicked state, I sigh, trailing my fingers up her spine. Yet I know I had to get rid of the smell of bleach from the bathroom, but for now, she is calm, and I will wait until she sleeps. My thoughts run rampant as she moans and wiggles, trying to get comfortable while locked to me.

'Who was watching the room?' I ask them through the mindlink. Everyone knows how Lycan women are, and to remove every scent from the room baffles me. She could have hurt herself or someone else. It is stupid on their part. I cringe, thinking of what would have happened if she had brought Abbie here while she was like that. She would never forgive herself if she hurt her.

'Us, the only time we left was to help set up the ballroom when you asked.' Gannon's mindlinks back.

"And you saw no one else up here.'

'No, everyone was helping, then Dustin and I went and got something to eat quickly, and I checked Abbie,' Gannon answers.

'Clarice?' I ask her, knowing she is listening in.

'Same with me. After I finished eating, I checked the door and it was still shut, and I smelt no scents up there."

'Where did Peter go?' I ask.

'He was with me until just before dinner and then slipped out the back to feed the horses, returned the same way 20 minutes later when we were finishing up,' Clarice answers.

'Can anyone verify he was down there?'

'Yes, because he came back with the gardener who helped him,' Clarice tells me. I sigh and shake my head.

'This is getting ridiculous,' I mutter.

'And nothing else happened that was odd?' I ask them.

'No, Abbie went into town and picked up fruit and veg with Clarice,' Gannon says.

'When?'

'This morning. But Abbie wouldn't have done that. She loves Azalea,' Gannon defends his future mate.

'I know that. I'm just trying to think of who had access to the room.'

'Just us, no one has been up here without signing in and out, and the only time we left, we ensured the floor was clear, and I just checked the cameras in the hall and nothing. Peter came up to clean the steps. He hadn't finished his punishment from Clarice, but he never went near the room,' Gannon tells me.

'Peter would never. He is just a boy, but we must be missing something,' I tell them.

'I will ask around,' Dustin says, and I cut the link.

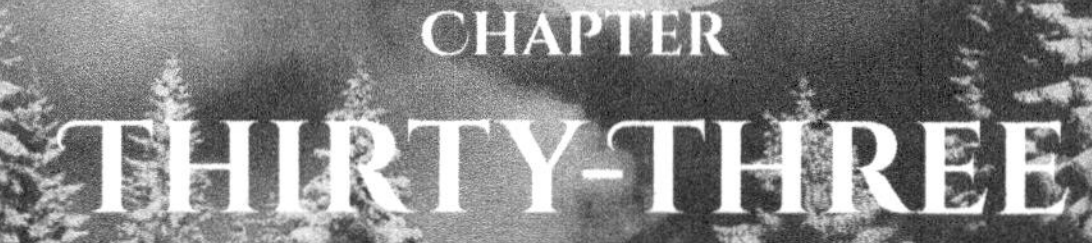

CHAPTER THIRTY-THREE

AZALEA

As I awaken, the midday sun streams through the open drapes, casting a warm glow upon my eyelids and coaxing me to open them. Squinting against the brightness, I survey the room, my gaze drawn to the windows. The sun sits high in the sky, its rays illuminating the space and a cool draft gently caresses my skin, sending a shiver down my spine. I notice the heavy drapes swaying in rhythm with the breeze.

Inhaling deeply, a sense of unease washes over me as I detect an unfamiliar scent in the air. It takes a moment for me to grasp the reason behind this disquiet, until it dawns on me that Kyson's intoxicating aroma is absent. The silence enveloping my den, devoid of his presence, leaves me restless. With determination, I shove aside the blanket and force myself out of bed, rushing towards the window, slamming it shut with a low growl.

Why would he leave it open? I snarl inwardly, catching a glimpse of my disheveled reflection in the glass. My hair is tousled, and I stand naked, yet traces of Kyson's scent linger faintly upon my skin. However, the den itself carries no hint of him, only my own fragrance permeating the space. An itch surfaces on my skin, amplifying my longing for my mate. With a sigh, I tear my gaze away from my reflection and startle when my eyes land on the grassy patch atop the hill.

Children are playing and rolling down the slope, having a rolling race to reach the bottom. A smile tugs at my lips as I observe Abbie and Clarice with the kids. Abbie sits at the top with Tyson nestled in her lap, while Clarice joins in the children, rolling down the hill along with them. Laughter rings loudly in the air, filling my heart with a longing to be down there with them.

Turning on my heel, I make my way to the closet, selecting a loose-fitting, long-sleeved dress from its hanger. Slipping into it, I relish the way the fabric cascades over me, concealing my growing bump. As I smooth my hand over my abdomen, I feel the firmness of my skin, evidence of the life flourishing within me.

Just as I finish dressing, the mindlink opens, Kyson's voice filtering through my thoughts.

'You're awake. I can come back up,' he offers.

'No need. I'm planning to join the children outside. What are you up to?' I inquire, tugging the dress down and ensuring its comfortable fit. My fingers instinctively caress my belly, I love the feel of it.

'Reviewing some files with Gannon. Are you sure you don't want me to come back?' Kyson asks.

'No, unless you need help? Shouldn't I be there,' I ask, realizing that perhaps my presence is required. After all, Abbie and Clarice seem to have everything well in hand.

'No, just take Trey with you. Also, don't forget about your ultrasound appointment this afternoon. I'll come fetch you beforehand,' Kyson reminds me.

'Are you certain?' I ask, slipping on a pair of comfortable sandals.

'Positive. Enjoy yourself. I love you,' Kyson says.

'Love you too,' I respond before severing the mindlink. Pulling my hair into a haphazard bun atop my head, I step out of the room and find Trey and Liam waiting outside my door.

"Afternoon, Azalea," Trey greets me as he stands by.

"My Queen," Liam acknowledges with a slight bow.

"Hey, Liam. Trey, I'm going to join Abbie and the children. Kyson wants you to accompany me," I inform Trey, he nods, offering me his arm. Looping my arm through his, we proceed towards the staircase that leads to the ground floor. Halfway down, my attention is drawn to Peter, kneeling on the steps, meticulously scrubbing the wooden beams of the guardrail with a toothbrush.

"What mischief have you gotten into this time, Peter?" I inquire, noting that the boy seems to find himself in trouble quite frequently lately. Peter glances up at me, a mischievous grin spreading across his face, revealing his pearly white teeth.

"I was just fooling around with the gardener and accidentally lobbed a mud pie at him. It missed and hit Clarice instead, and her freshly washed sheets," Peter chuckles.

"And why were you throwing mud pies in the first place?" I ask, attempting to stifle my own laughter.

"He threw one at me first! So he should be helping me clean these damn stairs! Honestly, I think Clarice punishes me just so she can avoid doing it herself," Peter pouts.

Shaking my head at his antics, I continue descending the stairs when Liam calls out above us.

"My Queen?" he addresses me from the top landing. Pausing on the middle step, I turn to face him.

"I need to shower and have a meal. I've been on duty since last night. I've called Dustin to take over for an hour. Is that alright?" Liam asks.

"Just go. He won't be long anyway. Besides, Peter will tell him if anyone comes up here," I say looking at Peter, who nods.

"You're fine. I will keep watch," Peter says, and Liam's eyes narrow at him on the stairs.

"It's fine. I will wait for Dustin. I was just letting you know, My Queen," he says.

"Seriously. Liam. Just go. Dustin will be here soon. What could happen?"

Liam for some reason, looks indecisive and is staring at Peter weirdly like it is the first time he is truly seeing him.

"Why did Clarice send you to clean these stairs?" Liam's voice grows cold, his gaze fixed upon the steps.

"Huh?" Peter says, looking up from his scrubbing.

"Why were you up here yesterday?" Liam asks him while tilting his head to the side. I have no idea what he is talking about, but Peter's brows furrow in confusion as he peers back at Liam.

"Pardon? I don't understand? Clarice sent me to clean the stairs," Peter says to him before glancing at me. He tosses his toothbrush into his cleaning bucket and his can of polish and rag while staring at Liam with fearful eyes. I walk back up the steps, wondering what has got into Liam because I don't like the way he is watching Peter.

"There are plenty of other staircases in the castle," he observes, tilting his head to the side. Trey shares my confusion, his brow furrowing as we exchange glances, questioning Liam's sudden shift in demeanor. It is then that a chill runs down my spine as I sense Liam's aura, distinct from Kyson's but still potent, emanating with an intensity that far surpasses that of an ordinary Lycan. Peter whimpers under its weight, visibly cowering in response, making me wonder if Liam is drunk.

"I dirtied Clarice's sheets," Peter stutters.

"That wasn't the question I asked," Liam growls icily, his voice dripping with menace. I watch in concern as he descends a step closer to Peter. At that moment, I make my way back up the stairs, eager to understand what has come over Liam and why he is scrutinizing Peter so intensely.

"Why these stairs?" Liam demands, pointing accusatory at them. "There are numerous stairways throughout the castle," he asserts, stepping down another level. Trey's eyes widen with alarm beside me, mirroring my own growing unease. It becomes apparent that something is amiss. His aura intensifies further, causing Peter to whimper under the weight of its pressure.

CHAPTER THIRTY-FOUR

AZALEA

"Liam!" I hiss urgently, my heart pounding as I rush to Peter's side. Beads of sweat glisten on his forehead, and his hands are clenched into tight fists on the steps. Panic courses through me as I take in the scene before me.

"Did you remove the scents from the King and Queen's room?" Liam demands, his voice filled with accusation. I gape at him, unable to comprehend his words.

"Liam! He's just a child! Stop commanding him!" I snap, my voice laced with anger. Peter's grip tightens on my arm, his eyes pleading with me, tears welling up.

'Kyson!' I call out through our mindlink, desperation creeping into my voice. But before I can receive a response, Liam's voice cuts through, pulling me back into the tense situation.

"My Queen, he cleans these stairs every day. Why would Clarice assign him the same task repeatedly?" Liam questions, his gaze shifting back to Peter.

"No... no, I didn't..." Peter gasps, his voice trembling with fear.

"What didn't you do? And why were you up here yesterday?"

Liam presses, motioning for me to come closer. But Peter clings to me tightly, his grip on my dress and arm desperate, as if I am his only lifeline.

'What is happening?' Kyson's frantic voice echoes through our mindlink.

'I... I don't know. Liam is accusing Peter,' I explain, my voice filled with frustration and worry. Trey growls protectively behind me, sensing the tension in the air.

"Answer me!" Liam barks, taking another step down towards Peter. His eyes flicker to Peter's trembling hands clutching onto me.

"Liam, calm down. He's just a boy," Trey interjects, trying to diffuse the escalating situation.

"And this boy will answer," Liam growls back, his voice dripping with authority.

"I was asked to bring lunch up and assist Clarice with her tasks. I didn't touch anything in the room. Clarice wouldn't allow it. She made me stand by the door while she handed me the baskets," Peter blurts out under Liam's commanding tone, unable to resist the power of his aura any longer.

"Why these stairs?" Liam probes further.

"Clarice told me to clean the stairs where she could see me," Peter blurts out, his words coming out in a rush.

"Clarice instructed you to clean them?" Liam asks, his tone slightly softer.

"Well, not specifically these stairs. Just anywhere she could spot me if she left the kitchen. These are the closest ones," Peter explains, his voice quivering with nerves.

"Why did you choose these stairs?" Liam asks, descending another step towards him.

"Liam! Enough!" I intervene, my voice filled with anger and disbelief.

"No. I was just thinking. And out of everyone we've questioned, Peter has never been asked," Liam says, his gaze shifting between Peter and me. Suddenly, his eyes settle on the tool bucket resting on the step in front of Peter. As he approaches, a stronger scent of liquor wafts towards me, revealing that Liam is intoxicated. Anger boils within me as I witness his drunken state.

"He's just a boy!" I exclaim, outrage seeping into my words. How could Liam take out his drunken ramblings on an innocent child? Peter looks petrified, his hands trembling as he clings onto me, tears streaming down his face.

"I was a boy once too, My Queen. And I had already killed someone long before I was his age," Liam retorts coldly, each step calculated as he moves closer to Peter. I glance down at Peter, who growls softly as I hear Kyson's voice entering the mindlink.

'My King, has Peter ever been questioned before,' Trey's voice cuts through the tension, breaking the silence as Liam continues his relentless approach towards Peter. The savage gleam in Liam's eyes frightens me, and I see Peter whimper in fear.

Gently prying Peter's fingers off my dress, I stand straighter and take a step up, placing myself between Liam and Peter.

'No, why? What has happened? Azalea, answer me! I'm on my way,' Kyson growls urgently. But before I can respond, Liam reaches for me, attempting to pull me to his side. In that instant, a sharp pain slices through my side, stealing the air from my lungs. Trey's ear-piercing scream reverberates behind me, freezing time itself. I see Liam's hands reaching out towards me, his eyes widening in shock, but I stagger back, my hand instinctively going to my side. My fingertips brush against the hilt of a dagger embedded in my flank, and my hands are suddenly soaked in warm blood.

Gasping for breath, struggling to breathe around the pain, I hear Peter's voice amidst the chaos. "That's for my mum!" he cries out as Trey tackles him to the ground. I try to reach for something to hold onto, to stay upright, but the banister gives way under my weight.

A scream escapes my lips as I realize I am falling, my body crashing onto the ground with a jarring thud. Agony engulfs me as pain radiates through every fiber of my being. My head collides with the stairs of the ground floor stairwell, the wooden railing crashing down upon me. Paralyzed and unable to move, I lie there, staring at the ceiling above and the floor above that, where Trey has subdued Peter.

Liam leaps from the second floor, his feet hitting the ground mere seconds later. But it is too late. Warm blood trickles down my neck, my head, and my back throbbing in agony. The taste of copper fills my mouth, making it difficult to breathe, and I choke on every attempt. It feels as though my entire body is tingling with pins and needles, the sensation pulsating in time with my rapid heartbeat.

My vision blurs, the world around me pulsating with pain. Liam's face comes into focus, his lips moving in frantic silence, as if he's screaming. But all I hear is the pounding of my own heart in my skull.

I feel myself fading, my vision narrowing into a tunnel. I am unable to move, and yet a strange warmth spreads between my legs, like I've wet myself. It's a peculiar sensation that inexplicably captures my attention more than the excruciating pain. It becomes the focal point of my mind, above all else. As darkness descends upon me, I'm still fixated on that warmth, even as everything slips away.

CHAPTER THIRTY-FIVE

KYSON

We had found a few things in the documents from the Alpha Dean's pack, such as Mr. Crux's name linking to multiple brothels in the state. It looked like he was helping traffic rogues because sizable sums of money had been sent to Alpha Dean's accounts when they suddenly stopped abruptly a few years ago and enormous debts started accumulating. Debts from Crux's casino.

As we sifted through the boxes, we found other strange things that didn't add up, which had me going down to the underground storage. Gannon and Dustin are pulling everything we have on Crux from the archives, and we set them on the huge wooden table in the storage room.

"While we're down here, gather all the staff records for me," I instruct them, their footsteps echoing as they return to the towering stacks of boxes before depositing them at my feet.

I delve into the piles of documents, searching for any trace of council records or vital information. "You two can begin with the staff files," I direct, my gaze focused on the task at hand. "Go as far back as fourteen years ago when the Landeenas were taken from us."

"So before Azalea's fourth birthday?" Dustin asks, and I nod.

"Yes. There must be a reason why someone is targeting her, and it's highly likely that the culprit resides within the castle grounds. Scrutinize every guard, whether under oath or not. Examine the records of all the cleaners, gardeners—every individual who has been on our payroll," I state, their hands eagerly sifting through the extensive collection of files.

After just a few hours of sorting, Gannon pulls out Trey's file once more, accompanied by another containing his medical records —proof that corroborated every detail he had shared with us. It becomes increasingly apparent that we needed to establish an efficient electronic filing system; the sheer volume of paperwork is becoming absurd.

A couple of hours later, I feel Azalea stir from sleep. She informs me of her intention to play with the children and I urge her to take Trey along. As I finish talking with her, my attention is abruptly seized by Gannon's interruption.

"Did you know that Ester had spent time in the Landeena Kingdom?" he questions. I glance up, momentarily breaking the connection with Azalea.

"What?" I reply, my curiosity piqued as Gannon extends a file towards me.

"For an entire year. Her parents reported her as a runaway, and she was eventually located in the Landeena Kingdom. Garret granted her permission to stay," Gannon reveals, his eyes fixed on mine.

"What year was this?" I inquire, my mind racing to make sense of this new revelation.

"The year preceding Azalea's abduction. According to the records, she left a month prior to the attack, following a falling out with Queen Tatiana," Gannon discloses, prompting me to read the contents of the file. I find it peculiar that Ester would venture there only to return a year later.

Despite our thorough investigation, no additional information surfaced, leaving me confused. It occurred to me that Ester's parents had once served my father, but I hadn't seen them in years. However, her grandfather contacted me seeking employment for Ester, and since they were former employees I gave her a job. While I was aware of her strained relationship with her parents—whom she had been primarily raised by—my involvement in their affairs remained minimal.

I try to pick my brain about why she has an odd relationship with her parents, trying to remember what their falling out was for, but I don't really involve myself with her.

I feel the mindlink open up moments later, Azalea calling me only to end the call abruptly. Almost immediately, Trey opens it up.

'My King, have you looked into Peter?' Trey inquires urgently, prompting me to establish a connection with him as well in an attempt to regain contact with Azalea.

'No. Why? And Azalea, bloody answer me!' I growl impatiently, my attention divided between Trey's words and Ester's files. As I comb through the documents, Trey's mention of Peter sparks a memory—I vaguely recalled Ester having a brother. In fact, her parents had adopted him! The realization strikes me with the force of a lightning bolt.

I knew she had an estranged relationship with her parents since they had adopted Peter! Peter! My eyes widen in realization.

"It's Peter!" I growl when Azalea screams through the link, and I race to get to her. My heart is hammering in my chest.

Dustin and Gannon are chasing after me, and I skid across the floors as I smash out of the cellar, my shoulder smashing against the doors, and into the kitchen's pantry before I race out of the kitchen. I lose my footing as I twist to head for the stairs at the same time. I hear someone scream.

My heart feels like it stops when I see a figure fall off the staircase, and I register that the figure is Azalea a second later. Her arms flail about just as the entire banister railing comes down after her. My feet try to get friction on the floor just as Gannon and Dustin burst out of the kitchen doors.

I sprint towards Azalea, but Liam is quicker, leaping after her. My heart constricts as her body collides with the stairs with a resounding thud, just out of my reach.

Time stands still as I watch in shock. Trey forcefully thrust Peter against the wall, his form crumpling unconscious on the steps. Paralyzed by disbelief, I can only stare at Liam, who screams for assistance, his hands pressing down on the knife embedded in Azalea's side. Blood gushes from her mouth and dribbles down her chin, jolting me back into action when I see Gannon and Dustin trying to move but are both unable. I rush to Liam's side as Azalea's eyes roll back, her body growing limp. I clutch her face desperately.

"Azalea!" I choke out, my voice laden with anguish. "Stay with me." But she succumbs to unconsciousness, her body slackening in my grip.

"Get a doctor!" I bellow, my command echoing through the air as Gannon and Dustin rush off.

"Stay with me, love," I beg, my voice trembling as I cradle her fragile form. Panic courses through me as I feel warmth seeping onto my knees. My eyes dart downwards, witnessing the crimson stain spreading across her dress, pooling between her legs and trickling down the steps.

"No. No, no, no! NO!" I cry out frantically, my mind racing to comprehend the severity of the situation. With every fiber of my being, I know that time is of the essence. Without hesitation, I slide my arms beneath her lifeless body, scooping her into my arms before sprinting towards the doors. Liam races ahead, forcefully shoving them open while urgently summoning the guards to unlock the gates.

Blood coats my arms—her blood—flowing from her head and also trickling between her legs. My clothes become saturated with her life blood as I bolt down the bitumen road, shifting while in motion. The sound of her weakening heartbeat, of our baby's, reverberates in my ears while I pray for its next beat. But she is still too early for any hope of a viable life to emerge.

My legs falter as the heartbeat ceases. Her pulse weakens, and I glance at her in my arms, I wait for that flutter, needing to hear it and tears blur my vision as I force myself to run harder when I don't.

The doctor's surgery come into view ahead of me, its brick facade a flicker of desperate hope. People stare in shock as the doctor bursts through his surgery doors, his medical gear clutched tightly in his hands. His eyes widen as he spots us, and he wastes no time rushing back inside, barking orders at his nurses to prepare a gurney.

Navigating through the corridors of the aging brick building, we reach a room where the nurses anxiously await our arrival. Carefully, I lay Azalea down on the gurney, her body appearing fragile and vulnerable. The doctor swiftly places his bag beside her, his sense of urgency palpable as he whisks her away. I move to follow, but Liam's firm grip on my shoulder halts me in my tracks.

"You'll just get in the way," Liam says, but I could heal her. I am about to say that when Liam speaks, seeming to know what I am going to say.

"Some things can't be healed, my King. Let Doc work," Liam says, and moments later, Damian burst through the surgery doors. He looks at me, his eyes then moving to Liam's hand holding my shoulder.

"Come on, let's wait outside. There is nothing you can do right now," Damian says, and I shake my head.

"Come on. Come have a smoke," Liam says, pushing me toward the doors, and am forced to take my eyes away from where Doc took her through the double doors to the day surgery area. Liam pushes me out the doors, nudging me and I reluctantly step outside, and he shoves his smoke packet in my hand, yet I don't light one when he pulls two from the packet and lights them, keeping one for himself and passing me the other.

"Azalea will be okay," Liam says, blowing smoke into the air. "She is tougher than she looks," he says.

"The baby?" I ask. Neither of them says anything. Even though I know that if she is alright, the baby isn't going to be. Which makes me wonder if Azalea will be alright after all.

The doctor confirms that when he steps out the doors twenty minutes later. He tugs his gloves off.

"Azalea?" I ask.

"Alive. She is still unconscious. I stitched her up. The bleeding stopped, but you could probably help that healing process," Doc says, and I nod.

"Our baby?" I ask, grasping on to any form of hope.

"I'm sorry, My King. The fetus didn't make it," he tells me. Fetus. I hated the way he said it, but she was just in her second trimester. My legs buckle under me, and I hit the ground hard at his words. My heart sinks and my stomach drops at the information.

I failed her! I should have figured it out earlier. Peter was a child and the last person I would have suspected! I failed her, and it cost us our baby and nearly her life! How do I tell her that?

"Azalea needs you, Kyson. Get up," Damian says.

"We lost the baby," I murmur, trying to wrap my head around everything.

"I know, but if you don't get up and get in there, you may lose her, too. Now up," Damian says, gripping my arm and Liam grabs the other; they haul me to my feet.

"One foot in front of the other. Come on, big fella. Your Queen needs you. Break later, but not in front of her," Liam says, pushing me towards the doors.

☽◯☾

It takes hours for her to wake up, and Damian goes back to the castle to retrieve some clothes, so I'm not walking around in just a hospital gown. I have just walked back into the room to find that she is sitting up. I feel nothing through the bond to tell me she has woken, and I only stepped out a minute to change quickly. Pinching the fabric of her hospital gown, she peers inside before rubbing her thighs. Her lips tremble, and she stares at her hands. Doc and I make sure to clean her up, so she isn't drenched in blood, but it seems like that is all she sees as she examines her trembling hands. Closing the distance between us, I notice her head rise, her eyes meeting mine. There is no emotion in her voice, and the bond between us feels nonexistent.

"Do you feel it?" she asks, halting my hand as it reaches towards her. I swallow hard and step closer, my fingers finding the back of her neck as they weave through her hair. Yet still, there is no response through the bond.

"I could feel it... feel it leaving me," she whispers, her vacant stare fixed on my chest.

"I know, love," I whisper back, but she remains frozen in place, staring off into nothingness.

"How about we get you home?" I suggest, hoping to elicit some kind of reaction from her. But once again, she says nothing, not even a blink. She is like an empty shell, and I fight the urge to growl. I will kill him, but first, I need to take care of her, but he will die for doing this to her once I find out why. Azalea has no reaction when I pick her up, none at all. I take her home and set her in her den, and she lays down.

Three days later

For three days she has remained in bed, refusing to eat or sleep. Doc came by yesterday and assured me that it is to be expected, but I can't bring myself to leave her side. The bond between us feels nonexistent, and it's as if she isn't even there, even though I can see her right before me.

Brushing her hair back, I attempt to move her up the bed so she can rest against me, but she slides right back down into her den, seeking comfort beneath the blankets as if they can shield her from the world.

Letting out a sigh of frustration, I set aside the book I have been reading to her and make my way to the bathroom. I fill the bathtub with bubbles and lavender-scented soap, crinkling my nose at the fragrance that I know she likes. Returning to the room, I retrieve one of my shirts from the closet. She is still dressed in that hospital gown, but I am determined to change that today. Baby steps.

Perhaps if I can get her to eat or speak, she will feel more like herself. Equipped with towels and a shirt for her, I check the water and wait for the tub to fill before turning off the faucet. Stepping into the room, I find her in the same spot as before, tangled in blankets.

With care, I untangle her from the fabric and lift her up, removing her gown as she sits on the edge of the bed. Goosebumps cover her skin, prompting me to strip off my own clothes before joining her in the bath. I settle her between my legs, and she remains motionless as I wash her hair and clean her gently.

We stay in the water until it turns cold, and then I lift her out, drying her off before slipping my shirt over her head. But it angers me when she simply rolls back into her den without any order or structure. Clarice has sent up soup hoping to entice her to eat but Azalea only rolls over in response.

Reaching for my whiskey, I take a swig straight from the bottle. It is the only thing that keeps me from losing my damn mind. The silence is suffocating, and absence of any sensation through bond is unbearable. I long for any reaction from her just to know that she is still with me.

My frustration grows as I glare at the disheveled den that obscures her from view, hiding her beneath layers of blankets. In a fit of anger, I accidentally drop the bottle, shattering it on the floor. I snarl at the mess I have made. Overwhelmed by my anger, I can't contain the shift any longer. I storm towards the bed, tearing at her den in a futile attempt to fix it. Instead, all I manage to do is tear apart the mattress. Growling with frustration, I collapse onto the bed. Just as I'm about to mindlink Damian to call Doc again, I feel movement on the bed, followed by her hand running across my fur and settling on my chest as she lays her head against me.

At first I am astonished, staring down at her in disbelief. It's the first time she has moved towards me since this ordeal began, and of course, it has to be when I'm not in human form. Part of me wants to shift back and revel in her closeness, but I don't want to risk her pulling away if she realizes what she has done. Turning my face towards her, I nuzzle her hair and let my calling wash over her. She snuggles closer, and with a sigh, I accept that it's something even if it isn't much.

A few hours later, she wakes up prompting me to shift back into human form. Immediately, she retreats back under the covers. In the following days, I notice that she only seeks my presence when I'm in my shifted state. It seems that being in my Lycan form provides her with some comfort. So, I spend most of my time in this state hoping to provide her with some sense of security.

As a knock sounds at the door, I move away from the bed. Today Azalea has mustered enough strength to help me fix her den. We change the sheets and tidy it up although she doesn't rebuild it like I had hoped. I had grown accustomed to its presence even though it's an odd habit for female Lycans. Nevertheless, I miss curling up in it with her.

Liam enters with strips of raw meat and cubed cheese and crackers that Clarice had sent up.

"Is she still the same?" Liam asks, and I nod wearily. It has been over a week, and still, she hasn't eaten. She is losing weight rapidly. This time, I've struggled lately every time I've attempted to make her eat while in my shifted form. The claws make it difficult, but she seems more at ease when I am in this state.

"I've been thinking," Liam says as I turn away from him. I pause and glance back at him.

"About what?" I reply, not wanting to entertain any thoughts about Peter or theories at this moment. My focus is solely on Azalea.

Peter is locked away in the cells, and I will deal with him when the time is right.

'About why she only goes near you when you're shifted,' he states, opening up the mindlink between us.

'You can't mate with her,' Liam continues, and a growl rumbles in my throat. I look back towards the bed before turning my attention back to Liam.

'Something to consider,' Liam says, leaving the room. I remain by the bed, propping Azalea up with pillows so she can sit comfortably. Accidentally, my claws nick her arm, causing her to flinch. Leaning down, I place a gentle kiss on the spot where I have broken the skin, watching as it heals before my eyes.

"Sorry," I murmur to her, but she remains silent, her gaze fixed on me. I pick up a strip of beef with my claws, only to fumble and drop it. Frustrated, I try again, but the same result occurs. She then reaches out and picks it up herself, her movements robotic and detached.

She eats half of what is on the plate despite my insistence that she eat more. Eventually, I set the plate aside and lay back down with her, eventually drifting off to sleep. It feels like all we do is sleep and read, and it feels wrong.

I long to hear her voice again. However, it is Trey's conversation with Abbie outside the doors that rouses me from my slumber. I quickly rise to my feet and catch sight of the fading sunlight through the windows. The children are playing on the hill; their laughter fills the air. As I make my way towards the door, a flicker of hope ignites within me. Perhaps Abbie can coax Azalea out of bed.

But as I open the door, reality sets in. Abbie can't help; she is still under her command. She stands outside, talking with Trey about how Azalea is doing. Liam is nowhere in sight, presumably having taken over guard duty of Peter. I half-expected Peter's grandparents to come searching for him, but no one had arrived or informed me otherwise.

Tyson is perched on her hip, playing with her hair as I open the door. She gasps, peering out the window at the children playing on the hill. A brawl starts outside amongst some of the older children. She thrusts Tyson at Trey, rushing down the steps to break it up. I watch from the window while Trey holds Tyson.

"Maybe go help her," I suggest, seeing her and Clarice both struggling to separate the kids that are determined to get the last hit in. Trey sighs, passing Tyson to me and rushing toward the stairs.

"Wait!" I call, and he stops on the steps. "Take the boy with you," I tell him, holding him at arm's length.

"You want me to help or not," Trey says, and I look out the window to see guards trying to help and sigh.

"Just don't take too long," I tell him, and he nods before disappearing. I perch the boy on my hip. Tyson is only small, tugging on my fur when he starts making strange grunting noises before wailing like he is being murdered and pointing toward the room.

"No, we can't go in there," I tell him as he starts wailing and thrashing in my arms. He kicks me in the balls, making me drop him, but I catch him before he hits the ground, setting him down gently. He rushes off, and my eyes widen in horror as I turn to find him in our room. Unsure how Azalea will react to him, I rush in. He is screeching and fisting air.

"What?" I ask him, trying to hush him while glancing nervously at the bed where Azalea is. She doesn't seem to hear him or doesn't care; I'm not sure. He screeches and grunts again.

"I don't know what you want," I tell him, trying to pick him up and remove him from the room. I shush him and peer out the window for Abbie who is scolding some of the kids.

"Your mother will be back soon," I tell him. He grunts, fisting his hands and squeezing them tightly.

"He wants the books," Azalea says, and I jump, looking at the bed where she's still sitting. Tyson also jumps at the sound of her voice and peers over at her. I set him down when he starts kicking his legs and moving towards the bookshelf. I point to each book when he goes crazy, grunting as I touch one with a picture of an apple on the side - *Snow White.*

I pull it from the shelf and hand it to him, about to escort him out when he rushes towards the bed. I chase after him, scooping him up before he climbs in only for him to bite me, making me let go with a growl.

As I reach for him again, Azalea sits up quickly snatching Tyson before I can. She sets him next to her, and Tyson opens the book smacking the pages while grunting and making strange noises - it's obvious what he wants this time; he wants her to read it. Azalea doesn't say anything but grabs the book from Tyson holding it out to me.

"He can read Tyson; you know I can't," she tells us just as Abbie returns, walking into a wall almost as she tries to cross the threshold. Azalea stares at Tyson brushing her fingers through his hair; meanwhile, Abbie mouths something to me wanting her son back.

"Can he stay for a bit?" I ask.

Abbie glances at Azalea who is brushing Tyson's hair, she nods before walking off. It's more than she had done before so I don't want her slipping back into herself. I open the book and start to read; eventually both Tyson falls asleep followed by Azzy.

Trey comes in a few hours later to collect Tyson for Abbie, and I expected her to roll away from me when I shift back now that the kid is gone. Instead, she moves closer and places her head on my chest. I kiss her forehead, tucking her closer.

Maybe tomorrow will be better, I think to myself. Either way, tomorrow, I have no choice but to deal with Peter. He has been in the cells for over a week, nearly two, and I want him gone for what he has done.

CHAPTER THIRTY-SIX

AZALEA

Nothing feels real, yet the searing ache in my heart serves as a constant reminder of its undeniable existence and it beats despite feeling like it's broken beyond repair. My mind, however, remains shrouded in a disorienting numbness, as if it has willingly retreated to shield me from the weight of emotions. It is both a blessing and a curse, it's a detachment that renders me irrevocably, undeniably numb.

But when I lay my eyes upon Kyson, a flicker of concern ignites within me. He drowns his sorrows in an endless torrent of alcohol, a desperate attempt to drown out his own pain. And still, he never strays far from my side. Through our bond, I can sense his anguish, intertwined with mine yet separate. It is a peculiar sensation, to feel his pain as my own and yet disassociate from it, acknowledging its existence while refusing to claim it as mine.

Yet, in this state of emotional detachment, I find myself indifferent to everything. I exist but do not truly live. The concept of living or dying holds no sway over me; they are mere notions devoid of meaning. I am adrift in a bubble of indifference, numb to the world around me and to my own existence. And yet, as the days stretch on, I realize that remaining anchored to this unfeeling place cannot be a permanent state.

As life continues its relentless march before my silent eyes, I am haunted by one question: is this all there is? Is this the extent of my existence, forever trapped within this barren emotional landscape?

Gradually, I lose sight of the man who is my mate, losing connection not only with him but also with myself. Perhaps it is because for so long I had no sense of self, and the prospect of our unborn child held the promise of an identity—a role I could embrace as a mother. That loss cuts deep, for with it, another fragment of an identity I long to keep slips away.

Questions gnaw at my every thought, rendering me paralyzed in their grip. Why did he feign friendship only to plunge the blade of betrayal into my back? How can he harbor such seething anger towards someone he claims to care for? Why did he strip away the one thing that was undeniably mine?

The weight of these unanswered questions threatens to suffocate me. They consume my every waking moment, leaving little room for anything else. Yet, as I return to awareness, uncertain whether I have slept or have been awake this entire time, the room comes into focus and I am faced with my sleeping mate beside me.

He stirs, instinctively drawn closer to me, his warm breath cascading over my neck as he buries his nose in my hair. Worry lingers within our bond even in his sleep, evidence of his desire to bring comfort. But I know that true comfort will elude me until I uncover the answers I seek. I want understanding, need it for closure, I need proof that I did not bring this upon myself. Though a part of me knows this truth, doubt continues to claw at my consciousness, insidiously whispering that perhaps I am to blame.

With a heavy heart, I summon the strength to remove myself from Kyson's protective embrace, sliding out from under his arm that drapes heavily across my waist. Crossing the room in silence, I reach for his robe, craving the familiar comfort of his scent enveloping me.

Clutching it tightly against my chest, I cast one last glance at his peaceful form before tiptoeing towards the door. Peering back at him, he remains asleep.

He might be mad, or maybe he won't be, I'm not sure. So much has changed and yet remains the same. Though I have seen yet another side of Kyson, multiple in fact over the last few days.

One that he loves me fiercely not leaving me alone despite his own anguish, two that he has a really bad drinking problem. I never realized its true extent until I was locked in a room with him for so long, it makes me wonder if that is how he drinks all the time.

On a few occasions, he drinks himself to oblivion. And on days when he doesn't, I can feel the tremor of his hands when he touches me. I feel his frustration as he fights the urge to find himself in the bottom of another bottle. One thing became apparent after the first week, the bottle always won in the end.

That is something we will have to address later, for now I need to move before I decide to crawl back in bed and wallow in my own misery, so I twist the handle and step out the doors to find Trey. He looks at me as if he is seeing a ghost when I slip out the door and close it gently. He appears hesitant when I move toward him before he grabs me, crushing me against his chest. His arms lock around me and I feel his nose in my hair, as he inhales my scent like he is hoping I am real and not a figment of his imagination. I sigh, and briefly hug him back glad that I haven't been too much of a burden on my guard that they've turned and now hate me.

"Thank god," he whispers before holding me at arm's length.

"Where's the King?"

He glances at the door behind me before clutching my face in his hands and leaning down to look at me, his eyes sparkle with sadness, endless hazel depths of worry stare back at me as he stares with worry.

"Sleeping," I say, though my throat hurts from hardly using my voice and comes out raspy.

"I shall wake him for you," he says, though I shake my head.

Kyson needs sleep, I know how little he has been getting, I know how exhausted he is, I also know he will feel like shit after how much he drank last night before he succumbed to it.

"Let him sleep, but I have a favor to ask of you," I tell Trey.

"Yes, whatever you need," he answers swiftly, while standing straight again.

"I want to see Peter," I admit. He opens his mouth no doubt to deny me but I hold my hand up silencing him.

"I need this please, I wouldn't ask if I didn't, and I know Kyson won't let me, and he believes he is doing it to protect me, but I need this," I plead, hoping he won't wake Kyson to tell him of my plans. Trey's eyes turn black and he looks torn but my blood is his sire, my blood he is oathed to.

"Can you at least tell Kyson? I am not comfortable going against him, he would see this as a betrayal," Trey pleads. If I do, he may lock me in the room, or just go kill Peter without questioning him.

"You won't, will you?" Trey sighs and rubs his temples. "At the very least, let me wake Liam to come with us, just to be extra safe," he says, and I agree, one can never be too careful.

We meet Liam in the kitchens, he is still in his pajamas, which sit low on his hips, his chest is bare and a tattoo of a beast clawing out of chest is tattooed on his skin.

He tugs a tank top on as he walks in making me wonder how close his room is to the kitchens. Shaking that thought away, he drops a hand on my shoulder.

"Lass, maybe you should let Kyson deal with Peter," he says, and I shake my head. I need answers then Kyson can deal with him.

"Aren't children off limits?" I wonder how it would be possible. Would Kyson break the very laws he swore to uphold?

"Not when it comes to treason, there is an exception to every rule," Liam explains.

I'm not sure how I feel about that, I'm not sure if I feel anything at his words. Trey walks ahead into the pantry opening up the door inside that goes to the stairs under the castle.

A chill rushes through me as we descend the stairs, and I stay close to Trey and Liam, using them like shields and they happily oblige as we navigate the winding tunnels before stopping at the cells. It's dark here with the dim lighting and two guards stand either side of the cell.

Trey snarls and Liam places his hand on my side as if he is ready to rip me from the place, yet my eyes are on the boy that sits huddled in the corner, looking like the weight of the world rests solely on his shoulders.

Peter, a boy I trusted and despite what he had done. Some part of me hangs on to the hope he will tell me it is all a joke and it wasn't him, that he hadn't taken my baby from me. He is a child himself; a child who took my own child from me. Seeing him so broken and scared only makes his young age that much more painfully obvious.

Peter looks up, and I move to the bars. His head snaps up to look at me and he hangs his head. His knees are pressed to his chest; he looks small and meek. Though looks can be deceiving, was all of it a lie? Everything? I liked Peter, I liked his energy, his carefree personality, his bubbliness but now I see a monster in a child's body, yet monsters hurt too. That becomes abundantly clear when he looks up, tears in his eyes that etch down his face and drip off his chin.

"I'm sorry, I... I didn't mean... I panicked," he sobs, and I look at Liam who is glaring daggers at him.

"Panicked? You drove a knife into her, that isn't panicking that is calculated," Trey snarls, hitting the bars and making him jump. The guards, I notice, step away from Trey, backing away from him as his body shakes violently. I place my hand on his arm and he calms some, glancing down at me.

Turning to the guard, I ask for the keys. Liam quickly grabs my hand to stop me and Trey presses closer to me like he will toss me over his shoulder for even thinking of going near Peter. He is detained, shackled with chains around his neck, ankles, and wrists; he isn't going anywhere.

"He can't hurt me," I tell them.

"He already has," Liam replies. I look at him and press my lips in a line. Yes, he has more than he will ever know.

"I want the keys, I am not talking to him through the bars," I tell Liam who looks at Trey. They hold some secret conversation, and Trey growls, but Liam lets my wrist go. But when the guard goes to hand the keys over Trey takes them.

"I'm coming in with you and you remain by my side and Liam by his," Trey says. I don't fight him on it, I know he won't budge unless I order him and I don't have the fight in me to debate it. I nod my head, and he unlocks the door. Liam walks in first and stands near the wall beside Peter who flinches at his closeness. Liam, however, just offers him a cold glare.

Trey refuses to step aside to let me in, and he grabs my arm when I try before pulling me to the opposite side of him; however, he doesn't close the door, probably in case something happens so I can run out. I go to sit on the steel bed but apparently that is too close because Trey grabs my arm, steering me to the far wall. Liam leans over and tosses the pillow over from off the bed to him and he catches it dropping it at his feet.

"If you want to sit you can but not near him," Trey says, and I sigh but sit on the pillow and lean against the wall. Though Trey remains standing, his leg brushing against my arm and I look up at him.

"Can you at least sit, it feels awkward with you standing," I tell him, and he looks down at me before looking over at Liam.

"He moves, I will break his neck," Liam says in more of a warning to Peter, but Trey sits beside me, though his entire body is tense.

Peter stares at the floor, sniffling and wiping his nose with the back of his hand. For a few minutes, I can't bring myself to speak. The air is thick with tension but eventually, I find my voice.

"Why?" I ask him, and his head lifts, his eyes snapping to mine.

"I didn't mean to, I.." He moves his hands and Liam has him by his throat instantly and my shriek makes him pause.

"He can't hurt me, he won't, will you Peter?" I ask. Peter chokes and sputters, his eyes bulging but shakes his head as best he can, and Liam lets him go, he falls to the ground gasping.

Peter pushes further into the corner away from him but his eyes return to mine after a moment.

"It was you that poisoned the fruit?" I tell him and he chews his lip and nods his head.

"You bleached my room?"

He nods again,

"He also unbolted the stairs banister, that's why he was cleaning them," Liam growls, and Peter flinches, cowering away.

"How did you get past the guards to get in the room," Trey asks him.

"I offered to clean the roof's gutters, the window was cracked," Peter answers and I press my lips in a line.

"Was it you that morning in the room? The window was open," I tell him, and he hangs his head and nods.

Trey snarls at him, and Peter visibly makes himself smaller.

"I just wanted you to go back to Landeena, to leave the castle, I didn't mean to kill your..." He looks at my stomach, and a tear rolls down his face, which he tries to hide as he glances away.

"Liam figured it out, and I knew they would remove me from the castle. I panicked and I went to take you hostage but then he lunged at me, so I stabbed you. I swear I didn't mean it, command me please, ask anything. I will answer whatever you like. It wasn't my intention to kill you but I freaked out."

"If you didn't intend to hurt her, why did you have a knife?" Liam asks.

"I always have it, it was my father's," Peter says.

"I thought you didn't know your father," I ask, and he shrugs.

"I've heard of him, apparently he wasn't worth knowing."

"So you know who he is?" I ask. Peter shakes his head.

"No, not even my grandparents know, just said he was a dead beat because he never came for me," Peter answers.

"You don't believe that?" I ask, curiously. I don't know why I am asking him, I shouldn't care, but for some reason I do.

"I don't know, but then you came along and the King made her leave, I just wanted to scare you, make you leave so she could come back, it was the only time I got to see her," Peter says.

"See who?" Trey asks, and Peter looks at the ground.

"She never comes to see me, she pretends I don't exist," Peter says, clearing his throat and wiping his face.

"At least here she has to speak to me, I would ask Clarice to let me help her, sometimes she would let me help her," Peter says, wiping his face and rubbing his bloodshot eyes.

"Then you ruined it, you made her leave. I just wanted her to stay," Peter says.

"Who are you talking about?" I ask. I haven't made anyone leave that I am aware of.

"My mother," Peter answers. Confusion washes over me, and by the looks on Liam and Trey's face, they are just as confused.

"Grandpa said one day she would come around, that she would see me and come get me but she didn't, so I got a job here to be near her," he says.

Liam and Trey exchange wary looks. I am just as confused. .

"Peter, who is your mother?" I ask, trying to figure out who he is talking about.

"Ester, and you made her leave me again. I was going to make her see, see that I could be good, that I wasn't like my father, that she could love me, and I wouldn't leave her," Peter says.

Ester is his mother? I am horrified by this news, but I am shocked more by the thunderous growl escapes from Trey. I jump at the sound, not expecting it.

CHAPTER THIRTY-SEVEN

AZALEA

"Liar! You are not that whore's son!" Trey growls, and Peter flinches as Trey goes to get up. I grab his arm, and it ripples under my hand just as Liam moves so quickly, he knocks the air out of my lungs, getting me out of the way as Trey shifts. Liam shoves me out the cell door, the guard grabbing me before I can fall, and Liam also shifts, pinning Trey to the wall.

"Calm down!" Liam snarls while Trey's eyes are on Peter, who whimpers in the corner, cowering away from him. I swallow, petrified, and my heart races as I watch Trey's nostrils flare, his face savage, and a deep reverberating growl rips from him, challenging Liam, who returns it with a deafening one. Their auras clash and batter one another, and are both potent and deadly, the testosterone in the room making me dizzy. I have to fight the urge to run to my mate, not liking the charged energy after days of only being under Kyson's calming calling.

"Choose wisely, Trey. I was coming around to not hating you. Challenge me, and you go back on my shit list," Liam warns, his tone ice cold and threatening.

"Trey?" I plead, and he looks at me. He puffs out his massive furry chest before shoving Liam who barely moves. After another tense moment, Liam releases Trey, who storms out of the cell and down the corridor.

Liam shifts back, standing in his naked glory before glancing around at Peter before looking at me.

"What the fuck was that about?" Liam says while I stare at the roof, still recovering from being knocked to the ground after my recent injury.

"Liam! Pants!" I squeak, not knowing where to avert my gaze without seeing that monstrosity between his legs.

"Oh! Sorry, my Queen, forgot you have only seen the King's twinkie," Liam says, clicking his fingers at the guard who chucks him a hessian bag. Liam holds it up and looks at it.

"Fucking pants, moron! What will I do with this? Have a potato sack race?" Liam asks. The guard rushes off, returning minutes later with shorts, while I stand awkwardly staring down the corridor. Once he has pants on, I turn to look at him. He is standing over Peter, who looks up, even more terrified than before.

"Now you'll tell me why Trey just fled," Liam says.

Peter looks at me before looking up at Liam. "I... I don't know, I barely know him," Peter stutters.

"You're asking the wrong person. Let's find Trey, but first, I want to go to town," I say, and Liam turns to face me, but my eyes go to Peter.

"I want to speak to your grandparents," I tell him.

"They didn't do anything! I swear! They aren't part of this," Peter begs, his eyes widening as fear graces his face; I'm not sure if he is scared for them or of them.

"I just want to speak to them," I assure him, though he doesn't deserve the reassurance. Yet, it's hard for me to comprehend Peter the boy in front of me, and the Peter that stabbed me as the same person.

"What? Why?" He says, looking at me petrified.

"Because if I am going to convince Kyson not to kill you, I need the information to back my reasoning."

"My Queen, Kyson won't let him live after what he did, and I wouldn't recommend telling him otherwise," Liam says. I chew my lip.

"Would you let him live?" Liam asks, and his aura slips out with his outrage at my idea.

"He is a child. I don't forgive what he did, and he will be punished, but I won't let Kyson kill him. That is for the Moon Goddess to decide. If I choose it," I tell him. Liam growls, clearly not agreeing, but I turn my gaze to Peter.

"I want your address, now," I tell Peter. He rattles it off, and I nod. I go to leave, only to pause and turn back to him.

"If you're lying to me, I will let Kyson decide your fate. I never made your mother leave. Kyson did. After he woke up to her trying to touch him in his sleep," I tell Peter. He gasps, clearly shocked by this news. Obviously, not all news gets around the castle or maybe it was kept from Peter since he is a child.

"Mom always had a thing for him," Peter admits, and I nod, not knowing how to reply.

"She shouldn't have done that knowing you were his mate," he adds.

"No. She shouldn't have but this is your chance, Peter. If you are lying, tell me now because if I leave here and find out you lied, I won't stop my mate from killing you," I tell him.

"I'm not lying. You can command me, though sometimes it doesn't work," Peter says, glancing nervously at Liam, and I look at Liam, who returns his gaze.

"Pardon?" Liam asks.

"Your command, it hurts but doesn't affect me as badly as the King's," he shrugs.

"So you lied when I commanded you? Faked it?" Liam growls but Peter nods his head.

"I thought you would let me go, but you didn't," Peter says, yet Peter has not shifted yet, so how could he resist it?

"We will figure that out later. For now, we should go. I just felt Kyson wake up, and I want to go before he comes looking for me. Kyson won't ask for answers. He will demand blood," I tell Liam.

"And Trey?" Liam asks.

"When we get back," I tell Liam before turning on my heel and walking out. The mindlink stirs as Kyson wakes, but I can feel he is pretty hungover.

'Azalea!' He says frantically through the mindlink.

'I'm fine. I am with Liam,' I assure him. I feel the tension leave him through the bond, relief flooding through me from him.

'Where are you? I will come to you,' he tells me as Liam holds me steady, helping me climb the stairs leading back into the kitchen. I stop just outside the pantry doors, waiting for Liam to lock the cellar door.

'I'm in the kitchen, but you should shower and wake up. Clarice will send up something for you to eat to help get rid of the hangover,' I tell him while looking at Clarice, who nods to me. She seems surprised to see me but doesn't comment on it, which I appreciate.

'That can wait. I'll be down soon,' Kyson says.

'Kyson, I'm fine. I just want to go into town. Liam is with me. I promise I will come to see you when I get back,' I tell him.

'Azalea!' He says my name like an order, daring me to challenge his word again, and I sigh, knowing he is already on his way to me. I can feel him getting closer when he appears in the doorway leading into the kitchen after a few minutes, there is no point running; he would chase me down so don't even bother to try.

Yet as he appears, the sigh that leaves him and how he rolls his shoulders tell me he needs to see me to ensure I am alright. His smell overrides my senses and is more potent than the robe I am wearing, which has me moving to go to him. He meets me halfway, pulling me into his arms, his hand going to my head while he wraps his arm around my body, his lips in my hair.

"You shouldn't have left without telling me. I woke up and thought..." he doesn't finish, and I don't question, not wanting to know where his mind had just taken him.

He sniffs me before burying his nose in my hair and then pressing it to my neck. A low thrumming growl leaves him, making goosebumps rise on my arms, and his grip tightens but not painfully, more like he is trying to remove the scent on me and replace it with his.

"Where were you?"

I know he knows, so there is no point lying.

"I went to see Peter. Liam and Trey went with me because I asked, and there were also two other guards down there," I tell him knowing Peter's scent is heavy down there; he growls, grabbing my face in his hands and turning it up to look at him.

"Out!" he growls, watching me. The room is evacuated under his order within seconds. Yet he doesn't let me go. Instead, he rests his forehead against mine and lets out a breath. I wait for the wrath, his fury. I can feel it through the bond as he fights the urge to break something, or maybe me. I'm not sure, so I don't push him.

After a moment he seems to calm himself down enough to speak. "Explain.... Please," he growls.

"You wouldn't have let me go," I tell him. He pulls his forehead from mine, looks away, and nods because I am right.

"I may have," he breathes out.

"You don't seem so sure of that," I tell him. I struggle to read him through the bond yet I press my face to his chest. He purrs, a sound I relish, calming and relaxing me.

CHAPTER
THIRTY-EIGHT

AZALEA

"I may have to prevent you from going without me," Kyson whispers, his voice barely audible. Relief washes over me as I realize he isn't angry, but the urgency of my palms remain. "Come on, I need to get changed."

"I am about to go into town with Liam," I reply, my words tinged with a hint of hesitation.

"Why? What is it that you want? I can send for it," Kyson asks, his face buried in my neck. His breath against my skin sends shivers down my spine, while his words stir a whirlwind of emotions within me. My heart races as he picks up on the turmoil within me, and a low purr escapes him as he traces his nose along my neck and jawline, tilting my head up to meet his gaze. I can't bring myself to lie. Not for Peter, not for myself either. Kyson stares, and even though his scent reeks of whiskey from last night, which should have made me wary, I tell him the truth.

"I need to see Peter's grandparents. He told me something important, something I need to ask them about," I confess, my voice filled with a mix of curiosity and guilt at the thought of hiding it from him.

"No!" Kyson growls, cutting me off abruptly.

"Wait. You haven't even let me explain," I plead, desperately wanting him to understand.

"I don't care what Peter said! It won't change anything. He won't escape from my wrath, and you won't alter my decision either! Whatever game he's playing that has made you curious and guilty, I won't entertain it. The answer is no, Azalea," Kyson declares firmly, causing my stomach to sink. I long for answers, for clarity, but Kyson's refusal feels like a barrier preventing me from achieving peace of mind.

Kyson nudges me towards the door, but I remain rooted in place. "Azzy, please. I don't want to fight with you, especially when you've just come back to me," Kyson pleads, but I need answers.

"Then don't make me," I respond, my voice resolute. Kyson snarls in frustration, pinching the bridge of his nose as his eyes squeeze shut. I watch as the hair on his arms bristles, sensing the internal struggle he wages against himself. He battles against the urge to drag me to our room and lock me away, torn between his desire to protect me and his belief that he has no other choice.

"Please," I plead, my voice softening. I don't want to defy him, but I need the truth.

"What for? What did he say to you that made you feel sorry for him?" Kyson demands, his tone laced with anger.

"I want answers about his parents. About why he did it," I reply, desperation seeping into my words.

"He did it because he is a fucking monster!" Kyson screams, his rage echoing through the air as he strikes the nearby bench. The sound of shattering glass punctuates his outburst, and he growls as he stares at his injured hand and the broken bowl beneath it.

"I ask, and you say no. I go, and I get punished for it. You leave me with no choices, Kyson," I say, my voice tinged with frustration. I reach for a tea towel, wetting it as Kyson extracts the glass shards from his palm. The pain makes him hiss, but I apply pressure, knowing that his healing abilities will mend the wound swiftly when the door bursts open.

"Out! She is fine. I won't fucking hurt her!" Kyson snarls at whoever just tried to enter before the door creaks shut.

"I need to go, Kyson," I whisper. Regardless of whether he agrees or not, I am determined to find a way.

"I wake up, and you are bloody gone and you went to the person responsible for killing our baby! So no, I don't want you running around after him," Kyson snarls.

I reach for his hand and start cleaning it. The way he says it makes me sound stupid for wanting answers. Kyson watches me and turns his hand over, and I pick another thick shard from the side of his palm.

"I'm fine, leave it," he snatches his hand away, and I sigh.

He mutters something unintelligible, and as I head towards the back to dispose of the tea towel in the laundry, but he catches my wrist. I turn to face him, finding his jaw clenched, although his grip remains gentle.

"Will you sneak off? Will you go behind my back if I say no?" he asks, his voice laced with concern.

"Don't ask me questions when you already know the answer. Don't make me feel like I have to lie to you," I respond in frustration.

"I want to know why," he states firmly.

"He said Ester is his mother, and the dagger he used to stab me with was his father's. I want to know who his father really is," I explain, hoping he will understand the weight of my curiosity.

"Why does it matter? He's a monster, and he's lying. Ester never had a child," Kyson insists, his voice filled with conviction.

"Are you sure?" I question, hoping to plant a seed of doubt in his mind.

"Even if she did, it changes nothing. He hurt you! He killed our baby! Nothing will stop me from exacting revenge," Kyson declares vehemently.

"Kyson!" I exclaim, my voice filled with frustration and desperation.

"No! He will pay for what he has done!" Kyson interrupts angrily.

"Then come with me! If you come with me, I won't have to go behind your back," I propose as a last-ditch effort, knowing that this moment could lead us down one of two paths. Either he will drag me to our room against my will, or I will go behind his back.

Kyson growls and stares at me intently, but I hold my ground. Why can't he see that I need this? That I need closure?

"I'll take you, but we leave if I don't like what they have to say," Kyson relents finally. I look up at him, resting my chin on his chest.

"You don't leave my side. You won't argue if I say we're leaving," he adds, his voice filled with a mix of protectiveness and possessiveness. I bite my lip but nod in agreement, and he dips his head lower, pinching my chin gently.

"And you eat first," he purrs, his breath caressing my face. "Then I will take you to see them. Just don't hide things from me."

"That should go both ways, Kyson. If you don't want me to hide things, then don't be a hypocrite and hide things from me," I retort, asserting my own need for openness and honesty.

"Come then. You can't go into town in that robe. Were you really planning on wearing it out?" he asks, a hint of amusement in his voice.

"It smells like you," I admit sheepishly, earning a kiss on the top of my head as he guides me towards the door. We eat hastily, both dressing quickly, and true to his word, Kyson accompanies me into town.

As we approach the old cottage on the edge of the forest, its worn walls covered in ivy, a faint flicker of light dances in the windows, casting eerie shadows. Stepping out of the car, I notice that the door hangs precariously from its hinges, while sounds of banging and crashing emanate from within.

In an instant, Kyson pushes me back into the car, his muscles tense as he prowls towards the cottage. Suddenly, a figure bursts through the doors, his body smeared with blood. Another man follows closely behind, also stained crimson. My breath catches in my throat when I recognize Trey emerging from the house.

"Trey?" Kyson questions, staring at him in disbelief. Ignoring Kyson's gaze, I step out of the car, my eyes fixed on Trey's distressed state as he paces back and forth, clutching at his hair. The commotion halts when a woman rushes out, grabbing the older man by the arm. She bears a striking resemblance to Ester, though her youthful appearance belies her true age. Lycan genes have a way of deceiving appearances. The woman clutches her chest upon spotting Liam and Kyson in her driveway.

"What is going on here?" Kyson demands, his voice firm and commanding. The woman's gaze shifts to Trey, who collapses onto the ground in a defeated heap despite not being injured himself.

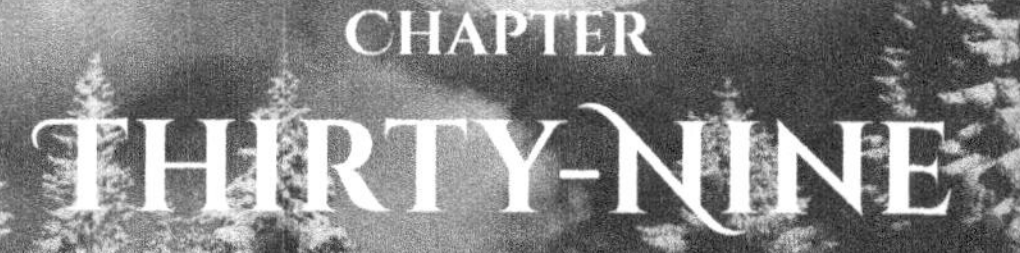

CHAPTER THIRTY-NINE

AZALEA

"I asked a fucking question!" Kyson snarls before turning on Trey. He stalks toward him when the woman calls out.

"He's my son!" she says, making all of us freeze. My eyes widen, and Kyson looks between the couple and Trey. Liam does the same, yet my eyes go to Trey.

"Ester, is your sister?" I ask him.

"That slut is not my fucking sister!" he growls menacingly, and Kyson roars back at him. Trey drops his head before baring his neck to me.

"I'm sorry. I didn't mean to speak that way to you, Azalea," Trey murmurs.

"Okay... Well, I am fucking lost here! Not what I thought you were going to say. Not gonna lie, but when I saw you burst through those damn doors, I, for a whole second, believed Peter was your son and that you never knew," Liam says, and Trey puts his head in his hands.

"He isn't, though. Right? Because that's a little fucked up. And bloody gross, man. Not that I am judging or anything, but... Fuck it!

Yeah, I am judging," Liam adds. Trey growls, glaring at Liam while my head is spinning, trying to figure it out.

"Is that what it is? Did you fuck your sister? Or is this bitch lying?" Liam asks, nudging his head at the woman. Kyson just kept staring back and forth. My neck was hurting from doing the same as I try to figure it out myself.

"I did not fuck that whore!" Trey growls.

"Wait! So Ester is your sister?!" Kyson snaps.

"She is not my sister!" Trey snarls.

"Will someone tell me what is going on here?" Kyson demands, finding himself caught up in the drama. I move toward Trey, but Kyson's arm wraps around my waist, stopping me as he pulls me against him.

"No. You remain by my side. I won't be taking chances with your life," he whispers. Trey glares at the woman on the small veranda when the woman speaks as she steps down the steps and onto the grass.

"Trey is my son," she says, and Kyson looks at Trey, and he nods.

"How?" is all Kyson says.

"My father raised me. My father was a Landeena guard," Trey says, glaring at the man who is beside the woman.

"She is my mother and it turns out Peter is my nephew. I am Ester's half-brother and that prick isn't my father!" Trey snarls.

"If I were. You wouldn't be a disrespectful little shit! I would've beaten that attitude out of you when you were younger. You dare come in here mouthing off and demanding answers we don't fucking have! We don't see Ester. She has nothing to do with us," the man sneers.

"And where is Ester? Does anyone know?" I ask. The couple look at each other but both shrug.

"Liam, go find her and bring her to the castle," Kyson says, although something else played on my mind. Why haven't they come looking for Peter? Did they care so little for him?

I place my hand on Kyson's chest and look at him. He sighs.

"My mate wants to ask you both some questions, though now I have a few of my own," Kyson says, looking at Trey.

"I will put on a pot of tea, My King."

"Trey will make it. I don't trust you," I tell them. They look outraged at my words.

"I suppose that is understandable after what that mutt did," the man says, and I raise an eyebrow at his words. Mutt? He would call his grandson a mutt?

"Brennon! Quiet! Go clean yourself up," the woman hisses at him, and he growls in retort but storms inside, and so does Trey.

"Hands to yourselves in there," Kyson snarls out the order, his aura erupting out, and his grip on me tightens when I nearly give way under it, not expecting it.

The woman across from us is brought to her knees under the weight of it, and the man dropped in the doorway of his house. Trey growls and grits his teeth. He nods, and Kyson releases Trey, who walks inside.

"Don't you pass out on me. My side, not my feet," Kyson growls, kissing my temple and holding me tighter. The man is fighting it when Kyson adds more weight to it. He screams, rolling onto his back.

"Submit Brennon, you old fossil," Kyson growls. Brennan whimpers, then yelps before giving in to the order.

Kyson releases him, and the woman on the ground is panting for air. She bares her neck to Kyson, and he growls but lets her up. She dusts her hands off on her brown apron.

Brennan, however, sits up, leaning against the doorframe, trying to catch his breath. "Prick just like your father." The man spits at him.

"Wrong, Brennon. I am so much worse than him. Test me again, and you'll find out how much worse!" Kyson snarls, leading me to the verandah.

"I'm Mavis, dear. It is lovely to finally put a face to the name," the woman says as she shows us to a small outside setting. I move to sit down when Kyson tugs me on his lap farther away from the couple as they take their seats.

"Why didn't you come looking for Peter?" I ask.

"He got himself in trouble. Broke the law, and went against everything we believe in," Brennan says, nodding to Kyson.

"Brennon was oathed to my father. A personal guard."

"Correct, and the boy broke a sacred law. A few of them in fact. Therefore, I accept the fate coming to him," Brennan says. Mavis looks at her hands and she says nothing though I can tell she feels for Peter.

"You would let him die?" I ask.

"Yep! I'd kill the little shit myself if the King asks," Brennon states.

"I can handle the boy myself," Kyson says, and Brennon nods once. I swallow. It sounds so cruel. Would no one fight for him? Though the woman's eyes are glassy, she remains quiet and submissive to her mate.

"And Trey?" I ask just as he comes out.

"Oh, mom got around, didn't you, ma?" Trey snarls, dropping a tray on the table. Brennan growls, his eyes glaring daggers at Trey.

"Watch your tongue, boy!" he sneers.

"Why? The apple doesn't fall far from the tree. Mom was whore. Ester is a whore ... "

"Enough," Kyson warns, and Trey presses his lips in a line.

"Oh, will you stop it? I never wanted you or your twin. Get over it. I was young and stupid, yet still, you blame me. Your father wasn't my mate. What did you expect? I bring some other man's bastard twin's home with me?" she asks.

Wow, I think to myself. *This woman is a nasty piece of work.* Trey shakes his head and scoffs.

"No. I am glad dad raised us. His mate was my mother and worthy of the title. You are pathetic!" Trey spits at her.

CHAPTER FORTY

KYSON

The situation is spiraling out of my grasp, slipping through my fingers like fine sand. Our visit to Ester's parents gives us little information. They seem genuinely clueless about the identity of Peter's father, yet I can tell Trey is hiding something, or maybe he too is trying to make sense of everything. According to Peter's grandparents, he had been left on their doorstep with a letter from Ester, pleading for them to care for him. It was an odd visit to say the least. Throughout the drive back home, Azalea remains unusually quiet, her thoughts hidden from me.

I can't fathom what she hoped to find by visiting his grandparents; all I know is that it leaves us with more questions than answers. Trey, on the other hand, sits in brooding silence, his gaze fixed on the passing scenery outside the window.

As the gates of our castle loom into view, Azalea turns to look at me. She knows that Peter's fate has been sealed by his grandparents, but I can't comprehend why she still wants to save him after everything he has done. Once we arrive back at the castle, I ask Liam to take Azalea back to our room. She glances at me, searching my eyes for something, but I have already shut her out.

I can see the unspoken question lingering on her lips, but she remains mute, choosing instead to open the door to head inside. Trey moves to exit the car, but I hold onto his shoulder firmly.

"Stay where you are," I command, keeping a watchful eye on Liam and Azalea until they disappear from sight. Only then do I release my grip on Trey.

"Why didn't you tell me that Ester was your sister?" I question him, my voice laced with an undercurrent of frustration.

"She's not my sister!" Trey growls, shaking his head vehemently.

"By blood, she is your half-sister," I remind him, trying to inject a sense of reason into our conversation.

"Not by choice. I should have killed her back in Landeena," he snarls, his voice dripping with bitterness.

"You have a twin. Is it possible that he is the father?" I probe further, a nagging doubt tugging at the corners of my mind, though I am reluctant to admit it.

"We're not some inbred family," Trey retorts, turning to face me directly in the passenger seat.

"She wanted to escape from her parents, and I can't blame her. You've seen what they're like. Her mother accidentally revealed that she had brothers, and that's when she came to us. We took her in. Little did I know that it would be the biggest mistake of my life," Trey confesses, his voice heavy with regret.

"How long ago was that?" I inquire, trying to piece together the timeline.

"Almost fifteen years ago," Trey replies.

"Peter is fourteen. Is it possible that his father is from Landeena?" I press, my mind racing with possibilities.

Trey falls silent, refusing to provide an answer.

"Was she already pregnant when she arrived?" I probe further, determined to uncover the truth.

"No, she wasn't. I didn't even know she was pregnant. She left a few months before the attack," Trey admits, his voice tinged with pain.

"Was she involved with anyone else during her time with you?" I ask cautiously.

"She's nothing but a whore," Trey spits out bitterly but also evades the question.

"You know that I plan on killing Peter, right? Will that cause any issues between us?" I question him directly, searching for any signs of hesitation or conflict within him.

Trey shakes his head firmly. "If you want, I'll do it for you," he offers coldly, his eyes glinting with an unsettling mix of detachment and hatred.

"And Ester?" I inquire further, needing to understand the depth of his feelings towards her.

"She's dead to me," Trey declares through gritted teeth, his anger palpable.

"I want Peter out of the picture, but I have a feeling Azalea will resist. Liam has taken her to our room. Do you have the stomach for it, or should I ask Gannon?" I ask, my words carrying a weight of finality.

"As I said, I'll do it for you," Trey replies, his voice devoid of emotion. The ease with which he accepts the task unsettles me, making me curious how he could instantly hate Peter more knowing he is his nephew, but there is no turning back now.

"Good. We're heading down to the cells while Liam distracts Azalea," I declare, my mind made up. Trey nods in silent agreement, though I know that my decision wouldn't have changed even if he had voiced opposition when another thought occurs to me since Trey was one of the King and Queen's guards there.

"One last question," I interject as Trey opens the car door. He pauses, turning to face me with a questioning look.

"Are you sired to Peter?" I ask, my voice laced with curiosity and a hint of trepidation.

"No, no, I'm not," Trey answers firmly.

"Is there a chance that this could be considered treason?" I probe further, seeking reassurance in his response.

"With Garrett, there's always that chance," Trey replies, venom dripping from his words.

His response confuses me; if he is sired to the Landeena bloodline, shouldn't Peter fall under that same sire if Ester was fooling around with the King? The questions continue to multiply in my mind, but for now, I have a pressing matter to attend to.

I will seek answers regarding this sibling rivalry and the intricacies of their lineage at a later time. As we step out of the car and approach the castle, the sound of heated arguing reaches my ears, reverberating through the corridor. It is Azalea, her voice filled with defiance as she turns her fiery glare towards me the moment I enter the hall.

"No! Don't think I can't sense your intentions, Kyson. We need to talk to Ester first. I won't let you harm him," she snarls, her words cutting through the air like a sharp blade. Can she truly be serious? This boy has taken the life of our child.

"I am not seeking your permission. I told you that nothing will stand in the way of me killing him," I retort firmly, my resolve unyielding.

"He's just a boy! Ester should..."

"Ester isn't here, and she doesn't have a say," I interject, redirecting my attention to Liam.

"Bring him to me," I command, watching as Liam hurries off to fulfill my orders. Turning towards Trey, I instruct him,

"Lock her in the room and wait until Liam returns. Then join us downstairs..."

"What? No! I won't allow this!" Azalea protests, stepping away from Trey's reaching hands.

"Azzy, go to the room," I urge, but she shakes her head adamantly, evading Trey's grasp.

"No!" she exclaims, slapping away Trey's hands. I gesture for him to proceed and he swiftly scoops her up, hoisting her over his shoulder.

"Put me down! You're sired to me, not him!" Azalea screams, thrashing against Trey's hold and delivering blows to his back.

"I'm sired to protect you and this is me doing that, you don't want to witness his death," Trey reasons with her, his voice tinged with a hint of sadness.

She continues struggling as Trey carries her towards our chambers causing quite a commotion along the way. Clarice emerges from a nearby room, her eyes widening in surprise at the sight.

"Kyson please! He's just a boy," she pleads, rushing over to me.

"What is it with you and her defending him?" I snap, my frustration boiling over

"Because no one else is. Not his family, not anyone," Clarice explains, her voice filled with compassion.

"He killed my baby, and nearly took the life of my mate! Your Queen!" I exclaim, my words heavy with the weight of grief and anger. Clarice flinches under the weight of my accusations, just as Liam emerges from the kitchen down the hall. Trey turns towards the stairs, but not before Azalea's gaze catches on Peter.

"Please! Please, Azalea! I didn't mean it! I didn't mean it!" Peter's voice echoes through the hall, his pleas desperate as he drags his feet in a futile attempt to resist Liam bringing him to me.

Anger flares within Liam, and I feel Trey grunt. Azalea lunges at Liam in a desperate bid to protect Peter, but Trey swiftly intercepts her, wrapping his arms around her waist and pulling her back.

"No! No, Kyson!" she wails, her voice filled with anguish. What is wrong with her? This monster has taken the life of our child, yet she will fight tooth and nail to protect the bastard.

"Please, Kyson," Clarice pleads, her voice filled with desperation as she stands beside me. I shoot her a glare, silencing her momentarily, only to witness a blazing fury erupt from Azalea. The intensity of her emotions sends a shiver down my spine as her aura erupts.

From the end of the corridor, I can feel her command resonating like a shock wave, bursting forth with undeniable force. "Let me go!" she demands, her voice carrying an authority that makes even Trey, who had been restraining her, release his grip under the weight of her command.

"You will not kill him! Not until I have spoken to Ester. Unhand him, Liam!" she orders, and Liam groans, struggling against her command. But in the end, he succumbs to her power, succumbing to her even from a distance. I grit my teeth in frustration; this is the last thing I needed – for her to discover her damn power over that insignificant mutt!

Peter attempts to flee, but I seize the back of his shirt and yank him towards me. His screams pierce through the air, assaulting my ears. Clarice whimpers, and even the guards and staff present seem to tremble in fear as I forcefully hurl him out the doors. He crashes onto the ground and skids across it before scrambling to his feet and fleeing.

My voice reverberates loudly as he tries to escape. "Freeze!" I command, and instantly he freezes in his tracks, straining against my order as I advance towards him.

"I warned you, Azalea, that I would do this. So if you wish to witness it, so be it," I inform her coldly, stalking towards Peter with determination.

But Azalea launches herself at me, her hands grasping onto my arms tightly. I spin around and seize her face in my grip.

Her tear-stained face reflects her desperation back at me. "He killed our baby. He almost killed you!" I remind her, and her eyes flicker towards Peter. Her Lycan side flares up, her gaze burning brightly before dimming in defeat.

"Please, don't make me do this," she whispers, her voice trembling.

"I'm not making you do anything. Just go inside and I will handle him, you don't have to watch," I insist, my tone firm. She shakes her head defiantly.

"We lost our baby," she murmurs, and I nod, closing my eyes momentarily to gather my thoughts.

"But that doesn't mean we should lose ourselves. We are not child killers. We are not monsters. At the very least, Ester should be able to say goodbye," she pleads softly.

How could she even suggest that? Peter never afforded her that opportunity. I open my eyes, finding her lip quivering as more tears spill over. I wipe them away with my thumbs and plant a tender kiss on her forehead, causing her to whimper. Deep down, she knows she won't change my mind.

"Go inside," I urge her, releasing my grip on her. She crumples to the ground, broken and defeated and I turn back to Peter.

"No! No, no, no, please! Please!" Peter begs desperately, but he remains frozen under my command. Suddenly, a scream pierces through the air, causing me to turn towards Azalea. However, it isn't her who screams. Azalea is still on the ground, sobbing uncontrollably as she turns her head to the side.

"Mom!" Peter's voice echoes in anguish, and when I follow his gaze, I see Ester standing just outside the gates.

Instead of looking at her son, her gaze is fixed upon Azalea. Trey rushes out the doors with a ferocious growl, and Ester jumps in surprise when Azalea rises to her feet with astonishing speed. It's a wonder she doesn't faint from the sudden motion. With a swift gesture of her hand towards Trey, Azalea unleashes her command, sending it surging out from within her along with an intense blast of her aura.

"Stop!" she roars, and Trey is thrown back against the doors as if hit with the weight of a force field. Her command sends shock waves through me and if it were directed at me, she would drop me. Her eyes glow brighter than ever, taking on an eerie look, an almost white light. They burn so brightly that it hurts my eyes to look at her.

Trey smashes against the doors, ripping one door off by the hinges completely as it crashes down beneath him. He grunts, and I stare, shocked. I knew the Landeena's and Azures have power, and have seen the way her father cheated in the trials. His command has the power to kill, and looking at Azalea, she has now just awoken it.

What terrifies me the most is the thought of her realizing what I am hiding from her. Her gaze goes to mine, just as Ester drops to her knees at her feet. I swallow guiltily, and she does not take her eyes from me, not even as Ester begs.

"Please! It's not his fault! Kill me. Please, let me take his place," Ester pleads, and Azalea pulls her gaze from me.

She is furious, and her entire body trembles with anger so hot I worry she will set the castle on fire with it.

The history books always told of the Landeena Power, and looking at her, I realize she holds her father's power and if she also holds her mother's, she will be a force of nature. No one could contend against a Landeena and she was born of not one gifted bloodline, but two. Both Landeena and Azure.

Azure the powerful, Azure the pure, Azure the great. So the history books read. Azalea is also Landeena. Their history books read similarly. Landeena the blessed, Landeena the beholder of divine power, Landeena our salvation, and now she had awoken it. Now she possesses what was suppressed, and I know without a doubt that I have some answering to do. And now she has awoken it, the entire werewolf, Lycan and Hunter communities would be after her.

But first, I have to take care of Peter before she turns her wrath on me. Shifting, she would struggle to hold power long enough to contain my beast, given she has already used a heap of energy she hasn't held before, which will wear her down and take a toll on her. So, I give in to it, letting that side take control. My claws slash down Peter's face. Ester screams, and I move to break his neck. My fingers wrap around his throat when Ester's words stop me, and so does Azalea's command.

"He is a Landeena!" Ester screams simultaneously as Azalea orders me to stop. Though, her shock had her dropping the command long enough for me to grip his throat tighter and cut his air off, before I am frozen under it again. My head pounding to the force of it as I try to fight it; she can overthrow me. However, she is using power she has no idea how to wield, and it would be straining on her until she learns to harness it correctly.

I growl, turning to Ester. "He has immunity! He is King Garret's son!" Ester cries, clutching onto Azalea's pants.

"Please! He is your brother! He's your half brother, please!" she begs, and I swallow, looking down at Peter my hands trembling as I squeeze his neck.

"Let him go," Azalea says, her voice trembles, her eyes flicking toward me. I growl at her and her eyes blaze with anger, and her next words slam against me with the force of a freight train.

"Let him go. I have already lost my child and I will not witness another lose hers! Let. Him. Go!" she commands, with tears trekking down her face. Yet her words are clear and unwavering.

I can feel her betrayal, her sadness, her anger, and her confusion. She is full of every emotion I can think of, but the biggest one is grief as she looks down at Ester, clutching her leg. My hand lets him go, and he gasps for air. Yet I am rendered powerless to kill him by her command when Azalea speaks, drawing my attention to her.

"I would do anything to be able to have my baby. You have a chance to hold yours. I will never get that chance. Your son took it from me. However, I would never wish that on any mother even after what you have both done," she tells Ester, who sobs. Azalea then looks at Peter.

"Go to your mother, Peter," Azalea whispers. I grit my teeth as her command overrides mine easily, and he rushes to her, falling at her feet. Ester clutches him tightly when Trey roars, getting to his feet.

Azalea turns to face him. His anger forces his shift as he lunges at his sister and Peter. Ester shifts taking on her brother to stop him from getting to her son. Azalea just stares at them before turning and walking off, looking defeated, and that's all I feel through the bond too. Her defeat, pain, anguish and grief when Ester tosses Trey aside and snarls. She bares her teeth at her brother before they both lunge at each other, ripping each other apart.

Peter screams for his mother, and I feel Azalea stop and glance at them while Peter sobs on the ground. I try to piece together what is happening and what isn't happening. She is defending the boy she refused to acknowledge, fighting her own brother for him.

Trey swings at her, his claws slashing her face when she ducks, and she stumbles back. Trey pounces on her, intending to kill her only for her to kick him off.

"All of this is your fault! Your fucking fault because you kept throwing yourself at his feet! You knew you were hurting her! You fucking knew who she was to me," Trey snarls, getting to his feet and stalking toward her.

"And then you decide to keep his bastard!" Trey snarls.

"I loved him!" Ester screams back at him only to receive a kick to the stomach that sends her hurtling toward the gate with a crash.

"He used you, and you nearly killed her for it! You nearly killed my fucking mate!" Trey says, grabbing her throat. He slams her Lycan form on the ground, her head crashing into the ground. Peter jumps on his back, only to be swatted away like a fly by Trey. Yet, once again, I am left feeling confused.

"She didn't want you, you idiot! She married the prick. Then you let him sire you to their daughter just to stay near her. You did the same thing, Trey! How is loving him any different from you loving Tatiana?" Ester screams back at him.

"I was her mate! You were his whore!" Trey screams when Azalea's voice reaches my ears.

"Enough," she says softly and everyone freezes. I watch as she sways on her feet. Liam grips her arm holding her steady, but her legs go out from under her as exhaustion takes her from using too much power too soon. Trey tosses his sister to get to her, just as I reach her.

"You awoke it, and you burned yourself out," Trey tells her, clutching her face as I scoop her up in my arms.

Whispering softly, her voice strained with pain, she rubs her temples, trying to alleviate the throbbing ache in her head. Trey moves towards her, concern etched on his face, but I instinctively growl, warning him to keep his distance. My attention shifts, scanning the surroundings for Ester, only to find her gone, vanished along with Peter.

However, as my gaze lands on the gate through which they escaped, a chilling sight meets my eyes. Countless faces peer in at us, their presence making me gulp nervously. They must have sensed her power, though I had not anticipated their arrival so swiftly. Armored and armed with Landeena swords, they have come prepared to fight for her.

"Find them. Bring them back," I command Trey and Liam firmly, my voice laced with urgency. Cedric, adorned in the Landeena crest upon his armor, walks through the gates, drawing wary glances from Liam and my men. He extends his hands towards Trey, offering the Royal Landeena sword. Kneeling before Azalea in my arms, Trey gazes down at her tenderly. Cedric is tethered to me, and the rest of the Landeena Lycans are tethered to him and have been since Landeena fell. I know what he desires, and a snarl escapes me at the thought. However, Azalea must sense their intentions too because she nods to Trey, signaling him to accept the blade. As he runs the cold steel across her palm, her eyes blaze like beacons.

"You won't harm them, any of them," Azalea whispers determinedly, fighting to remain conscious within my embrace. "You do, and I won't forgive..." Her words trail off abruptly as she collapses in my arms, her body limp. Trey grips her wrist tightly, bringing her bleeding palm to my lips in an attempt to staunch the flow. Swiftly, I run my tongue over the deep gash, seeking to heal her wound. Trey then takes her hand and presses it against my chest.

"Bring them to the castle," I command Liam, frustration evident in my voice. He nods in understanding, but I curse inwardly at the realization that I forgot to specify they must be brought back alive. Frustration turns to anger, and a low growl rumbles through me as I redirect my attention towards Cedric and the others. They all kneel before me, swords held firmly in their hands looking so out of place in today's world, sure my men used swords but modern times there are easier ways to kill a man, and we don't need weapons to do so. With Cedric's blade now stained crimson with Azalea's blood.

Cedric locks eyes with me, unflinching in the face of my snarl. He was her father's former Beta, though age has rendered him unfit for that title now knowing Garret was as old Lycan bloodlines began. I know Cedric must be too, though he barely looks older than 50, yet it takes centuries to look his age. Eventually, Azalea will have to choose another successor.

"We renounce our allegiance to Valkyrie Kingdom and pledge ourselves to Landeena Kingdom!" they declare in unison, their voices resonating with unwavering determination.

Cedric rises, lifting his sword high, and the others follow suit. Gripping the hilt with one hand while grasping the blade with the other, they all trace their hands along its edge, crimson liquid drenching their skin before making their solemn pledge.

"We pledge our allegiance to Azalea Ivy Landeena, the Landeena Empress, the true Empress of the Kingdoms. I bleed for Landeena, I fight for Landeena, I die for Landeena, we are Landeena and our Empress has risen and so has the Landeena Guard. We pledge to serve and protect the rightful heir of Landeena." they drop their arms and fall to one knee, swords at their front before continuing.

"When the Empress rises, we rise with her, and when she falls, we too shall fall." Their words echo with unwavering loyalty as they pledge their lives to protect her. Suddenly, I jolt as their tethers to me snap, and Azalea inhales deeply, her connection with them now established.

And all I can think is now her bloodline has awoken, how am I going to keep her safe from the rest of the world, all while keeping her safe from herself.

About the Author

Join my Facebook group to connect with me

https://www.facebook.com/jessicahall91

Enjoy all of my series

https://www.amazon.com/Jessica-Hall/e/B09TSM8RZ7

FB: Jessica Hall Author Page
Website: jessicahallauthor.com
Insta: Jessica.hall.author
Goodreads: Jessica_Hall

Also by Jessica Hall

AUTHORS I RECOMMEND

Jane Knight

Want books with an immersive story that sucks you in until you're left wanting more? Queen of spice, Jane Knight has got you covered with her mix of paranormal and contemporary romance stories. She's a master of heat, but not all of her characters are nice. They're dark and controlling and not afraid to take their mates over their knees for a good spanking that will leave you just as shaken as the leading ladies. Or if you'd prefer the daddy-do type, she writes those too just so they can tell you that you are a good girl before growling in you ear. Her writing is dark and erotic. Her reverse-harems will leave you craving more and the kinks will have you wondering if you'll call the safe word or keep going for that happily every after.]

Follow her on facebook.com/janeknightwrites

Check out her books on https://www.amazon.com/stores/Jane-Knight/author/B08B1M8WD8

Moonlight Muse

Looking for a storyline that will have you on the edge of your seat? The spice levels are high with a plot that will keep you flipping to the next page and ready for more. You won't be disappointed with Moonlight Muse.

Her women as sassy and her men are possessive alpha-holes with high tensions and tons of steam. She'll draw you into her taboo tales, breaking your heart before giving you the happily ever after.

Follow her on facebook.com/author.moonlight.muse

Check out her books on https://www.amazon.com/stores/Moonlight-Muse/author/B0B1CKZFHQ

Made in the USA
Monee, IL
02 August 2024

63151382R10156